A Marquess Scorned

Tales from The Burnished Jade
Book 4

ADELE CLEE

This is a work of fiction. All names, characters, places and incidents are products of the author's imagination. All characters are fictitious and any resemblance to real persons, living or dead, is purely coincidental.

No part of this book may be copied or reproduced in any manner without the author's permission.

A Marquess Scorned
Copyright © 2026 Adele Clee
All rights reserved.
ISBN-13: 978-1-915354-60-0

Cover by Dar Albert at Wicked Smart Designs
Dragonfly motif by Vika Glitter via Pixababy

A Marquess Scorned

Chapter One

A mile west of World's End, Chelsea

Few men could stand at the gate of a graveyard at night without feeling the chill of dread. Fewer still would look upon old stone and unkempt gardens and find a measure of peace. But Gabriel knew the dead did not lie, deceive or disappoint. *That* wickedness belonged solely to the living.

Yet his thoughts were not on those resting beneath the hallowed ground. Every thought since turning his horse onto this lonely road centred on a woman still very much alive.

A stranger, all things considered.

A stranger with a secret.

Was that what fed this unwelcome obsession? The mystery. The puzzle. Or was it the enigma herself, with hair of burnished copper, and a mind like a labyrinth of hidden passages he longed to explore?

He tethered his horse to the post, his gaze straying to the quaint cottage next door, its red brick choked by creeping ivy. Faint candlelight slipped through a gap in the curtains, proof

Miss Woolf was not yet abed. The graveyard pressed close, as though death kept watch over its solitary mistress. Yet something compelled Gabriel to intrude. If he could help her unravel the riddles of her life, perhaps he might forget his own.

He moved to the rickety garden gate, noticing the length of string tied to a strip of rusted metal, a makeshift alarm. Sensible for a woman living alone in the wilds of World's End, though it spoke of fear rather than foresight. He lifted the latch with care, the faint rattle carrying into the night like a warning bell.

The curtain twitched.

Doubt gripped him. He should have sent a note, but he wanted to catch her unawares and see her unguarded reaction. Why the devil had she moved here? Why had he, a marquess with unlimited resources, struggled to find her address?

The reason became clear when she wrenched open the door, levelled a pistol at his heart, and drew back the hammer. Trust Miss Woolf to greet him with steel in hand. He ought to have been alarmed. But some dark part of him admired her nerve.

"Raise your hands, sir. High enough so I can see them." She firmed her grip to banish the tremble and stared down the barrel. "State your name and your business. Be quick. Out here, we shoot trespassers."

He raised his hands to shoulder height. "Gabriel Montague Saville. Marquess of Rothley. Friend, not foe. And fellow lover of morbid poetry."

Her gasp sliced through the cool air. He suspected she had known all along and only wished to prove she could defend herself.

"Lord Rothley?" Her voice carried doubt as she stepped

to the threshold, scouring the gloom as if unwilling to take him at his word. "Most men look the same in the shadows. Tell me something about yourself, something I would know."

He bristled, torn between offence and amusement.

He was nothing like other men.

That she could not recall the subtle edge of arrogance in his voice, or recognise that no other man in London bore shoulders as broad as his, frankly, grated.

"We accompanied friends to Cheltenham last month and stayed at the Duck and Dog. We witnessed a duel in the walled garden. Afterwards, I escorted you back to your bedchamber."

The moment was seared into his memory. Nothing short of death would eradicate the image of her copper hair tumbling in waves about her shoulders, and the knowledge she wore nothing but a nightgown beneath her pelisse.

"Good heavens. What are you doing here?" Miss Woolf didn't lower her pistol or offer him a gracious welcome. "It's almost eleven o'clock. Do you make a habit of calling uninvited after dark?"

"Madam, I could knock on any door in town and people would be tripping over themselves to let me in. Must we have this conversation on the doorstep?" He glanced at the graveyard, certain no gossips lurked behind the headstones. "Surely you're not concerned about your reputation. There's not another living soul within half a mile."

The lady angled her pistol towards the shadowed cottage beyond the hedgerow. "I'm not entirely alone here. Mrs Hodge was the housekeeper at Canfield Manor before she retired. She's used to dealing with intruders."

The woman also had a loose tongue. While his friend

Gentry treated her chest ailment, Mrs Hodge had gossiped about her new neighbour.

"I'm struggling to think what would bring you charging out here on horseback." Her gaze shifted to his imposing black stallion. "Is there trouble at The Burnished Jade? Is Joanna unwell?"

"The countess is fine." Which was more than could be said for his nerves. "Miss Woolf, I'm not a pedlar hawking brushes door-to-door. Might we speak inside?" He stepped closer, daring her to deny him. "I wouldn't be here were it not important. Now—"

"*Fetch the master!*" came a shrill voice from inside.

"*She's got a pistol!*" came another.

"Ah, your feathered footmen." He ought not be surprised. He'd heard Miss Woolf had acquired two African grey parrots to serve as protection. But protection from whom? "I hadn't realised you meant to train them for sentry duty."

"Better feathered footmen than none at all." She stole another glance down the eerie lane. "They keep intruders guessing."

"So, I'm right in thinking you live here alone." Rutland's comment slipped into his mind: a woman with her intellect and beauty would make the perfect poet's muse. Damn it, the man was not wrong.

"Is that why you're here? To play night watchman?"

"You know why I'm here." He advanced to the door, closed his hand around the barrel, and eased the pistol from her grip. Her fingers resisted for a heartbeat, as though testing his strength, before she yielded the weapon. "May I come inside, Miss Woolf?"

She swallowed hard. "I'm in my nightclothes."

Must she remind him? He kept his gaze on the weapon in

his hand, not the elegant column of her throat, and tried to recall why he'd come. "Fetch your wrapper. I'll wait at the door."

A moment passed before she returned, shrouded in a dowdy grey wrapper she'd fastened in a double bow. The glow of the candle in the chamberstick she carried drew his eyes to her full lips, proud cheekbones, and the copper hair bound in a braid.

Still, this felt like an illicit liaison, and he imagined slamming the door shut behind him, pinning her to the wall, and crushing his mouth to hers.

For heaven's sake, man, pull yourself together!

For this plan to work, he had to preserve indifference. But the fact he was miles from home late at night proved he was anything but. Damn the devil. God willing, he'd be over it soon.

"It's rather late." She stepped back and beckoned him inside. "I trust this won't take long."

"Time tarries for no one, Miss Woolf. It buries us all in the end."

"Then let us not waste more of it at the door."

He crossed the threshold, stooping beneath the low lintel, and entered the sitting room, a fraction the size of his dressing room at Studland Park. It seemed the fire had died an hour ago, though the open book and blanket on the chair said she had been absorbed in its pages.

He didn't need to glance at the gold-embossed title. A parrot perched in the corner croaked, "*The paths of glory lead to the grave.*"

Gabriel found himself smiling. "You're reading Thomas Gray."

She glanced at the book as if it were a familiar friend. "Indeed."

"What passage keeps you up so late?"

Her gaze fell to the dying embers. "The idea that beauty and wealth are meaningless. We all return to the earth in the end. A sobering thought, even for the proudest of men, my lord."

Her reply sounded much like a veiled attack.

"We all have a place. The mistake would be believing some of us are better than others." He'd be damned before he felt ashamed of his title. "We all know pain, Miss Woolf. We all know heartbreak."

Her mouth curved in wry amusement. "Even a man as confident as you?"

"Impressions deceive." He gripped the barrel and returned the pistol. "I believe you know that better than most. Who are you hiding from?"

A mocking laugh escaped her. She turned away, setting the pistol on the mantel as if she might need it again soon. "Must we revisit the same questions? Surely someone so enigmatic detests sounding like a bore."

A bore? Of all insults, trust her to pick the worst.

"I've been called many things, Miss Woolf. Murderer. Rake. Libertine. But never a bore."

"Perhaps *relentless* is the better word. Few men possess your intellect for seeing beyond the ordinary."

Pride stirred despite himself. The King's praise had never touched him as hers did now. "No one could call you a bore. One minute you belittle me, the next you bestow your good opinion. A man might grow dizzy."

"You are quite confounding."

"I've been nothing but honest."

"*What tripe!*" a parrot squawked.

That accursed bird.

Miss Woolf laughed, a rare sound, for sadness hung behind her eyes like a mourning veil. Though he was drawn to her solemnity, the lightness in her voice stole his breath.

"Forgive me. They can be terribly rude, though rarely wrong, much to your discomfort, I suspect."

He seized on her reply. "You speak as if you believe them." Men had lied to her before, and he wondered who. "Ask me anything, and I'll answer honestly. You've no cause to be afraid."

"Afraid?" She lifted her chin, a silent gauntlet tossed down. "Very well. Are you here because you imagine our mutual love of poetry means I might share your bed?"

He didn't laugh. "No, Miss Woolf. I have no wish to bed you." It was the greatest lie he'd ever told. But desire was fickle. "Though I am concerned for your welfare. You moved house without telling a soul, not even your closest friends."

"You found me."

"And was left staring down the muzzle of a pistol." He'd been surprised, not shocked, and darkly intrigued by her audacity. "You failed to attend the recital at The Jade on Tuesday. People were worried."

Namely him.

Her throat bobbed, and when the lie came she delivered it with remarkable aplomb. "I was feeling under the weather. And one cannot summon a hackney so easily out here."

"Then why move to World's End?" He considered the peace, the stillness, the gentle hoot of an owl and the soft whisper of wind in the trees. "I see the appeal, but it's hardly practical for a woman living alone."

The thought needled him. No maid to keep watch, no

companion to stand guard. Yet she always arrived at The Jade wearing an impeccable gown, each one the work of an expert modiste. Money enough for finery, but not for protection. Everything about her was a conundrum.

She stared at him, lips as tight as a miser's purse.

"I've been frank with you," he lied again, frustration rising. "At least grant me the courtesy of explaining your predicament."

The silence stretched, heavy with unspoken truths. He could almost hear her sifting through them, deciding what she might share. He fought the urge to leave, wondering why the devil he bothered at all.

"I have port, my lord. Would you care for a glass?"

Ah, alcohol. The oldest diversion in the book, besides sex. "I make it a rule never to refuse a drink in tense situations, though I must insist on pouring."

Her lips curved faintly. "You don't need to play the marquess here. As you can see, it's not a Mayfair drawing room."

No, though he rather liked the quaint intimacy of it.

"If we're to be friends, Miss Woolf, there's one thing you should know about me. Gallantry runs in my blood." He strode to the small wooden table, where a bottle stood beside two mismatched glasses and no decanter. The sight jarred. She dressed with unerring taste, yet served port in something chipped and common.

"Yes, I've seen the proof firsthand. You saved that poor boy from Rosefield Seminary. Yet you have secrets too. If gallantry runs in your blood, why do people believe you killed a man?"

His fingers froze on the bottle, the past like an icy draught down his spine. If tonight were to proceed as intended, he had to tell her the truth. "You're friendly with the Countess of Berridge and visit her ladies' club often. Has she ever mentioned her brother Justin?"

Saying the name stiffened every muscle. The question remained: was his death an injustice or a cunning betrayal?

"Yes, she mentioned him once. He was your friend at Cambridge, I believe. His body is interred at St Michael's churchyard."

Gabriel filled a glass with port and tossed it back, the burn doing nothing to soothe his ire. "That's not his body. Probably some vagrant used as bait to trick a man. He's alive, though where he's been for a decade remains a mystery." He'd refused to stand at the grave, certain he'd be mourning a lie. Not a day passed that he didn't wrestle with the blasted riddle.

Miss Woolf edged nearer. Whether from curiosity or relief that she wasn't under scrutiny, he couldn't tell. "Why would it not be him?"

He poured her port and handed her the glass, careful not to touch her fingers. "The remains found in a hidden shelter in the woods were inconclusive. The coroner based his decision on Justin's clothes, height and build."

She sipped her drink while he poured himself another. "Did he mention going there? Was it somewhere he frequented?"

Gabriel faced her. No one had asked him these questions in years. "The fact he never mentioned it at all is what's most odd. We were as close as brothers."

Her slight shrug said that was of no consequence. "Families lie to one another. It's those closest who often harbour the darkest secrets."

He pondered her words. "Is that why you're hiding

here? Because of a disagreement over inheritance? I was told you keep your heirlooms somewhere safe and anticipated the robbery at your previous lodging house." The thought of any man laying a hand on her set his blood alight.

"Robberies occur frequently in London," she replied dismissively, taking a quick nip of port.

"Rarely to the same person twice. Are you here because of family troubles?"

"I have no family."

"Dead or estranged?"

"Does it matter?"

"Yes."

"Why?"

He held her gaze. "Because you're afraid, and I need to know whose neck to wring. Give me a name, and they shall trouble you no more."

Her laugh held no mirth, only deflection. "And why would you wish to protect me? We've only ever exchanged pleasantries."

"Some would say talk of graveyards and death is hardly pleasant."

"We see things differently than most."

"Which is exactly why I'm here."

"To pry into a lady's personal affairs?" She set her empty glass on the table. "To scare me half out of my wits at night?"

"To help you." And in the process he might help himself. With his closest friends married, what was left but to use his privilege for the greater good? "Because I know how it feels to tackle problems alone." Loneliness was a foe he knew too well.

"There's safety in solitude." She turned from him, taking

the open book from the chair and snapping it shut. "I've learned to rely on myself. I'm not your responsibility."

"We can change that."

She didn't ask how. The shutters were already drawn, barring his entry. "It's late. I appreciate your concern, but I think you should go." She glanced towards the window as if she'd heard the sudden creak of the gate. "A horse of that calibre is bound to draw attention on the open road."

He almost laughed at the irony. He could buy a stable of fine Arabians, own any house of his choosing, have any woman he desired—except this one, and the one his father denied him a decade ago. He was a marquess with blood bluer than the King's. Yet here he was, practically pleading for Miss Woolf's attention. Perhaps this sudden need to help her was nothing more than proof the past had not beaten him.

The thought was sobering.

He straightened to his full height.

Despite the plan, he'd not sacrifice his dignity. "If I leave now, I'll not approach you again. This is the last time I shall ask. If you want my help, demand it now, and you shall have my proposal."

She gripped her book of morbid poetry, hugging it to her chest. Uncertainty clouded her cornflower eyes. "Your proposal? I warrant you're an astute man, but how can you help me without knowing the problem?"

"By offering a solution that will restore the balance of power." His tone carried the kind of certainty that brooked no argument. "No sane man in Christendom would dare challenge you if you accept."

Her brow furrowed. She tightened her hold on the book, her fingers fretting at the edge of the pages. "Why? What are you proposing?"

He allowed the silence to stretch just long enough to make her uneasy. Then, as if it were the most obvious thing in the world, he said, "Marriage, Miss Woolf."

Chapter Two

Olivia stared at the formidable man who towered above her in the modest cottage, his shoulders broad beneath the sweep of his coat, his presence impossible to ignore. "I beg your pardon. I thought you said marriage."

"I did. A convenient arrangement to suit us both."

Her mouth fell open. Of all the reasons for his visit, marriage was the last she'd expected. "But that's absurd. You're a marquess." A striking one at that. He could have his pick of society brides.

"You make it sound like a problem, not a solution."

"It's unthinkable. Quite ludicrous."

The man had lost his wits. Yes, they could converse on all manner of subjects, but he was stern and steadfast in his opinions. He despised liars, and she had barely spoken an honest word since they'd met.

"Why? Lord Gillingham married his housekeeper. And you're a respectable woman with titled friends." His midnight eyes darkened, as unreadable as ever. "Do you think I give a damn what people say?"

"No, which is why I wonder if this is an act of defiance. Perhaps you wish to add *rebel* to your long list of monikers." But why choose her as his accomplice? "What point do you wish to prove? Because whatever it is, I want no part of it."

Instead of biting back, he grinned.

"You find my opposition amusing, my lord?"

"Delightfully amusing. Few women have the courage to berate me. That bodes well for the future."

Heaven help her. Had he woken this morning with pebbles for brains? "Besides the obvious—"

"Which is?"

She waved a hand over his impressive physique, searching for the right words. "I cannot lie with a man who means nothing to me, no matter how handsome he might be."

"Nor shall I force myself upon you. Should you agree, a relationship based on friendship and mutual respect will suffice. I have estates scattered across the country, though I must insist you make Studland Park your home for the foreseeable future."

"Studland Park?" It sounded like a stable for thoroughbreds, yet here he was, choosing the common hack.

"My estate in Islington. A vast house with over two hundred rooms, though I've never bothered to count them."

Two hundred? She glanced around the humble sitting room and felt faint. "Surely you know I cannot accept." She reached for the arm of the chair and sat before her knees buckled.

He fell silent, the brooding weight of it heavy in the room.

Something in his expression, a flicker of vulnerability beneath the control, made her confess what she'd sworn to conceal. "You were right. I am hiding. I cannot do that while living as your wife in a grand mansion."

He gazed at her from under hooded eyes. "Believe me, I can end your torment, by whatever means necessary." The quiet severity of his words struck harder than a judge's gavel. "Is that not what you want, Miss Woolf? A man to protect you? A man who would die to keep you safe?"

She knew better. Men were vipers hiding behind polished words and fine tailoring. Still, the marquess struck her as more honourable than most. "I could never live with myself if you were harmed."

"You truly think I can be broken?"

"No, you look strong enough to fight an army." Her gaze betrayed her, drawn to the breadth of his arms beneath the fitted coat. "But we both know strength of mind matters most."

"You'll meet no one with wits sharper than mine."

What was this about? Boredom? Loneliness? He could have his choice of titled daughters, but still he lingered here. They said he was haunted by his past, and so was she. Perhaps he sensed a kinship, though she could not imagine herself his marchioness, jewels at her throat and silk upon her skin. Such pretence would dull her spirit, corrode her soul.

"A man with your generous heart deserves someone worthier," she said, certain he would one day regret being burdened with her misfortunes.

From the corner of the room, a parrot squawked, "*Show him the door!*" as if fate urged her to be rid of him.

He tsked at the birds before facing her, uttering the words every woman longed to hear. "What if I want it to be you?"

They pierced her defences, a dangerous whisper to the part of her that longed to believe him. Her resolve faltered, if only for a heartbeat. "Trust me. I'm not who you think I am."

"None of us are."

"A marriage without love will be a prison sentence."

His lips curled in a bitter sneer. "Love is a death sentence. You're intelligent enough to know that." He paused, his gaze sweeping the modest room. "Name your terms. There is nothing you could ask of me that I would not give you."

"Except love." That much was certain.

"When the poets wrote about love, they were high on opium."

"And yet you loved someone once." Only those who had been hurt were so dismissive. "Perhaps *you* should be honest with me. I'm not the first woman you've offered for." Though this was hardly a proposal of marriage, more a conundrum of sorts.

A muscle in his cheek twitched. "I was in love once, or so I believed. But she accepted my father's bribe and was never seen or heard from again. There's nothing quite like the sting of betrayal. It still throbs when least expected."

She wasn't sure which cut deeper, his father's duplicity or the woman's treachery, but it gave her a reason to enforce her refusal.

"It sounds like you're still in love with her." People often spoke in the past tense to dull the pain. "Am I your revenge? Nothing more than a token to prove you've moved on?"

She had been used before. Never again.

He studied her for one unnerving moment. "You're the air in a smoke-filled room. Somehow, I find it easier to breathe around you."

Heavens, the man was a thief in the night, out to steal a lady's sanity. But she knew better than to fall for his flattery. "Because you seek a purpose and think I fit the mould."

Perhaps he couldn't see it, but men of rank needed something to possess. Now that his friends were married, was the Marquess of Rothley looking for a pet?

"One day your lost love might return to you." She moved towards the door. "Perhaps then you'll find the answers you seek." She squared her shoulders, summoning what strength she could. "Good night, my lord. I plan to cancel my membership at The Burnished Jade. I will be leaving London soon. I doubt we'll meet again, but I wish you well."

He shook his head as if confused. "Leaving London? Where will you go?"

"As far as money allows."

"What about the friends you've made? The ladies at the club are fond of you. They'll be distraught if you leave."

She closed her eyes to the memories and the bonds of sisterhood. For the first time in her life she truly belonged, yet the past had caught up with her, leaving her no choice but to flee. "I cannot think about that now."

"There must be something I can say to change your mind."

He could swear he would never regret making the proposal, never grow to hate her in time. But that would be another lie among the many. "No. I am resigned to my decision. Please, don't ask me again."

His deep sigh almost made her falter. He looked at her for a long moment, then reached into his coat pocket. "Permit me to contribute to—"

"No!" She clamped her hand around his wrist, stalling him. The air shifted, thick with the dangerous undercurrent that always left her feeling unmoored. "Allow me some dignity. I don't need your charity."

The stalemate lasted for a heartbeat or two.

Long enough for her to imagine what it might be like to

know him better, to test his resilience, to find hope where there was none.

He withdrew his hand from his pocket and bowed with polished grace. "Wherever you are, Miss Woolf, know you always have a friend, and a place to rest should you need one."

She managed a smile. Miss Woolf wasn't her name, but it reminded her to scent danger before it struck. "That's very generous. In return, please accept this book." She offered him the volume of poetry, her companion in troubling times, pressing it firmly into his hands. "A reminder that friends may be found in the least likely places."

He smoothed his large hands over the board and glanced at the spine, his dark eyes softening. "There's nothing quite like a gift that means something. I'll not forget it. Good night, Miss Woolf."

When he left, the place felt empty, though the spicy scent of his cologne lingered, conjuring visions of a distant market in Marrakesh. The fragrance would fade, but not the memory she wished she could forget.

Strange, that he said good night, not goodbye.

Her eyes burned with tears she refused to shed.

It was foolish, but she hid behind the curtain and watched him mount his horse. He paused on the lane, scanning the graveyard and house before nudging the animal into a trot and vanishing into the gloom.

Still, she remained there, staring into the shadows, her pulse thrumming with unease. It was foolish to think she was safe out here. Somehow the marquess had found her, and in her shock she had failed to ask how. If he could track her, others could too.

"*Good riddance!*" a parrot screeched.

"Be quiet, Figaro." She didn't share the bird's sentiment. She wanted to trust the marquess. The title, the wealth, the comfort of a grand house meant nothing. But she would sell her soul for a measure of peace.

Instead, she would spend her life looking over her shoulder, with nowhere to call home, no way of discovering why the past still haunted—

A sudden thud of hooves on the lane shattered the thought. Her heart leapt to her throat. Had the marquess returned, unwilling to accept her refusal?

Hope guttered like a dying candle as she strained to see through the blackness, catching only a glimpse of a chestnut horse passing beneath a sliver of moonlight.

The rider kept his gaze ahead and continued on, swallowed by the night. The silence that followed pressed all the heavier, and she wished she wasn't so alone.

Last night she might have settled in the chair, believing herself safe. Tonight, fear stood at her shoulder, and she reached for the pistol on the mantel instead of the blanket.

Dread knotted in her stomach. She crept to the front door and scattered tacks along the threshold, as she had done every night since the first attack at her lodging house in Clerkenwell.

She knew what the blackguard wanted. The valise. He would fight to the death for it, but she had hidden it in the one place no mortal man dared to venture.

Instinct made her snuff out the candle and move cautiously to the window, keeping to the edges of the room. Her senses betrayed her: the rustle of leaves became footsteps, the groan of boughs became the creak of the back door.

Then the darkness shifted beyond the gate—subtle at first, but the shadow thickened to flesh before her eyes. A figure emerged from the night: tall, athletic, dressed head to toe in black. A beaked half-mask hid all but his mouth and the hard line of his jaw.

He had come.

Her faceless pursuer.

The devil who haunted her dreams and every waking hour between.

She turned to the African greys, resting quietly on their perch, and whispered, "It's time for the play to begin. The countess will care for you now."

At the clap of her hands, the birds broke into chorus, shrieking every phrase they had ever learned. *"Time for an encore. Take a bow. Who's there? Close the door. Hush now."* On and on they went as she slipped out through the back door and hurried down the garden path, every step mapped in her mind.

The graveyard loomed ahead, an eerie wilderness of stone crosses and moss-cloaked memorials. She passed through the rusty iron gate, opened earlier to silence its groan, and entered the domain of the dead.

The air smelled of damp earth and decay, yet tonight it was her sanctuary. She made for the mausoleum, its crumbling grandeur rising like a forgotten Roman temple, and hid behind a column. A line from Shelley came to her: *here peace dwelled, wrapped in silence*. A reminder there was nothing to fear. At least, not until the devil's call sliced through the chill night air.

"I know you're out here." The gate creaked, then came the measured clip of boots on the cobbled path, the cold click of his hammer. "This time, there'll be no second chances. There was nothing but pauper's paste in your box of jewels."

She remained as still as those in the coffins, head bent, breathing into her chest to avoid the telltale mist in the air.

"Give me what I want, and I'll let you live." The voice came from her left. No, from her right. It was impossible to tell. "I know you have it."

The irony was that she didn't know what trinket he sought among those packed into the old leather valise. She suspected he didn't either. The thought chilled her to the bone. What if the thing he wanted wasn't there and he hunted her forevermore?

The sudden crack of a twig confirmed he was close.

What to do? Run? Remain rooted? Pray?

Her mind raced through every scenario, but a shadow lunged from the right. A gloved hand seized her wrapper, yanking hard, dragging her onto the path.

Her pistol discharged amid the panic, the deafening clap ringing in her ears as the shot went wide. The acrid swirl of smoke and sulphur did nothing to deter her attacker. He wrenched the weapon from her hand, flinging it aside, then closed his fingers around her throat.

"Tell me where it is." The reek of liquor filled her nose as he squeezed tighter, thumbs pressing on her windpipe. "I know he gave it to you."

Desperation gave her strength. She would not die here. Not tonight. She twisted, driving her knee into his groin and wrenching herself free.

He let out a guttural cry, doubling over, and she stumbled to her feet and ran. Branches tore at her sleeves. She slipped on mossy stones, but the gate gaped ahead, and beyond stretched the dark lane.

A sinister laugh followed. "There's nowhere to run. Save

your legs and your breath. I'll wring the truth from you, even if it takes until morning."

Though her heart hammered and defeat seemed inevitable, she hiked up her nightclothes and ran until her lungs burned. Behind her, the devil jogged, confident he would catch his prey.

Then the thunder of hooves shook the ground beneath her feet. A muscled black stallion burst from the gloom, rearing as its rider fired a warning shot into the night air.

Olivia blinked, caught between shock and wild relief.

The marquess had returned. He'd come back for her.

"Miss Woolf," he growled, settling the beast with utter mastery. "Put your foot in the stirrup. Give me your hand. Now! Hurry!"

There was no time to protest. She reached for him as he leant down, his iron grip seizing her wrist and hauling her up as though she weighed no more than a child. She landed hard against him, swamped by his size and the solid breadth of his chest. His arm locked around her waist, holding her steady as the stallion surged forward.

Her attacker roared behind them, the crack of a pistol splitting the night. The ball sang past, harmless, yet close enough to make her flinch against the marquess' coat.

"Get down!" Lord Rothley barked, forcing her to shrink lower against him as the horse thundered along the lane. "And for heaven's sake, hold on."

She clung to him, cheek pressed to his chest, arms locked tight about his waist. The fierce rhythm of his breathing reminded her how close she had come to dying.

"What made you come back?" she asked, afraid she might never let go of him, knowing she owed him her life now. He could ask anything and she would have to agree. She was forever in his debt.

"A sick feeling in my gut," he said, cursing her attacker and promising to end the man once he was caught. "It was as if I felt your fear calling me. If I'd ignored it … if I hadn't turned back …" He muttered another profanity.

"It helps not to dwell on what might have been."

A mirthless laugh escaped him. "I've spent my entire life failing to do exactly that. It's the bane of my existence."

"We're alive. That's all that matters."

"Yes, but not free of the torment." He paused, the next words almost apologetic. "I may have led him here. In coming to offer sanctuary, I almost lost you in the process."

Lost her? He made it sound like they were star-crossed lovers, bound by fate, as if nothing mattered but finding each other. If she were not careful, this man might slip past her guard.

"None of this is your fault." What mattered now was where to go and what to do. "I'll need to ask the countess to take care of the birds while I devise a plan."

She felt the weight of his gaze before he spoke. "Rest now. We've a long ride ahead. We'll discuss this once we're home."

"Home?" She swallowed the lump in her throat. The only home she had known burned to the ground when she was fourteen. She had not stayed in one place longer than six months since.

"Studland Park." He gave her no chance to protest. "My offer still stands. Let me help you escape your past. In turn, help me escape mine. I'll afford you every freedom. You have my word."

She sat with that thought, trying to imagine how a marriage of friendship might work, but every problem she could conceive surfaced. "I wasn't raised to hold such an elevated position."

"Yet you're the most graceful woman I know."

Oh, this conversation was more dangerous than pistol fire. "Says the man accused of keeping a harem of women in his cellar. People don't invent such things without reason."

"That's something you must judge for yourself. We'll discuss it over a late supper, in the safety of my drawing room."

They reached the King's Road tollhouse, a modest brick cottage not unlike the one she had left behind. Even now she pictured the felon rifling through drawers and cupboards, desperate to uncover the item that eluded them both.

"We need to rescue the birds tonight."

"I'll have my coachman ride out," the marquess said, drawing his stallion to a halt at the tollgate. He slid his hand between them, his fingers brushing her body with a husband's familiarity, and drew a coin from his pocket. "Trust me, no one wants to meet Kincaid on a dark road."

A shutter opened, the gatekeeper's face ghostly in the lamplight. Rothley passed him a penny without a word. The man ducked his head, raised the bar, and they were away again.

"You have a house in town. Can we not rest there?" The plea was born of a need to put some distance between them, to gather her wits.

"I can protect you better at Studland Park."

"How far is it?"

"Six miles. An hour's ride, if I keep a steady pace."

An hour pressed so close she could feel each breath and

shift of muscle? An hour to decide how to repay her debt to him without risking her heart? It would feel like a lifetime.

Even this late at night, they drew looks from those souls still abroad. What must people think? "The gossip will be rife tomorrow. They'll say you kidnapped a maiden in her nightclothes and paraded her through the city."

"You'll be the latest addition to my non-existent harem. I can add devil and despoiler to my litany of sins."

Sadness crept into her heart. He had saved her life and did not deserve their censure. "The only name that springs to my mind is hero."

His sharp intake of breath matched her own. It was a foolish thing to say. Now he would think … she didn't know what he would think, and so held her tongue all the way to Islington.

She must have closed her eyes, for she started at the sound of his deep, steady voice. "We've arrived at Studland Park, Miss Woolf."

They were already halfway up the long, sweeping drive when Olivia raised her head and almost slipped from the horse in shock.

Studland Park rose from the darkness, a vast palace of pillars and pediments, built for gods, not mortals. It stood as a monument to irony. With its countless sash windows, one might expect clarity, yet for a decade the marquess had battled in the dark. Candlelight spilt from every room, though the chambers lay empty. He rarely entertained guests. Few people were welcome here.

The house was nothing but an illusion.

A gilded cage.

A prison masquerading as his sanctuary.

"Don't be alarmed," the marquess said, sensing her

unease. "Like its master, the house is far less intimidating than it appears."

Strange that a man so perceptive couldn't see what was plain to her. Sadness clung to these majestic walls as it did to the air about him. He didn't terrify her. He intrigued her, as a line of poetry did, a mystery begging to be unravelled. What lay beyond these walls and his words fascinated her more than it should.

"Things are never as they seem."

"Including you?" he said.

"Including me. You would be wise to return me to World's End." It was only right she should give him fair warning. "The last thing you need is another burden. The wrong company won't ease your loneliness."

He snorted. "Is that what you think I am? Lonely?"

The hollow look in his eyes spoke of a man more isolated by wealth than enriched by it. "Yes, and so tethered to the past, you're in danger of ruining your future."

He offered no quip, only brought the stallion to a halt before the grand entrance, its columns soaring skyward, too vast for mortal hands to have raised. A footman hurried down the steps, livery gleaming, his buttons as polished as his bow.

The marquess made no move to dismount. He kept her locked between his powerful arms, bent his head, and whispered, "I need you to cut the tethers. I need to leave the past behind. We both do."

He spoke with finality, as if he believed this moment might determine the course of their lives. How did one change such a stubborn man's mind? How could she explain she was no one's saviour?

"Help Miss Woolf down, Albert. Take her arm. An hour in the saddle can unsettle anyone."

The footman bowed low. "My lord."

He moved swiftly to her side, supporting her as she slid to the ground. But aching muscles were not the problem. The chill breeze tugged at her nightclothes, and she found herself longing for the solid warmth of Lord Rothley's chest.

Dismounting with ease, the marquess patted the stallion's neck and stroked his nose. "Tell Lumsden to take extra care of Hector tonight. We've put him through his paces. There's a discharged pistol in the saddlebag. See it's cleaned and returned to my case."

"Yes, my lord."

And then the marquess' hand was at her back, guiding her up the broad staircase towards the great oak doors. "I know it's late. But we must come to an understanding before we retire tonight."

Perhaps he might come to his senses. Perhaps she might persuade him that marriage was a foolish endeavour. That the solution to one problem might well ruin their lives.

They entered the hall, and she almost lost her footing. She didn't know where to look: at the gleaming marble floor, a mosaic of cream, black and gold, at the Roman statues standing in silent judgement in their grand alcoves. It was magnificent, yet left her cold. Beneath the splendour, she felt only sadness for the man who called this place home.

"Thank goodness you're back, my lord." A slender, dignified woman of middle years hurried forward, a lace cap set neatly over dark hair. "I've been pacing the hall for half an hour."

The marquess arched a brow. "I'm not a boy in shorts, Mrs Boswell, though I am glad you're not abed." He glanced at Olivia. "Miss Woolf will need a room prepared, and we'll require a light supper in my private drawing room. A simple collation will do."

Mrs Boswell paled. She cast a glance at the door to her left, as though the Beast of Blackwall were locked inside. "My lord. There's something you should know. You must prepare yourself."

"From your grave expression, I take it disaster has struck. Speak, Mrs Boswell."

The woman pressed her hand to her chest. "You have a visitor, my lord, waiting in the antechamber."

The marquess frowned. "A visitor? At his hour? Is it Daventry?"

Mrs Boswell's gaze flicked to Olivia, softening in silent apology. "No, my lord. It's ... It's—"

"Spit it out, Mrs Boswell."

The poor woman never had the chance. The antechamber door opened, and a vision of golden hair stepped gracefully into the hall. Her beauty struck like a blow. When she smiled, the world seemed to hold its breath. She dropped into a deep curtsy and said, with devastating familiarity, "Hello, Gabriel."

Chapter Three

Gabriel froze. He had faced ambushes, fought alongside friends in their darkest hours, endured the deepest betrayal, but nothing unsettled him like the sound of his name on this vixen's lips.

While he'd spoken of cutting ties to his past, she had walked into his house and announced herself proudly. Were it not for his need for answers, he would have instructed Mrs Boswell to march her out and bolt the door.

"Miss Bourne." He would be damned before he called her Kate. "What an unpleasant surprise. If you're here to explain your absence, you're a decade too late."

She smiled, the coquettish smile that had once fooled him into believing her lies, back when he was young, blind, and far too trusting. "I see you've not lost your talent for bluntness."

"Do not profess to know me, madam. You have no idea what manner of man I have become." And God willing, she never would.

Her gaze slid to Miss Woolf's nightclothes, and her smile

sharpened. "It seems the gossip is true. The mad marquess steals women from their beds in the dead of night and—"

"I came of my own volition," Miss Woolf countered.

The devil's own wrath surged in Gabriel's veins, but his temper abated the moment he set a hand to Miss Woolf's back. "Mrs Boswell will escort you to my private drawing room and wait with you there. I shall be but a moment."

Miss Woolf hesitated. She had defended him to a stranger, so why did he sense she would run at the first opportunity? The contradiction both frustrated and intrigued him. Could she not see their burdens would be lighter if shared?

He cast his housekeeper a knowing look, and she gestured for Miss Woolf to follow. "I'm sure you'd welcome a seat by the fire, ma'am."

Of all his rotten luck. Tonight was about solving her problems, not mastering his own. Any doubts she had about a marriage of friendship were probably gathering now, dark as a coming storm.

He watched Miss Woolf disappear through the door, his plans for the future likely vanishing with her.

"What do you want, Miss Bourne? More money?"

"Of course not."

Her hair caught the light, a halo of gold framing cherubic features. But she was no angel, only the devil who had betrayed him.

"How much did my father pay you to leave London?" How much had it cost to buy her loyalty, her integrity, to turn every loving word into a lie?

She moved towards the antechamber as if she owned the damned house. "May we sit and talk like civilised adults?"

"About what?"

"I've moved back to the manor. My aunt is ill—"

"And you're set to inherit Wynbury Hall. I know." They would be neighbours, forced into the same circles, the same church pews, when he bothered to attend. The thought was unbearable. "I asked a friend to make enquiries once I learned your aunt was bedridden." And Daventry had come up trumps.

"Please. May we sit, so I might tell you my plans and answer any questions you may have?" She smiled, like a puppet trained to entertain. "Should we not attempt to clear the air?"

Clear the bloody air? He would rather choke on it.

Yet the need to know what his father had said to her plagued him still. Nothing in his cutting statement—*Miss Bourne has shown her true colours*—revealed how easily she had been bought.

"Very well." He gestured to the antechamber and followed her inside. She sat in the red velvet chair beside the fire. He settled opposite, still on edge, as he had been since the day she disappeared. "If there's to be any peace between us, you will tell me what he paid you."

Her composure wavered, the faintest crack in her poise. "Gabriel, you must understand, my father was facing penury and had fallen out of favour with my aunt. You know she held the purse strings, and still does. Everything depends on her whims. She used every—"

"How much, Miss Bourne? And this time, address me with the respect befitting my title."

A blush rose to her cheeks, cheeks he had once stroked with the backs of his fingers as if they were the rarest thing in the world. But that had been a naive boy's fantasy. Now the sight made him grip the arms of the chair, battling the fury within.

"The marquess gave me ten thousand pounds, my lord." Her voice held a trace of shame. "And my father the same. In all, he paid twenty thousand so you would be rid of me."

The news struck like a blow to the gut, stealing his breath. The act had destroyed his relationship with his father, yet it might have been the greatest gift the man ever gave him.

"And where did you go?"

"To France."

"Alone?"

"My cousin lives in Lyon. I'm sure I mentioned her."

"You told me she lived in Avignon."

"You're mistaken, my lord."

No. She was lying.

And he was already tired of this conversation. He was no longer in awe of her beauty. It was merely a mask. Rubies and rouge could not hide a deceitful heart.

"Are you not going to ask if I'm married?" she said, catching him unawares. "If I wept for months when my father forced me to leave England? If I'm still in love with you?"

"No," he said flatly. The past was dead, and he had no interest in resurrecting it. A man had to draw a line somewhere, and his was here, with her, with what she had done ten years ago.

She flinched. "Then you are as cold as they say. You always had such a generous heart. You were kind, forgiving, the most—"

"I still am to those who deserve it."

His thoughts turned to Miss Woolf. She had stood in her humble cottage and refused the chance to become a marchioness, refused his money. She wanted peace, not him, and she had been honest enough to say so. What she thought of him now, heaven only knew.

He rose abruptly. "I'll have a footman see you home. I would hate for you to get lost en route."

Miss Bourne was on her feet, her fingers clamping around his wrist like a viper's coil. "Please, Gabriel. I made a mistake. If we're to live in such close proximity I need your forgiveness ... your friendship."

He let her hold him, waiting for a flicker of the old emotion, some spark to prove he wasn't dead inside. Nothing came. No warmth. No longing. Her treachery had robbed him of the ability to love, to feel joy, to know happiness.

"You have my forgiveness, purely because you taught me a great lesson and saved me from making a grave mistake." The words tasted bitter, for lessons bought with betrayal were the hardest to stomach. "But you lack all the virtues I seek in a friend."

Miss Bourne looked wounded. "Is she your friend, that woman in her shabby wrapper? Do you make a habit of rescuing strays? Or is it only the desperate who can abide your coldness now?"

He did feel something then, something other than anger. A desire to protect Miss Woolf, a woman he barely knew. But he'd be damned if he understood why.

"What I do is not your concern."

She stared at him, incredulous, as if she had expected to walk back into his life as though she had never been away.

He tugged his arm free of her grip and yanked the bell pull. "Albert will see you safely home."

"There's no need. I'm not a child," she snapped, buttoning the open pelisse he had barely registered. "I know these grounds well enough to walk home in the dark."

"Even so, I must insist."

She was at the door, her disappointment plain. "Mrs Boswell seemed to think I would be welcome."

Another lie. Mrs Boswell was not merely his housekeeper but the closest thing he had to family, a true confidante. She knew his darkest thoughts, his faults, his failures. "Good night, Miss Bourne."

With an irate huff she swept out, the oak door slamming in her wake. His anger boiled. He kicked the side table and damned every wicked woman who ever lived.

It was not the sight of Miss Bourne that riled him, but her accursed timing.

He braced his hands on the marble mantel, mastering the urge to lash out. "Welcome, indeed? The bare-faced cheek of it. Who the hell does she think she is?"

A light tap on the door brought Mrs Boswell.

Before she could speak, he swung around, irritation hardening into resolve. "Twenty thousand pounds. That's what my father paid to be rid of those devils." In part, the truth eased his bitterness toward the parent he believed had ruined his life. "I suspect she named her price, and my father couldn't count the notes fast enough."

Mrs Boswell's pained expression surely mirrored his own. "Forgive me, my lord. I should have turned her away, but—"

"You've watched me battle the past long enough to know I needed answers. And you were right." Though of all the infernal nights to call. "Did you know she had returned to Wynbury? No, of course not. You would have told me."

Mrs Boswell stepped forward. "I believe Miss Bourne arrived in Islington earlier today. They say her aunt won't last the week."

Merciful Lord. He hoped the woman rallied, but fate was determined to make Miss Bourne his neighbour.

"About Miss Woolf," Mrs Boswell said, her name bringing a measure of calm, though wolves were meant to chill the blood, not steady it. "She—"

"Will be staying for the foreseeable future. It's a complicated matter, but I'll explain properly in the morning. I trust you made her comfortable."

God knew he had fought hard enough to get her here.

Mrs Boswell winced as if she had stubbed her toe. "As to that ... she's gone."

The calm broke. "Gone?" A rush of alarm gripped him, fiercer than anything Miss Bourne had ever stirred. "Gone where?"

"Miss Woolf left. I tried to stop her but—"

"You let her walk out of this house? Alone? At this hour? Have you lost your senses?"

"What was I supposed to do, my lord? Chain her to the chair?"

"You were supposed to persuade her to wait." He strode to the antechamber door. "Which way did she go?"

"Through the front door." Mrs Boswell hurried after him, words tumbling as she tried to keep his pace. "I didn't want to disturb you, and Miss Woolf insisted there was no need for her to stay. She was adamant."

It wasn't his housekeeper's fault. "The lady is headstrong, and you were unaware of our plans. I'll look for her. If I've not returned in fifteen minutes, send the servants to search the grounds."

Independence might be a virtue, but if he could not command one woman beneath his roof, how was he to protect her from the vultures beyond it?

He burst through the door and flew down the steps, the drive stretching before him. Gravel crunched beneath his boots as he broke into a sprint. Hopefully, she'd not reached the road.

He scoured the darkness as he ran, then caught sight of a figure to his right. "Wait!" he called. The woman turned. It was Miss Bourne.

Cursed saints. It had to be her.

"Why should I wait? Your rudeness was unthinkable," she complained. "I know you're hurt, Gabriel, but as I've explained, I was forced into an impossible situation. It has been a decade. Can we not move past the follies of youth?"

He groaned inwardly. There was no time to dally. "Never mind. I mistook you for someone else."

He took flight again, ignoring Miss Bourne's muffled protests. A laugh escaped him as he ran. He had pictured their reunion often, but never thought he'd be so dismissive.

The drive curved ahead, the imposing gates visible in the distance. Then he saw her, the woman who could make a suave man run like an errant schoolboy. She stood beneath an ancient oak, leaning against the trunk as she shook a stone from her shoe.

Relief came first, then a pulse of excitement, an attraction born of her love of poetry and their shared disappointment with the world.

"Do you make a habit of midnight rambles, Miss Woolf?" He stopped before her, resisting the urge to brace his hands on his knees and steady his breath. "Or do you delight in watching me race down the drive like an escaped bedlamite?"

"I take no pleasure in watching you lose your dignity." She slipped her foot into her shoe and gave a satisfied nod. "You've had a dreadful shock. Should you even be outdoors?"

"No, I should be sipping brandy in the study, but you've forced me to play the errant knight twice today."

"Forced you?" Her teasing tone proved all was not lost. "You were born to play the role. Poor Hector has probably been in training since the day he stood on four legs."

"Were you not grateful I was there to whisk you away on my charger?" Though he jested, the memory chilled him to the bone. He had saved her life—of that there could be no doubt.

"No words could ever express my gratitude."

His mind ran amok then, likely due to exertion, and he conjured a host of scandalous images, all the wild, wicked ways she might thank him. But friends did not make love on a desk, nor in the stables, nor in the great marble bath in the west wing.

"Come back to the house." He made it sound like a suggestion, not a command or plea.

She glanced at the sprawling facade as if it were as hellish as Newgate. "There's something you should know about me."

"Yes?" At last, an answer to the hundred questions that plagued him daily.

"I am no one's charity case. No one's pet. No one's pawn in a scheme to wound an old flame. You used me to make your point with Miss Bourne. But some of us have real problems to—"

"So that's what you think of me? A man who plays games with women's lives?" It said more about her dealings with other men than her knowledge of him. "If I wished to make a point with Miss Bourne, I would not use you to do it."

"It's of no consequence now." She drew her wrapper close about her throat, as though arming herself for departure.

"I hope you get the answers you seek, my lord. Again, I shall bid you goodnight."

She turned, and his heart dropped to his stomach.

He had endured Miss Bourne's rejection. He could endure this as well. But despite his better judgement, he could not watch Miss Woolf walk out of his life.

"Don't go." He was at her side in a second, closing his hand gently around her arm. "Miss Bourne answered my questions. That's the end of the matter." A decade of uncertainty laid to rest in the crypt.

Miss Woolf's eyes met his. "She's exceptionally beautiful. I see why you've carried her in your heart all these years. She's not someone one easily forgets."

It was not her beauty he remembered, nor her touch, nor her laughter. It was her treachery, the wound that had hollowed him and left only bitterness in its place.

"My heart is barren, Miss Woolf. Betrayal stripped it bare. First by the friend I respected, then by the father I loved, and finally by the woman I planned to marry. What remains is resentment, nothing more."

She closed her eyes. Something he said had touched her, whether a nerve, her heart, or some old wound, he could not tell.

When she opened them, he saw the same crippling sadness that plagued his own soul. "No good can come of this. Surely you can see that. Let me leave, my lord, before it's too late."

Let me? Did she feel this inexplicable connection, too?

"Come back to the house," he said again, firmer now. "Nothing has changed. We will discuss this marriage of friendship, and you may trust I would die before I saw you harmed." He paused before issuing a fact she could not deny. "You cannot deal with this alone."

He watched the fight leave her with a resigned breath. "I will return with you tonight, in the hope that sleep restores our clarity. But there are things I cannot tell you, and it would be unfair to let you believe otherwise."

He had won the moment, not the war. Her words left a lingering uncertainty, yet one truth was clear: Miss Bourne no longer held dominion over him. That ghost was laid to rest. Whatever secrets Miss Woolf kept, she was willing to compromise. And for now, that was enough.

They walked to the house in companionable silence.

"Mrs Boswell is like family," he said as they mounted the steps. "It's important she understands why you're here. I never lie to her, though I can avoid the subject if you prefer."

"No. I would rather she hear the truth than jump to conclusions."

"And what is the truth?"

She cast him a sidelong glance as they entered the hall. "That you saved my life and offered to marry me because it suits us both. We're still considering our options."

"Put as succinctly as ever."

Mrs Boswell was pacing in the hall. A smile of relief brightened her countenance when she saw them. "Thank heavens. I was about to raise a search party."

"Miss Woolf will be staying." He braced himself, fearing his housekeeper might succumb to a fit of the vapours when she heard the rest. "I've asked her to marry me. We've decided to take a few days to see if we suit."

Mrs Boswell pursed her lips to hide a beaming smile and blinked away tears. "That is wonderful news. Truly splendid."

"No one must know I am here," Miss Woolf said quickly, almost too quickly. "It's vital it remains a secret for now."

Mrs Boswell made the obvious assumption. "Yes, of course, ma'am. You may be certain the staff are loyal to a fault. Your reputation is safe within these walls."

"Tell Molière we have company and to amend the menus accordingly." He arched a covert brow at Mrs Boswell when she failed to stop grinning. "It's been a long day. Miss Woolf would like to retire once her room is prepared."

"Certainly, my lord. The Peacock Room in the guest wing is ready. I took the liberty of leaving a fresh nightgown on the bed. One never knows when guests might arrive half-frozen or in need of a bath."

Gabriel almost smiled. Mrs Boswell's excitement was uncharacteristic, but perhaps it was contagious, for there was something oddly satisfying about having Miss Woolf in his house.

"Follow me, Miss Woolf," Mrs Boswell said.

The woman was a step ahead when he interjected, compelled by the need to escort Miss Woolf to her chamber himself. "You may lock the doors and retire. I shall show Miss Woolf to her room. If I can still remember the way."

"Of course, my lord." Mrs Boswell grinned again.

He shook his head faintly. The woman had the air of a matchmaker. Soon she'd be inviting the vicar to join her for tea.

They climbed the staircase, the plush red carpet cushioning their steps, the gilt balustrades gleaming in the candlelight. Portraits stared down from the high walls, rows of ancestors in silks and armour, their painted eyes following every move.

Miss Woolf's gaze flicked from the chandeliers above to

the endless rise of steps, a tension in her shoulders betraying how easily splendour could smother.

"They're merely things, Miss Woolf," he said, reading her silence. "Objects collected over the years, ornaments to distract a family from its troubles. Gray was right. Strip this away and there's no difference between us."

"The more we have, the more we think we need," she said.

"A curse of the aristocracy."

He led her through the endless corridors, their footsteps the only sound, yet memories invaded his mind. Wild parties. Incessant laughter. Drunken songs and licentious acts, nightmares for a young boy. Some wounds were not soothed by wealth, nor time.

He glanced at Miss Woolf. In her, he saw civility, intelligence and grace. Perhaps that's why he clung to her friendship.

"Ah, here at last." He paused at the guest chamber, opened the door, and stepped aside. "The Peacock Room, named for its exotic wallpaper. The bird is a symbol of new beginnings. Fitting that you should sleep here tonight."

She entered the candlelit room, passing close enough to stir that same whisper of familiarity he'd felt at The Burnished Jade. "It's a beautiful room," she said, crossing to the hearth to warm her hands. "I'm sure I'll be comfortable, if not a little lost."

"You'll be safe. That's all that matters." He drew her attention to the bell pull. "The maids are on hand should you need anything." He paused, wanting to ask if she'd read the new anonymous poem, and what she thought of someone baring their soul in such a raw confession. "Good night, Miss

Woolf. Do I have your word you'll remain here until morning?"

"You have my word." She returned to the door, her gaze lingering on him a moment longer. "Good night, my lord."

He stood in the corridor as she closed the door and turned the key. After the terrifying events of the evening, he should have gone straight for the brandy decanter. Instead, he found himself smiling. After a decade of shadows, the house itself seemed to draw its first steady breath.

And, remarkably, so did he.

Chapter Four

Olivia woke to stillness, not to the cries of London's costermongers, nor to birds singing in the boughs of the oak tree outside her cottage. To nothing but a quiet peace, the likes of which she had never known.

For once, she hadn't scrambled to the window to study every passerby, nor paused in doorways, terrified the devil might strike. Her attacker would need to breach the iron gates, force his way through the house, and hunt a labyrinth of rooms to reach her. There were plenty of places to hide, countless routes of escape, and a dedicated staff ready to come to her aid.

But her troubles were far from over. She could not remain in the Peacock Room, with its gilded walls and opulent furnishings, forever. And looming over her was the lord's shocking proposal.

Even now, lying in a bed large enough for five, the events of last night seemed like a strange dream. Marriage to a marquess? To Lord Rothley? The most perplexing man she had ever encountered. Stern yet kind. Indifferent yet attentive.

Cold, yet so warm she had burned when pressed to his hard body.

He had saved her life and offered her sanctuary.

What confounded her most was why?

She feared her first thought was correct. When spurned by a beautiful woman, a man sought a means of retribution. By his own admission, he was tethered to the past and the incomparable Miss Bourne. Where would that leave her when they rekindled old feelings, when they remembered why they'd fallen in love?

Yet despite all her doubts, she needed him. To her astonishment, he professed to needing her too, and a marriage built on friendship was surely preferable to being an inconvenient wife. But friendship demanded honesty. She would have to reveal something of the truth. For within the valise lay the key to escaping her pursuer.

She rose abruptly, the chill in the room sending shivers down her spine. Drawing back the curtain, she looked out across fields bathed in morning light. The peaceful scene stirred memories of her beloved home in Lewes, and with them came the piercing ache of all she had lost.

Then she saw him, the indomitable Marquess of Rothley, striding across the grass in an open-necked shirt, his greatcoat billowing in the breeze as he threw a stick for a grey, shaggy dog the size of a pony.

Something in the easy power of his movements, in the unexpected playfulness with the dog, tightened her chest, and she couldn't tear her gaze away.

"Is this who you truly are when the world isn't watching?" She pressed her hand to the cold pane, longing to know. He seemed a different man beneath the reserved facade, a truth she craved but was afraid to uncover.

She might have lingered at the window until he vanished from sight, but a knock on the door made her start. Her heart leapt to her throat as the knob turned slowly, then she remembered it was locked.

"Miss Woolf? Are you awake? I have the valise."

Though she recognised Mrs Boswell's voice, the last word made her draw a sharp breath. *The valise? Her valise? Impossible.*

"Just a moment." She opened the door to the cheerful housekeeper, pasting an innocent smile when she wanted to snatch the bag and make sure it wasn't the one she had hidden in the coffin.

"I thought it best to bring it up myself." Mrs Boswell entered, setting a brown leather valise on the side table, embossed with Lord Rothley's initials. "His lordship insisted on packing your things himself. I can't vouch for what he chose, but if anything is missing, you can blame him."

Olivia swallowed. "Lord Rothley returned to World's End? When?" She recalled a distant clock chiming two before she finally succumbed to sleep.

"Last night. He took the carriage and brought back the birds. They're keeping the staff entertained in the servants' quarters."

As the housekeeper opened the bag, a trace of the lord's exotic cologne escaped. Good heavens. He'd packed her undergarments into his own valise. He would have searched her cupboards, rifled through drawers, and touched her stockings.

"Did he say what he found there?" She closed her eyes against a vision of ransacked rooms and books tossed aside. Mrs Hodge would demand an explanation, seeing as she owned the quaint cottage.

"You'll need to speak to his lordship." Mrs Boswell withdrew a folded petticoat and gave it a brisk shake. "He's asked to see you in his study at midday."

"I shall need directions." It was easier to navigate the warrens of Shadwell than the corridors of Studland Park.

"His lordship's quarters are easy enough to find." She laid the garment on the bed before searching the bag for stockings. "The study is next to the drawing room where you sat last night. You'll find the library there. All part of the small cluster of rooms he keeps to himself in the east wing."

"The library?" She had forgotten about the books. A house as magnificent as this would surely boast a vast collection, with cases rising from floor to ceiling. "Do you think I might borrow a volume or two?"

"There's the Great Library," Mrs Boswell said, pride warming her tone. "More than twenty thousand books, some dating back to the thirteenth century." She tucked more garments under her arm while rooting one-handed through the bag. "Then there's his lordship's personal library, where he keeps his own collection of poetry."

Olivia's lips curved. An entire collection? It would be akin to standing before a confectioner's window, every treat an impossible temptation.

"His lordship said you're free to browse the shelves and select something to read, on condition you discuss your choice during dinner." Mrs Boswell rummaged deeper into the bag and grumbled beneath her breath. "Trust a man. He's forgotten the one thing no woman can do without."

"A pocket pistol?"

"No. A corset."

Olivia's breath caught. Without a corset, she might as well be half-dressed. And yet last night she had clung to Lord

Rothley, wearing nothing more than a nightgown and wrapper.

She forced a smile. "Pay it no mind, Mrs Boswell. I shall manage without, and will keep mostly to my room."

The housekeeper tutted. "Are you in half-mourning, Miss Woolf? Both dresses he's packed are grey. Best the staff are made aware."

"Not anymore, but I prefer to blend into the background."

Fewer people noticed a drab woman walking the streets. It was easier to vanish in the crowd. In safe places, she had dared to wear blue, but nowhere felt safe anymore.

Mrs Boswell's eyes went to Olivia's hair, and she smiled. "I'm not sure you could ever blend in, ma'am. You bring brightness to a room without trying."

The words caught Olivia off guard. She had never seen herself that way. And yet, there had been something in the marquess' eyes when he looked at her hair. Something that made her pulse quicken.

"Few ladies could hope to outshine Miss Bourne," she said.

The housekeeper practically snarled. "I can't imagine you would be overshadowed by anyone. Goodness comes from within. And yours shines clear as day."

She swallowed hard against the sting of tears. "That's the kindest thing anyone has ever said to me, Mrs Boswell. But his lordship hardly knows me."

Guilt rose unbidden. Mrs Boswell didn't know she was dealing with a fool, a woman too trusting by half. Olivia would be branded a felon if the truth came to light. It was why she had to know what secret lay within that dratted valise.

"Despite what happened years ago, his lordship is an

excellent judge of character." Mrs Boswell spoke with calm assurance. "He's rarely wrong in his assessments."

But he was wrong about her. He would see it in time.

"If he's welcomed you into his home, then there's no greater proof of his faith." The housekeeper held Olivia's gaze, the look like a silent plea. "I only hope you appreciate his efforts. One more disappointment, and I fear the darkness will claim him forever."

Olivia feared it was already too late. The darkness in Lord Rothley was not mere melancholy but a hard edge honed by betrayal. It made him dangerous and, dare she admit, all the more compelling.

"I owe him my life, Mrs Boswell. A debt I shall endeavour to repay."

Mrs Boswell's smile carried a fragile kind of trust. "May I ask something of you, Miss Woolf? Something that stays between us?"

"Of course."

The housekeeper reached for her hand, her clasp firm. "If you're thinking of leaving, will you inform me first? Or at least write his lordship a letter explaining why, so he's not left wondering?"

There was something raw in her voice, a sadness buried deep. It was plain this woman cared for the marquess as a mother does a son. For a moment, Olivia envied him that devotion.

"Should I need to alter my plans, you'll be the first to know, Mrs Boswell."

The woman's relief was palpable. "Let me help you dress. You can eat while you wait for his lordship to return from his walk."

"Thank you, but I can manage." She had dismissed her

maid a few weeks ago. The risk to life was too great, and trust grew harder by the day. "I've grown accustomed to being independent."

Yet she would be dead had Lord Rothley not come when he did.

"Very well. I daresay you'll find the task easier without a corset. I'll leave you to wash and change. A maid will be up shortly to see to your room."

"Thank you, Mrs Boswell." The housekeeper was already halfway out the door when Olivia felt compelled to say, "If I do decide to leave, it will be because I cannot bear to disappoint him."

"Then I expect you'll be here for some time." Mrs Boswell's smile softened. "If you'd like peace to think, might I suggest you choose a book before he returns from his walk? Otherwise, he'll want to hear the reasoning behind every choice."

Keen to see the library, she dressed in haste. The corridors proved harder to navigate than Mrs Boswell had claimed, each one a near reflection of the last. She stopped a footman to ask the way to the east wing, for she had passed the same grumpy-faced man in a portrait twice, and he looked no more welcoming the second time.

She found the drawing room from last night. The footman had said the library was the last door on the right. With a quick breath, she tapped lightly and slipped inside.

Excitement fluttered in her stomach, for this was no ordinary room. Narrow yet impressive, it rose from floor to cornice with shelves of leather-bound books, a sanctuary of secrets waiting to be uncovered. A fresco ceiling of cherubs in gold and blue arched overhead, and a tall sash window cast pale light over the solitary chair.

"This is marvellous." She trailed a finger along the spines. "Pope's *Essay on Man*," she whispered. "Goldsmith's *The Deserted Village*. Byron's *Childe Harold*."

The last name lingered on her tongue, conjuring the image of a dark, restless wanderer. Yet Lord Rothley reminded her more of Byron's *Corsair*. Formidable, untamed, and bound by his own relentless code.

"It's an impossible choice," she murmured, her hand trailing over the carved panel as her eyes wandered the spines. A haven of words where she could lose herself for hours.

That's when she noticed the bookcase set askew, behind it the faint, steady trickle of water. Could it be a secret door?

Curiosity tugged her closer. She pressed, and the panel yielded, releasing a draught laced with the marquess' scent, warm spice threaded with musk, worldly yet unmistakably his. The very air declared this was a gentleman's domain. One man's in particular.

Through the half-open door, she glimpsed him at the washstand. Bare-chested. A towel fastened around his lean hips. Water slid over the ridges of his torso as he reached for a cloth.

Her breath caught. She ought to turn away, yet her gaze lingered. No wonder they said he kept a harem of women. A man of his size and strength must have a hunger that never waned.

Broad shoulders caught the morning light, every line of muscle a testament to his power and command. His back, straight as a blade, belonged to a man who bent to neither fortune nor fear. Even the ease of his movements revealed control and an unyielding resolve.

She had come upon a private moment, yet it was impossible not to look, impossible not to feel his allure. She could smell his cologne on her clothes, as consuming as his presence now.

"Miss Woolf?" His low voice broke the hush, as if he had known she was there all along. "Admiring the view?"

Merciful Lord.

She fought the urge to bolt. "Forgive me. I thought you were out walking. I heard water and feared a leak. It would be a tragedy if the books were damaged."

He turned to her, amusement flickering in his obsidian eyes, though her gaze kept straying to his chest. "A leak? On the ground floor?"

"Someone with your wealth might have modern plumbing."

"No pipes, Miss Woolf. Only water, steam, and a man with nothing to hide."

Why wasn't he reaching for a robe?

Why wasn't she leaving?

Because their battle of wills left her as breathless as any embrace.

"That's not entirely true, my lord. A towel still guards your modesty."

A faint smile touched his lips. "Modesty is a fragile thing. One careless tug, and the towel is gone." He raised a challenging brow. "Tell me, Miss Woolf. Are you afraid? Would you hide your eyes or hold your ground?"

She stepped into his room, squaring her shoulders, determined to prove a point. He was a master of intimidation, but she would not yield. "I was almost strangled in a graveyard. I believe I can endure your scandalous behaviour."

"Scandalous? Says the woman bold enough to appear in a dress without a corset."

"You forgot to pack one."

"How careless of me."

"I confess I was surprised, for a man so astute."

"Call it an oversight. I've not undressed a woman in years. I'll endeavour to be more attentive in future. Shall I send a maid to town? I would hate to think you lacked ... support."

"On the contrary. It's the first time in years I've felt free."

His gaze dipped to her breasts. A flicker of triumph warmed her chest, followed by a heat that burned deeper, coiling low. For all his intelligence and distinguished drawl, he was dangerous.

She arched a brow. "If you're done teasing me, my lord, perhaps you'll put on a shirt so I may concentrate on our conversation."

A light twinkled in eyes of black satin. "I'm a gentleman, Miss Woolf, and this situation has far exceeded the bounds of propriety. Wait for me in my study, and we'll continue this thrilling conversation there."

It was entirely the right thing to do.

So she inclined her head, her composure intact, though her pulse raced like she'd won a private battle. "Have you eaten?"

"Not yet."

"Would you prefer if we spoke at the dining table?"

"That depends on what secret you mean to tell me. I'd rather not choke on kippers and coddled eggs."

She shifted uncomfortably, and not because he had a physique to rival a Greek god. It was the weight of his gaze, the unspoken expectation. He would demand the truth, and once spoken there would be no turning back.

"Then I shall ask Mrs Boswell to prepare a basket so we

might eat on the road. There's an important item we must recover."

His gaze sharpened. "Am I permitted to know where we're going?"

"Back to World's End."

He gave a low hum. "You have a talent for leading me in circles, Miss Woolf." The smile that touched his lips held a spark of amusement. "Very well. I shall meet you in the mews in half an hour."

"Shall I ask Mrs Boswell to summon your coachman?"

"No. You will inform her of our arrangements." His mouth quirked as his gaze ventured over her dull grey dress. "A marchioness in training never asks. It unsettles the staff." His voice dropped, smooth as velvet over steel. "Remember that, should you choose to be my bride."

A marriage of friendship had been a fool's notion. He'd been a greater fool to voice it. Perhaps the encounter with Miss Bourne had unsettled him, yet his thoughts strayed to the woman in his carriage and the fact she had seen him near naked.

Passion unravelled men and made rakes of them. Miss Woolf had spent one night beneath his roof, and already he had behaved like a libertine.

She could never know how close he'd come to letting the towel fall, how often he had tempered his desire when her gaze lingered and her lips parted. That curious look in her blue eyes would haunt his dreams.

"Are we to spend the journey admiring the hedgerows from opposite corners of the carriage?" he said, keen to put all amorous thoughts far from his mind. "Or will you explain why I failed to collect this important item when I rescued the parrots last night?"

"I wasn't thinking clearly last night."

He hadn't thought clearly since she clung to him as Hector thundered along the dark lane, her hands hot on his back, her body pressed so close he memorised every forbidden curve. And now, in the morning light, the sun caught her copper hair, unshielded by a bonnet he had neglected to pack, its brilliance seared into his mind.

He forced his gaze away. "Be honest. You weren't ready to make a confession."

"You're right. I have everything to lose, and the thought of sharing secrets makes me nervous." She licked a trace of butter from her lip, and he almost groaned aloud. "Besides, such things are best tackled during daylight hours."

Yet she seemed cloaked in shadow.

"Strange. You put me in mind of Geraldine in *Christabel*. So much of you is shrouded in mystery. Will it always be that way, I wonder?"

Any man who got too close to Geraldine found himself undone. After this morning's encounter, he was already losing ground.

"You fear you'll repeat past mistakes?" she asked.

He gave a derisive snort. He feared nothing but looking like a fool. Yet here he was, striving to trust a woman when he had every cause not to. "Doesn't everyone?"

"Sometimes we suffer for other people's mistakes and are fooled into thinking they're our own. That is certainly true in your case. The sin was not yours to bear."

Ignorance was no excuse. He should have seen the signs.

"A man cannot live without faith in someone." She delved

into the basket, took a cold sausage roll wrapped in a napkin and cut it in two, offering him the larger half with a quiet smile. "To lose faith entirely would be tragic."

He took the roll, sat back and studied her. "You mean I'm a stronger man for putting my faith in you, Miss Woolf?"

"We both have much to lose."

"Yet you intend to keep me in the dark to some degree."

"Only if I feel it's in your best interest."

"Shouldn't I be the judge of that?"

She fell silent, long enough for him to think she would say nothing at all. "I shouldn't admit it, but I'm afraid. Afraid for myself. Afraid for you. I don't want to be the reason you spend another decade believing women can't be trusted."

He was in danger of that regardless. "Then let's make a pact to share information when necessary." Trust was a commodity he had never bartered for—until now.

She gave a thoughtful nod. "I can do that."

It felt like a minor victory, though victories seldom lasted. Friendship demanded honesty. "Let's begin with something simple. What are we hoping to retrieve from the cottage?"

"Nothing. What we need is in the graveyard."

Hell. This woman piqued his interest at every turn. "Something you buried deep in hallowed ground?" He was confident his coachman had a spade and they wouldn't need to claw at the earth with bare hands.

"No, in the mausoleum."

Why the devil had she hidden it there?

"Something stolen, perhaps?" Why else was the villain stalking her? Whatever she had taken, he was willing to kill to reclaim it.

"No. Something my father left me for safekeeping."

"Is your father alive?"

"He died a year ago."

"My condolences. Though something tells me he didn't die peacefully in his sleep."

Her grave expression warned of something sinister, but he was not prepared for her confession.

"He was found dead in the woods." She hesitated, then described a murder scene all too familiar, for he had envisioned it every day for a decade: a body identified by nothing more than his personal effects. "He was buried in Cambridge, though he left me a letter insisting I disappear and never visit his grave."

The woods again. Another body stripped of its identity. Another grave built on lies. Ten years had passed since Justin's death, yet the wound still bled.

His fingers tightened on the seat. "Was he found in Cambridge?"

"A mile outside, near the village of—"

"Coton?"

"Yes, in a hideout used by gamekeepers."

He swallowed, but the tightness remained. Was that why he was drawn to this woman? Because fate had a cruel sense of humour?

Silence settled, the past pressing down on them both. Ten years of pursuit, and still the culprit eluded him. Her fear was not without cause.

"How do you support yourself? Did your father leave you an annuity?"

Money left trails.

Money revealed loyalties.

The ghosts could wait. They needed to focus on the facts.

"Are you in contact with other family members?"

Answers existed, and he would wrest them free.

She looked at him keenly. "I shall tell you, but when the time comes for me to question you about the past, please remember I have been forthcoming."

He inclined his head in acquiescence.

"The answer to your questions is no. No solicitors. He was quite firm. No documents to trace." Furrows lined her brow. Clearly, she had spent the last year as confused as he was now. "No trail to follow. Just a pouch of sovereigns, a handwritten poem and an old iron key."

"A poem and a key," he repeated, curiosity edging past his control. His gaze stayed on the iron clasp of her hands rather than her eyes. "Do you have them with you?"

"My lord, I came to you wearing little more than a nightgown," she said, though he didn't need reminding. "I was told to memorise the poem and burn it. The message hidden within it brought me here."

He straightened. The urge to hear the poem was almost as compelling as the need to learn what she had hidden in the mausoleum.

"Here? Meaning London?"

"The poem is entitled World's End."

Written in the graveyard style, it was hardly surprising.

"I visited a place in Buckinghamshire first, a hamlet by the same name, and scoured every graveyard within five miles, convinced my father meant for me to find whatever the key unlocks."

He was impressed. To destroy her only proof and sear it into memory took intelligence as well as courage. He understood the torment well enough, the burning need for answers, whatever the cost.

"And your search for World's End led you here to London?"

She drew a slow breath. "Yes, but please don't think ill of me when I recite a line or two of the poem."

"Why would I think ill of you?" His admiration had reached new heights, though he knew disappointment would clatter in like a late stagecoach.

She composed herself, then recited with quiet grace:

*"The air is thin, the light a grudging lure,
the burnished jade, a deathless dream still pure."*

Gabriel stilled. Symbolism he'd expected. But here, the message was plain. "You think your father meant for you to visit The Burnished Jade?" The words implied the club was not simply a destination—but the secret itself.

"I don't know what my father's motives were. But in leaving me with the valise, he placed me in grave danger."

"Perhaps he knew it was your only security?" he said.

"Perhaps." She gave no more and turned to the window as the carriage rolled to a stop outside her cottage. "I'll need to visit Mrs Hodge while we're here and offer some explanation for my leaving."

"Tell her the truth."

"Which is?"

"You're marrying, and the proposal was unexpected."

She worried her lip. "You may change your mind. I'm not sure you'll even consider me a friend when all is said and done."

There it was. The warning that should have chilled him, yet it only drew him closer. What was it about her that fascinated him? Her clothes carried his scent, and that thought stirred something primal.

The carriage rocked as Kincaid climbed down from his

box. They had come to World's End in an unmarked vehicle, his man dressed for highway robbery. This was no time to look weak.

"You're certain you want to do this?" she said as the Scotsman waited for Gabriel's nod before opening the door and lowering the steps. "I fear once we leave here, our lives will be inextricably woven together."

The thought of their lives bound stirred something dangerously close to desire. Yet he would do well to remember she had been keeping secrets for months, lying to her closest friends. That her kindness might be an illusion.

"There is one thing you should know about *me,* Miss Woolf. I have a passion for puzzles. Now show me what you're hiding in that damned mausoleum."

Chapter Five

She had told him more than she ought, yet he was easy to talk to, and one question had led to another. How long before all her secrets came tumbling out? Not long, she feared, because her thoughts kept straying to the memory of his broad chest, and the subtle intimacy that lingered between them.

It did not bode well for the future.

Friends did not look at one another's mouths while eating French pastries. Friends did not draw a sharp breath every time their knees brushed. And anyone who had spent time in a carriage with Lord Rothley knew his thighs left no room for escape.

The man in question turned to his coachman, a fellow who matched his master in brawn but lacked his finesse. "Follow us into the graveyard, but be on your guard." He scanned their surroundings, gaze narrowing. "There's a chance we're being watched."

"Aye, if there's anyone lurking, I'll haul them out by the scruff."

"Should you encounter the fiend, I need him alive."

"But I can rough him up a bit, so long as he's breathing?"

"Aye," Lord Rothley teased. "But dinna break him before I get my answers. Leave him a face his mother would still ken."

They spoke like comrades-in-arms, not master and servant. For Olivia, it was a revelation. She had always seen Lord Rothley as strong, intelligent, and possessed of a wry sense of humour. But here was something new. A playful side she had never witnessed before.

"We need to enter the cottage to retrieve the key to the mausoleum," she said, making for the rickety gate. "And I'd like to pack my things first in case we're forced to leave in a hurry."

Lord Rothley jerked his head. "You left the key behind?"

"I was in nightclothes, and the villain would have searched me, expecting to find it. Better to hide it in plain sight."

His brow lifted, as if faintly impressed by her reasoning. He drew an iron key from his waistcoat pocket. "You'll need this. I locked the back door when I left last night."

Something in his tone betrayed him.

"My attacker has been in the house, hasn't he?" She shuddered, fearing it wasn't a question but a grim certainty. What had he touched? What had he taken?

"Yes." His fingers closed around her arm, the gentleness at odds with his words. "We found drawers and cupboards ransacked, chairs overturned. He was likely searching for your mysterious object."

Doubtless, the place was a shambles. But the thought vanished beneath the warmth of his hand, the steadiness of his touch, and the unsettling truth that she didn't want him to let go.

"There's a cart approaching," Mr Kincaid said, sounding like an escaped felon hiding from the watchmen. "Best get the lady out o' sight."

The marquess released her, and she felt all the colder for it. He steered her along the narrow path to the rear of the house and stood guard as she opened the cottage door.

She braced herself, barely able to look as she passed through the small kitchen. But the chairs were pushed neatly against the table, the cupboards closed, the stone floor clutter-free.

Lord Rothley cleared his throat. "The intruder was almost mindless in his destruction. We put right what we could, in the hope of sparing you any distress."

She pictured him, weary in the dead of night, fixing a problem not of his making. "I'm extremely grateful. I must thank your coachman."

"Kincaid tidied the rooms below. I dealt with the disorder in your bedchamber."

The confession hung in the air for a heartbeat. How long had he been there? Folding her nightgowns, fingertips grazing the silk that warmed her skin.

"I ought to blush, but you've already rifled through my stockings."

His mouth quirked. "You might rephrase that. It gives quite the wrong impression to anyone listening."

"There's no one here but us." Yet she could not shake the sense of unseen eyes, of a villain who would stop at nothing to find the valise.

"Then you should know I've touched all your belongings."

"All except my corsets, it seems."

"No," he mused. "I touched those as well."

These playful exchanges reached some desolate place inside her. It was surprising that a man as sombre as the marquess could bring light to her darkness.

"I'm sorry to say you'll need to handle them again. We must pack with haste, fetch the valise from the mausoleum, and leave here before the devil returns."

"The valise?"

"I'll explain once we reach Studland Park."

They moved to the stairs. The tacks she'd scattered across the threshold were gone. "You swept the hall?"

"Kincaid did. I was too busy with your petticoats."

Pushing aside the image of his hands on her undergarments, she mounted the narrow stairs. He followed, casting the steps in shadow, his nearness causing an odd flutter in her belly.

She held her breath before entering her chamber. The space was neat, almost as if a maid had set it straight, yet a beast had prowled through her domain, and she wasn't referring to the marquess.

As they packed her clothes into the portmanteau, the marquess asked, "Where are the gowns you wore to the recitals at The Jade? I see nothing here but serviceable dresses."

"I hired them from a second-hand dealer in Covent Garden. Borrowed some from the countess. I left my father's home with nothing but the few belongings I could carry, a pouch of sovereigns and my mother's jewels." And a message to run and never look back.

His mouth tightened. "A father should protect his daughter, not feed her to the wolves. This whole business reeks of neglect."

Her throat constricted. Anger rose, not at Lord Rothley

but at the memory of the man who had failed her so completely. "I'm a stronger person for it," she said, though she was so tired she could sleep standing. A wave of heat swept through her, and she pressed a hand to her brow. "Is it hot in here? I'm finding it a little hard to breathe."

"No, it's so draughty one wonders how you slept at night."

Perhaps it was the daunting prospect of opening the coffin that made her head spin so fast she felt dizzy. "Let's hurry. I'll take the bonnet in the bandbox. That should suffice."

"What about the key to the mausoleum?"

"It's here, hiding in plain sight." She plucked the key from the armoire door and tucked it inside her glove.

He gave a hum of approval. "Ingenious. Who would think to take the key when the door is already open?"

"Precisely."

"You should have been a spy, Miss Woolf." He lifted her portmanteau as if it weighed nothing and headed for the door. "You certainly think like one."

She laughed lightly, hoping it hid the frisson of panic. If only he knew the truth: she'd grown up in a house where secrets were daily fare, her father the greatest conspirator of them all.

Outside, Mr Kincaid loaded her luggage, then did as his lordship requested and readied both pistols he'd taken from the walnut box beneath the seat.

The Scotsman fell into step behind them, the gate groaning as they entered the deserted graveyard. "They say the earth weeps when a man dies. Dinna look like it weeps much here."

In the cold light of day, the place looked less like hallowed ground and more like a neglected garden, with headstones leaning at odd angles, grass growing wild between the paths. A blackbird trilled from the yew, heedless of the silence that hung heavy over the stones.

Fragments of memory burst through her mind: gloved fingers at her throat, the horrid bird mask, her stumbling, scrabbling to her feet, the fear that every breath might be her last.

She gripped Lord Rothley's arm, and he started as if he'd heard a coffin creak. "Forgive me. I feel a little unwell."

"After what you endured last night, it's to be expected." He drew her hand tighter around his arm. "Lean on me."

Lean on him? She felt like collapsing and relinquishing every burden. But the less he knew, the better. Though keeping secrets from this man was akin to holding back the tide with her bare hands.

"Do you recall anything about your attacker?" he said.

"You mean his build or hair colour?"

"Yes. Anything to help identify him."

She tried to concentrate, but her thoughts were hazy, like a fog slowly closing in. "It all happened so quickly."

"You must tell me if you remember anything."

"I will," she said, for it was one vow she could keep.

They stopped before the mausoleum, and as she drew the cold metal from her glove, she wondered again how her father had come by the key.

"I shall ask you one last time, my lord. Will you not turn back and forget you ever met me?" He risked his life for someone unworthy. Did that not make her as wicked as Miss Bourne? "I fear this won't end well for either of us."

He surprised her with an amused snort. "Nothing in my life has ended well, Miss Woolf. Why should this be any different?"

"Perhaps your pessimism is the problem?"

"Shall I try to be more cheerful?"

"Yes. Because if we choose this path, I'd rather our days be filled with hope than regret."

He laughed, almost to himself. "I know what hope looks like to me. Though on that score, I doubt we think alike."

To her, hope was a day without worry, a day when something other than sadness filled her heart, when she might glimpse the marquess at his washstand and feel every nerve tingle to life.

"So, the valise we need is inside the mausoleum?" he asked.

"I hid it there for safekeeping. I'm certain that's why my father gave me the key. The poem speaks of a place of secrets, and where better to hide one than a coffin?"

"A coffin?" He drew his head back. "You opened a casket?"

"I had no choice."

"Did he say what he wanted you to do with the valise?"

She shook her head. "Take it and run, I suppose. Will you wait here while I fetch the bag?"

Mr Kincaid chuckled. "Wait here? You're askin' the most inquisitive man in England to bide outside? Not a chance, lass."

"As you can see, Miss Woolf, I'm but a puppet, and my coachman speaks for me."

"Aye, and I've nae been wrong yet."

She glanced warily about and stepped towards the iron door, but the marquess claimed the key, intent on playing the gentleman. The hinges groaned under his hand, releasing a rush of cold air, sharp with damp and decay.

Three tombs lay within. Two were fine stone, angels etched upon their lids, the inscriptions speaking of devotion.

"Mr Lucius Hathaway and his beloved wife," she murmured.

"And the other?" Rothley nodded to the crude wooden casket on the floor. "Their servant, perhaps?"

"There's no inscription. I searched there first because I lacked the strength to move the stone."

Without another word, he crouched beside the coffin, his trousers pulling taut over his thighs as he set his broad hands to the lid and heaved. The wood creaked in protest. Olivia's stomach clenched, her pulse quickening as she watched, praying the bag was still inside.

Dust drifted as the lid gave way. Inside lay a long, shapeless form swathed in a grey shroud, the fabric brittle with age. Nestled at the bottom, tucked beneath the folds of cloth, was the battered leather bag.

Her breath caught. Relief warred with dread.

That bag was the bane of her existence.

"I cannot believe you dealt with this issue alone," Lord Rothley said, removing the valise and swiftly replacing the coffin lid. "Why the devil didn't you accept my help? I offered countless times after the robbery at your lodging house."

Oh, she had longed to clasp his hand and say yes. But he was a marquess, and she the daughter of a spy. And the countess' words had forced her to keep her distance.

If Rothley asks, you should dance with him. After all, he needs to know there are good, honest women in the world.

But she had deceived them all—even her closest friends.

Tears gathered behind her eyes.

She longed for an end to the nightmare. And the more

time she spent in his company, the more she suspected he might be the one to save her.

"Miss Woolf?" His deep voice pulled her from her reverie. "Are you ready to leave? Is there anything else we need here?"

He used the word *we* again, as if fate had bound them together.

"No, just the valise." She pressed her fingers to her brow, surprised by the heat of her skin when the mausoleum was ice-cold.

"It's light. Are you certain what you need is in here?" He weighed the bag in his hand, a faint rattle sounding as the contents knocked together.

"Quite certain. It's empty but for a handful of curious things. We'll examine them together once we're safely back at Studland Park."

There was an odd glint in his eyes. Perhaps intrigue. Or perhaps he was simply unused to being included in a woman's plans.

They left the mausoleum, locking the door behind them.

Mr Kincaid eyed the valise in the marquess' hand and gave a wry grin. "Best hope the soul in that coffin doesna come knockin' for what's his. Folk say the restless never sleep easy. 'Tis a bad omen, make no mistake."

Lord Rothley shot his coachman a sharp look. "That will do, Kincaid. The valise belongs to Miss Woolf."

The coachman looked at her and frowned. "Are ye well, lass? Ye look like ye've been toastin' your cockles on the fire."

"I'm quite well," she lied, though her head throbbed and the ground seemed to tilt beneath her feet. "It's nothing a little rest won't cure."

Lord Rothley's hand closed over her arm, steady and unbearably hot against her already fevered skin. "Kincaid is right. We'll not remain here a moment longer."

She didn't argue. Her eyelids felt heavy, her chest tight. Perhaps she'd caught a chill from the long ride to Islington last night.

They were about to climb into the carriage when Mrs Hodge came hurrying along the lane, waving and calling Olivia's name. Heavens, her mind was so clouded she had forgotten to visit her landlady.

Olivia mustered a smile as the lithe, pinched-faced woman drew near. "Mrs Hodge. I was about to call and return the key to the cottage."

"Return the key? You're leaving?" Concern furrowed her brow as she studied the marquess with obvious unease. "You never mentioned a trip when you agreed to the contract."

"No. My aunt is taken ill, and I've been summoned to Brighton." The lie came easily. She was proficient at something at least. "The rent is paid until the end of next month, and you may keep my deposit."

She dared not glance at Lord Rothley, though she sensed his eyes upon her, measuring every word.

"And these gentlemen are friends of yours, Miss Woolf? I only ask because I thought I heard shots fired on the road last night, and there's talk of strangers roaming these parts."

"There's talk in town of highway robbers." Lord Rothley spoke with cool authority. "We're tasked with delivering Miss Woolf safely to Brighton." He paused, his gaze sharp upon her. "I'm told you were the housekeeper at Canfield Manor."

"That's correct. I retired last year."

"Then you worked for Sir Randall Ferguson?"

"For fifteen years, sir."

He offered no introduction, perhaps because he had no desire to watch the elderly woman fumble. "Then you know his sister, Lady Mayberry."

"Sadly, she passed twelve months ago, from consumption."

Lord Rothley looked faintly satisfied. "Yes. Sir Randall kept her wolfhound. What the devil was the beast called?"

"Kaiser, sir."

"Kaiser, yes." He turned to Olivia. "Do you have all your belongings, Miss Woolf? Would you care for one last look around the house?"

"No. I have everything." She pressed the key into Mrs Hodge's hand. A sudden faintness swept over her, whether from the year's strain or the daunting task ahead, she could not say.

"Do you have a forwarding address, Miss Woolf? Just in case any correspondence arrives for you."

"You may forward it to Burkes Bookshop on Aylesbury Street, Clerkenwell. The proprietor is a friend and knows how to reach me."

Lord Rothley cast her a pointed glance but held his tongue.

"Well, good luck to you, dear. The road here is lonely at night, and living beside a graveyard unsettles most folk. I'll pray your aunt makes a quick recovery."

Mrs Hodge bid them good day and returned to her cottage.

Once she was out of earshot, Lord Rothley said, "I cannot decide whether to applaud your talent for lying or be troubled by it."

"It's not difficult to lie, my lord, when lives hang in the balance." And the less Mrs Hodge knew, the safer they'd all be. "Do you think we should have told her about the beast in the mask? After all, she lives out here alone. He may return, seeking answers."

"I'll have one of Daventry's agents keep watch for a few days. If the villain is still hunting you, we'll know."

Her pursuer was relentless, intent on recovering the item her father had stolen, whatever the cost.

"He could be watching us now." She kept her gaze fixed on the man who was afraid of nothing but his memories. "What if he's waiting for the right moment to strike?"

"Trust me, Miss Woolf. He'll not harm you again."

She wanted to believe him. His words rang with conviction. Men feared him, and he seemed not to care if he lived or died. Strength like that might become a refuge, and that frightened her more than the man in the mask.

A marriage of friendship was an attractive prospect. Yet why would he sacrifice the chance of finding love? And what right had she, a woman cloaked in lies, to even wonder?

The question lingered, leaving her head spinning. Shadows gathered at the edges of her vision as her world began to slip away. She tried to draw breath and resist the darkness, but her strength failed. Her knees gave way, and she collapsed into Lord Rothley's arms.

Chapter Six

"For heaven's sake, Gentry, I hear you. But Miss Woolf has barely opened her eyes in two days. It isn't natural." Gabriel pressed his fingers to the bridge of his nose, but it did little to ease the tightness behind his eyes. Patience had never been his virtue. "There must be more to it than exhaustion."

Gentry glanced at Miss Woolf sleeping peacefully in the poster bed, surrounded by plumped pillows and images of blasted peacocks. The faint aroma of herbs lingered in the still air. "You'd be surprised how often I've seen this. A problem builds, the mind won't rest, and the body gives out. She needs sleep more than medicine."

"What about the mausoleum? She breathed in the rot when I opened the coffin." Dust and a sour damp had risen as the lid shifted, clinging to their throats. They were so intent on recovering the valise that neither had shielded their mouths. "Or will you tell me miasma doesn't cause disease?"

Gentry put a reassuring hand on Gabriel's shoulder. "You were only there a few minutes, though I wish to God you'd tell me why. And you said Miss Woolf felt unwell before she entered the crypt."

"She complained of being hot, and she seemed unsteady." Anger rose in him like an unstoppable tide. She would not be in this state if she'd accepted his help sooner. He had offered countless times. And what was in that damnable valise? He'd give his right hand to know. "I suspect the long ride from World's End didn't help."

In the silence that followed, Gentry merely arched a brow.

"What?" Gabriel pressed. The man observed him as if he were a patient in need of dosing. His friends Dalton and Rutland would doubtless share the same concerns, which was precisely why he hadn't told them, either. "I've broad shoulders, and we've been friends for over a decade. Speak your mind."

"You rarely keep secrets, certainly not from me. You've burdens of your own, a matter that needs—"

"You refer to Miss Bourne's sudden return." Ten years spent praying for answers, and now he'd sooner see her crawl back beneath the stone.

Gentry's gaze drifted to the woman lying still beneath the coverlet. "I mean you should examine why you feel compelled to take on Miss Woolf's troubles."

Gabriel could almost hear the unspoken concern beneath his friend's calm tone. He knew what Gentry was thinking, that loneliness had driven him to take desperate measures. "My interest in Miss Woolf has nothing to do with my closest friends being married."

"No? You spent three nights at Fortune's Den last week."

"And half the lords in London are still cursing my luck."

"You've not done that in years. Not since—"

"Forgive me. Last I looked, I was a grown man of thirty."

"Who, despite rampant gossip, doesn't keep a harem of women lounging in the grand salon. If people discover Miss Woolf is staying here, she will have no choice but to leave town."

Not if I marry her.

The retort burned on Gabriel's tongue, but he swallowed it. Fate had mocked him once; he would not tempt it again. Miss Bourne had made a public fool of him, and he would not wake to find himself abandoned a second time.

"She needs help," he said evenly. "She can't tackle this problem alone. But we'll wait until she recovers before we make any arrangements on her behalf."

He understood Gentry's need to make sense of this debacle. As a rational man, Gabriel should have questioned his own logic, too. But the moment Miss Woolf entered his thoughts, reason deserted him.

As if to prove the point, Miss Woolf moaned softly and shifted in her sleep. The sheet slipped, the thin fabric of her nightgown drawing taut over the gentle rise of her breasts. For a moment, Gabriel felt like the man people claimed him to be—a creature ruled by appetite. Yet this woman stirred something that defied such definition, something that blurred the line between friendship and folly.

Gentry's voice cut through the silence, sharper than usual. "Tell me you see this isn't right."

"Says the man who married his herbalist in my chapel to save her from being sold to the highest bidder." He crossed to the bed and pulled the sheet higher to cover Miss Woolf's modesty, his hand steadier than he felt.

The quip left Gentry verbally stumbling. "What are you saying? That you plan to marry Miss Woolf? When did you decide this? Was it when Miss Bourne entered the fray?"

"Be careful. You're close to crossing a line, and you know how bloody-minded I can be."

"Fine." Gentry reached for his black leather case. "Give her barley water and let her sleep. A light broth when she wakes, nothing heavy. Keep her cool, and she'll regain her strength." He snapped the brass clasp shut. "If you need anything, you know where to find me."

The tension was palpable.

"I'm not a man who keeps score," Gabriel said. He was a man who valued loyalty above all else. "But I've stood by you in your darkest hour, risked my life more than once. I only ask that you trust my judgement now."

Gentry's gaze lingered on Miss Woolf before he inclined his head. "Others fear challenging you, but friendship grants me that privilege. Your welfare is, and always will be, my concern."

The words cooled his temper. "When Miss Woolf wakes, she alone will decide what's best."

He was not about to dictate her choices. One man had already made her suffer enough, and he had no intention of doing the same.

"I would encourage her to contact her friends, particularly the countess. Let them know she is safe. They've been worried about her the last few days."

"Certainly. In the meantime, reassure them all is well."

But all was not well. A man meant to kill her, and Gabriel had no notion why. Her past was a blur, like a view through a misted window. Miss Woolf embodied everything he despised: secrets and evasions. Yet for all she withheld, he was already ensnared.

"There is something you can do for me." Gabriel felt no shame in asking. "Miss Bourne's aunt, Mrs Culpepper. Speak to her physician. What's her prognosis? Is she expected to last the week?"

Gentry eyed him with a calculating expression. "Would you like me to learn more about Miss Bourne? Whether she seeks a reconciliation or something else? If you're the real reason she's come home?"

Gabriel's mouth curved, but there was no humour. She had returned for the same reason she'd left—for money.

"No need. The moment she accepted my father's bribe, she ceased to exist to me." She could come crawling on bended knee, and he would not offer his hand. "Loyalty is the foundation for anything lasting."

He had watched his parents' marriage crumble like cracked plaster at the first whisper of adultery. He'd seen the craving for love wielded like a weapon of destruction. He refused to suffer the same fate. Better no love at all than a bond built on betrayal.

"I'll call when I have news," Gentry said, gripping his case. "Miss Woolf should begin to improve, but send for me at once if she develops a rash or a fever."

Gabriel nodded. "Thank your wife for the tisane. I won't ask you to lie, so tell her the truth."

"I would if I knew what the devil is going on here." Gentry gave an amused hum as he let himself out, leaving Gabriel alone with his thoughts and the woman who refused to leave them.

If only his friend knew he had spent two days staring at a battered valise, fighting the urge to pry it open and unearth its secrets. Or that he had ridden to town that morning to press the Archbishop into granting a special licence.

He moved to the end of the bed and watched Miss Woolf draw slow, even breaths. Something about the sound soothed him. Still, he whispered, "What is it you're not telling me, woman?"

What did the blackguard want from her?

And where the blazes was he now?

The questions plagued him until a discreet knock broke the silence. Mrs Boswell entered, carrying a pitcher of water and a stack of clean towels.

"Still no improvement?" she said softly, setting the pitcher down and draping the linen over the rail. "Mr Gentry seems to think it's exhaustion. Perhaps the herbs his wife sent will serve as a restorative."

"Perhaps."

What would he do if she never recovered?

He had not allowed himself to think that far ahead.

"I can sit with her for a while." Mrs Boswell wet a cloth in the porcelain bowl and came to the bed, dabbing Miss Woolf's forehead with the linen. "Have you tried moistening her lips with brandy? A little nip can do wonders for the constitution."

"I daren't risk hindering her recovery. And there's no need to stay. I'm sure you have enough to contend with. I have nowhere else to be."

Mrs Boswell schooled her expression, as she had the night she'd led him back to bed when he was ten and had stumbled upon his parents' orgy. "There's a pile of unopened letters on your desk, along with the surveyor's report from Eaton Chase. And Mr Davies sent the accounts for you to review when you're ready, my lord."

"They can wait."

Neither spoke for several seconds. The silence stretched taut as a held breath.

He knew why.

"Have you news to impart, Mrs Boswell?"

His housekeeper smoothed the sheets and cast a furtive glance at the woman in the bed, as if Miss Woolf had the power to bring empires to their knees. "The chapel has been cleaned, as requested. Fresh flowers placed in the vases."

Gabriel dipped his chin. "And you've informed the vicar I may need him at a moment's notice?"

"Mr Collard knows that if he values your patronage, he will be on hand night or day."

"Excellent. Though I sense your disapproval." He lifted a staying hand before she spoke. "You fear this will end in disaster. That, despite all I have done to avoid past mistakes, I am blind to the dangers."

"It's not my place to pass comment, my lord."

"Yet you know damn well I want to hear it."

Her lips thinned. When she spoke, it was scarcely above a whisper. "Must you marry her now? Could it not wait until you know her better? A week or two might make all the difference."

He gave a hollow laugh. What could be more absurd than marrying a stranger? "I gave my word. I offered her the protection of my name. The arrangements are merely a precaution. The lady is free to decide her fate when she—"

A sound from the bed cut him short.

Miss Woolf stirred, her long lashes fluttering. In a hoarse whisper, she breathed, "Water … please."

Mrs Boswell reached for the carafe on the side table and poured cooled barley water into a glass. "Just a sip, miss. Enough to wet your lips."

Miss Woolf's hand trembled as she steadied the glass. She lifted it, the rim brushing her mouth. Gabriel watched the cool liquid glisten against her lips before she swallowed, her throat working with the effort. His heartbeat quickened, and he told himself the rush of feeling was nothing more than relief.

She lowered the glass, her gaze wandering about the chamber. Confusion clouded her features as she took in the carved panels, the heavy drapes, and the parade of peacocks. "We're at Studland Park? The last I recall, we were at World's End."

Gabriel stepped forward, eyes fixed on her. "That was two days ago. You've barely stirred since."

"Mr Gentry diagnosed exhaustion," Mrs Boswell said, setting the glass back on the side table. "He seemed certain you would recover."

"Two days ago? Good Lord." She clutched her chest, panic flashing in her eyes. The thin nightgown offered little defence, and her gaze flicked to him, as though recalling how near he stood. Awareness quivered in the space between them before colour drained from her face and her eyes swept the chamber, sharp now, searching.

Gabriel knew what she sought. The valise.

"It's safe," he said to reassure her.

Her fingers sought Mrs Boswell's sleeve. "Might I trouble you for something to eat?" The question came gently, as though she were unaccustomed to asking for favours.

"Do you mean to remain abed, miss?" Mrs Boswell asked, patting her hand. "You would be wise to do so."

She drew a weary breath. "I shall eat first and see how I feel."

Gabriel caught the faint tremor in her voice, but also the resolve beneath it. "I shall dine here with Miss Woolf. Have Molière send up his onion soup."

Miss Woolf made no objection. Why would she, when the

only thing that mattered was the bag she had hidden at the foot of a corpse? Indeed, Mrs Boswell had barely closed the door before she pushed herself upright.

"Where is the bag? Did you open it? Tell me you didn't touch anything." She eyed him cautiously. "I suppose you're shocked, angry, perhaps disappointed the contents were less intriguing than expected."

"On the contrary." His gaze slipped to the three pearl buttons at her throat, undone to reveal smooth porcelain skin, then lower to the copper strands brushing her collarbone. She looked bed-tumbled, and the sight roused thoughts forbidden to a man sworn to celibacy. "It's the smallest things I find most intriguing. But I haven't opened the valise."

She frowned. "Why? It's not locked."

"I know."

"You've not peeked inside?"

He gave a short snort. "And betray your trust? How am I to prove I have honourable motives if I falter at the first hurdle?"

Her gaze slid over him. "Few men possess your strength —your strength of will, I mean." Yet her eyes caught on the breadth of his chest, just as they had at the washstand when she'd paused in the doorway, breathless at the sight of him bare.

She was a formidable adversary in this game of resolve. For the first time in years he felt like a man, flesh and blood, not a marquess bound by duty. He would be wise to eat his soup downstairs.

"How would you like to do this?" The words slipped out clumsily, and he cursed himself for it. They lacked the precision he prided himself on. "Shall we eat first?" His jaw tightened. "Eat before we open the valise? Assuming you feel well enough."

Her throat worked tirelessly before she said, "It's not too late to bundle me in a hackney cab with that dratted bag and forget you ever met me."

It was too late. His last chance to do something honourable. He might have lectured her on what it meant to make a vow, how faith was all he had left. Instead, he reached into his coat pocket, withdrew a folded parchment, and handed it to her.

"What's this?" She took it, her pale fingers shaking as she realised he'd used the weight of his position to make demands of the Archbishop. "You obtained a licence?"

"You're an intelligent woman, Miss Woolf. Do I strike you as a man who makes worthless promises?"

"No, but—"

"You must make the choice now." A knot twisted in his stomach. Her answer shouldn't matter, but it did. The realisation unsettled him, though his voice remained composed. "I can summon Kincaid. He will take you anywhere you wish to go. Scotland. Dover. A ship bound for the Americas."

He stopped there, letting her weigh the options.

"And the alternative?" she asked quietly. "I sense there is one."

His gaze held hers. "If you stay, we will marry in the chapel today." He spoke like a man of Parliament, calm, each word measured. "I need certainty, Miss Woolf. But as your husband, know I will not rest until those hounding you are caught. It strikes me as something we must do together."

She barely moved, barely blinked. "Ours would need to be a remarkable friendship to withstand a loveless marriage and the shame of infidelity."

"Infidelity?" The word tasted like poison. He had seen what deception could do, how it seeped into a man's veins and corroded everything decent in him. "Let me be clear. You will take no man to your bed. I'll not have cuckold added to my list of monikers."

She laughed, though a frown creased her brow. "Not me. I could hardly expect you to remain faithful. Do you not possess that animal instinct to mate?"

Her blunt retort caught him off guard, stirring an almost unbearable need to devour her smart mouth. "Celibacy sharpens a man's mind. I have no wish to squander my wits on fleeting pleasures. What I value is constancy, and I see the same in you. You crave security, Miss Woolf, as much as I crave loyalty. Together, we might yet find both."

Her gaze dropped to the licence in her hand, which she waved as if the words were flimsy. "What if one of us isn't strong enough to keep our bargain?"

"Then I will be strong enough for us both. You will not fall while I stand beside you."

She raised her chin. "You assume I'm the weak one."

This was what he needed, a woman unafraid to challenge his opinion. He had known that about her from their first meeting.

"I assume nothing. I know your strength, which is why I choose to share the burden." He bowed. "I shall leave you to consider your options, and trust you will choose reason over the folly of romantic love."

He had reached the door before she said, "Wait." She cleared her throat. "What if you realise you still love Miss Bourne? She's captivating. Beautiful enough to hold any man under her spell. It will be torture living so close."

He turned, his gaze unflinching. "Miss Bourne holds no

claim on me. Whatever she was, whatever spell she cast, ended ten years ago. Do you think me so cruel as to bind you to a lie?"

"Love catches people unawares."

"The capacity to love was stolen from me years ago." He drew a breath, loss tightening his chest, and for the briefest moment he wondered if it was entirely true.

Miss Woolf surprised him. She cast back the bedclothes and crossed the room in her nightgown, her bare feet sinking into the rug. He forced himself to remain still, though his eyes betrayed him, taking in the loose hair at her shoulders, the shift of cotton at her hips, the bare skin where the neckline gaped. This was not the time to think of her as a woman.

"I won't have it said I deceived you." She pressed the licence into his hand, her fingers closing lightly over his. "I fear my father was a spy and that he may have committed treason. I have not spoken of it to another soul." She drew a slow breath, as though the admission had cost her dearly. "Take time to consider your options, my lord. I shall await your decision."

Her confession should have shocked him, but it didn't. Men did not stalk graveyards or fire pistols on public lanes unless the stakes were high.

If she meant to persuade him to relent, she achieved the opposite. Did she not know he thrived on truth? That this show of trust touched him in ways kisses never could?

There was only one course left, and he would not waver. "Then we must marry without delay."

Chapter Seven

Madness was not a fleeting state of mind.

Barely two hours after agreeing to Lord Rothley's proposal, Olivia stood in the corridor outside the private chapel, preparing to marry the marquess. Vases of roses and honeysuckle crowded the marble console tables, their sweetness almost suffocating. Stone-faced ancestors watched from the canvases, their stares a silent rebuke.

She breathed to calm her pounding heart. She should leave, gather her skirts, run until her lungs burned. No good would come of this. One wrong move would invite ruin. But her attacker had seen Lord Rothley. If she fled, he would be the target. And against all reason, she believed he was the only man who could protect her from danger.

"You look quite the part," Mrs Boswell said, pressing a small posy into her hand, pink roses and peonies woven with myrtle. "The flowers bring a touch of colour." Her gaze moved over Olivia in quiet appraisal. "If you'd prefer, I could search the trunks in the attic. Perhaps there's a pastel gown that would suit the occasion. I'm sure his lordship will wait."

"That won't be necessary." Though green or lilac might flatter her hair, nothing would make her feel like a bride. "This is to be a union of minds. I doubt his lordship cares what gown I wear."

The words sounded braver than she felt. Her pulse quickened at the thought of standing beside him, bound by vows, not affection.

"Make no mistake, ma'am. His lordship sees more than most. Nothing escapes his notice."

Yes. At times, he looked at her with such intensity it seemed the world had stilled.

Mrs Boswell cupped Olivia's arms, her smile reassuring. "Passionate affairs dwindle like summer blooms, but a solid friendship brings comfort for a lifetime. Keep that in mind when you're troubled with doubt."

Yet as the words settled, another thought intruded, a need to know whether the recent gossip held weight.

"Is it true that Miss Bourne raced to the house when the vicar was summoned?"

A maid had let the secret slip while dressing her hair, warning that Miss Bourne's aunt had eyes and ears in every corner of the parish.

Mrs Boswell's lips thinned. "She begged for an audience, but his lordship refused and had Mr Kincaid see her back to Wynbury Hall."

"Why did she come?" Olivia asked, unsettled by Miss Bourne's sudden return and what it might signify.

The older woman arched a knowing brow. "Why does any woman chase what she can no longer have? Pride and vanity." She paused, casting a quick glance towards the chapel door. "May I offer a word of advice, Miss Woolf? I speak for the good of all in this house."

"By all means." The housekeeper's insight would prove invaluable in the trying days ahead. "If I'm to live here, I shall need your guidance and support."

Mrs Boswell's kind eyes brightened. "Today, you will become the Marchioness of Rothley, a position most ladies only dream of. You possess the quiet grace and dignity, ma'am, but to thrive you must learn to command." She lowered her voice. "Miss Bourne must come to know her place. And you must keep her there."

Unease prickled at the mention of Miss Bourne, yet Olivia lifted her chin. "One step at a time, Mrs Boswell. Let me reach the altar first, but I'm grateful for your advice."

A discreet cough drew their attention. An under-footman waited in the chapel doorway, pristine in his livery, a quiet emblem of the house's order. "His lordship wonders if you're ready, ma'am."

She pictured him pacing, restless as a brewing storm, and gripped the pretty posy as if the fragile stems were an anchor. "I'm ready." Her pulse quickened with dread and anticipation, but a marchioness did not falter under pressure. Not beneath Lord Rothley's gaze.

Whispering a silent prayer to her mother for guidance, she stepped into the private chapel, braced for the chill of loneliness and the emptiness of vacant chairs. Instead, the man at the altar filled the space, leaving no corner untouched by his presence.

She scarcely registered the vicar in his black cassock and starched collar, gripping his worn Bible. He raised his hand for the congregation to stand, then faltered, remembering no one cared if their lives were ruined.

Oh, she'd be damned to the fiery pits of hell for this. And

yet she moved towards the man who would be her husband, one measured step at a time.

He watched her with a gleam of satisfaction in his midnight eyes, his gaze roaming over every inch of her, as if friendship were the furthest thing from his mind. She would need her wits. A man like Rothley could conquer with a glance, yet would surrender to no one.

"Miss Woolf." He bowed, then eased the posy from her hands and offered it to Mrs Boswell. With a light, unwavering touch to her elbow, he guided her towards the altar.

They had barely begun, and already she was forced to make a confession. "Miss Hawkins," she corrected. "Miss Olivia Frances Hawkins." One could not begin married life on a lie. "I adopted the name Woolf when needing courage to run from the pack."

He didn't mutter a curse or appear disappointed. "I appreciate the late vote of confidence. Not that it matters. From this day forward, you belong with me."

With me. Not to me. An important distinction.

"Anything else you wish to confess before we begin?"

"Not presently." Though she might have admitted to being breathless at the brush of his hand, reassured by the steadiness of his grasp, thrilled by the awareness that passed between them.

"And what of you, my lord? Do you have anything to confess before we begin?" He might start by explaining why he'd deliberately left her corset unpacked. Or why he seemed so determined to wed a commoner.

His gaze lingered on her, like a cardsharp weighing the odds. "Only that I've felt a strange restlessness since the day we met."

The admission appeared to unsettle him as much as it did

her. Was it akin to the same pull she had felt while watching him at the washstand?

She forced all romantic notions from her mind. "Then we must hope friendship proves a potent remedy."

"Indeed."

The vicar coughed discreetly, but Lord Rothley stilled him with a raised hand. Drawing Olivia aside, he bent his head, his whisper grazing her ear and setting her pulse racing. "Be assured, what happens here will be spoken of in every fine house from London to John o' Groats. We must give the gossips no reason to doubt our eagerness."

She turned to him, realising too late how shockingly close their mouths were. He had taken a nip of brandy before the ceremony, its earthy essence rich on his breath. That he had needed to steady his own nerves proved strangely empowering.

"You want us to lie? Pretend this is about desire, not necessity?"

His laugh said he recognised the hypocrisy. "Yes."

"But you care nothing for people's opinions."

"I merely wish to shield you from malice."

Yet she sensed his concern was not only for her but for himself. This marriage was his way of silencing Miss Bourne and breaking free of the past. Did she not owe him that much, at least?

Against all caution, she said, "Then I suggest you take my hand and kiss my palm as though you cannot help yourself. And be certain the vicar sees it."

His mouth curved in the faintest hint of a smile. She stilled as he took her hand and turned it, his gaze never leaving hers. When his lips brushed her palm, heat surged through her. The kiss lingered a fraction too long, a claim disguised as devotion. The vicar might see reverence, but Olivia felt only the shocking intimacy of a man who could undo her with the press of his mouth.

Her life might be in danger, but so was her heart.

From nearby came Mrs Boswell's soft sigh.

Deception was a fool's game. Someone would suffer for it.

"That should appease the vicar," he said. Yet something in his stare said it wasn't enough. "Perhaps a chaste kiss once we've exchanged vows."

A kiss with mouths?

The question rose to her lips, yet she only nodded.

He led her back to the altar, but one brief, intimate moment had shifted her world. His pull was magnetic, and she was helpless iron caught in its field.

Keen to hasten the proceedings, the vicar read from his open Bible. "Dearly beloved—"

She almost choked. No doubt the parrots in the basement would squawk *what tripe* before he reached his next breath.

The vicar spoke with the gravity of a man certain heaven was listening. "Forasmuch as marriage is a holy estate, ordained for the procreation of children ..."

Children? Olivia's mind betrayed her with a vivid image of the act itself, of the marquess dropping his towel, of what it would mean to lie with him. Heat rose in her cheeks, and she gave herself a stern reminder: friends did not share a bed.

She listened to the vicar's exhortation on love and commitment, though the warning was plain enough. Marriage was ordained as a remedy against sin, and the Lord might punish those who sought to deceive Him.

"Who giveth this woman to be married to this man?"

The question stumped them both.

"Miss *Hawkins* is an independent woman," Lord Rothley snapped, his jaw tight. "There's no transfer of ownership here, Collard. She comes to me of her own free will."

She brought no dowry, no bride price, no land or connections, only a pocket full of lies and the threat of the noose. Still, he took her hand in his as though daring the world to challenge his choice.

Mr Collard dabbed at the sweat on his brow and hurried on, addressing Lord Rothley. "Wilt thou love her, comfort her, honour and keep her in sickness and in health?"

He didn't flinch or falter but spoke with confidence in his ability to provide. His coal-black eyes softened to a rich brown as he said, "I will." Then, with quiet conviction, "You have my protection, for as long as I draw breath. You'll want for nothing."

Except love. Children. A heart filled with joy.

Olivia felt the vicar's beady eyes settle on her, the silence stretching until he spoke. "Wilt thou take this man to be thy husband, to love, honour, and keep him in sickness and in health, so long as ye both shall live?"

The words echoed through the chapel, a vow meant to last a lifetime. But lifetimes were for other people. They would be lucky to survive the month.

She lied, mouthing oaths that sounded like impossible dreams. "I will."

Lord Rothley's broad shoulders eased, as if he had been holding his breath for a decade. The mood shifted when it came to reciting his personal vow. His voice deepened, warm with promise, as he spoke the words, "to have and to hold from this day forward."

The phrase brushed over her like a caress, a whisper

meant for her alone, too intimate for ceremony, too real to be mere pretence.

Then it was her turn to repeat the vicar's words. She looked up at Gabriel, into dark, unyielding eyes that glinted like burnished amber with each vow she spoke, as though her promise had kindled something in him.

They bowed their heads in prayer. Olivia lowered her gaze, her own thought rising in silence.

Lord, grant me but one sign this was your plan.
Let it not be a mistake.

The vicar cleared his throat and opened the prayer book. Lord Rothley placed a plain gold band upon the page, and the blessing was spoken so softly Olivia hardly heard.

Then the marquess took the ring and slid it slowly onto her finger, his hushed hum of approval drawing her deeper under his spell.

She stared at the simple band. No jewel sparkled, no crest proclaimed ownership. It was unadorned, a token of trust rather than possession. In a world steeped in deceit, its simplicity felt almost sacred.

Perhaps this was the sign she had prayed for.

And in the next breath, they were pronounced man and wife. "Those whom God hath joined together, let no man put asunder."

Mrs Boswell clapped in delight, then drew in a sharp breath as Lord Rothley caught Olivia's chin between his fingers and tilted her face to his.

"A seal upon our vows," he murmured.

The world stilled. His mouth met hers in a kiss innocent enough for the vicar's eyes, yet warmth coursed through her until her knees weakened. His breath mingled with hers, the kiss a contradiction, innocent in appearance, yet the slow, intoxicating slide of his mouth spoke of desire simmering beneath the surface.

The air between them vanished. A low sound escaped him, half sigh, half growl, before he drew back sharply and mastered himself once more.

Olivia dragged her gaze aside and found Mrs Boswell staring, wide-eyed, her expression caught somewhere between surprise and confusion.

The vicar produced the parish register, and they sat at the table to sign their names. Her hand wavered only once before she wrote, the black ink binding her to him more surely than words ever could. Lord Rothley added his name with firm, decisive strokes, and the witnesses followed in turn.

When the book was closed, he straightened and addressed Mrs Boswell. "See that the vicar is served tea. I wish to spend a private moment with my wife."

Despite the heat of their kiss, Olivia knew the private moment amounted to opening the valise and examining its contents.

When at last they were alone, she drew a breath and said, "Now that we've dispensed with formalities, I suppose we should retire to your study and get to work."

His mouth curved. "You mean to test your husband's abilities so soon?"

"Is that not the role of a wife, my lord?"

His gaze sharpened. "Gabriel. You will call me Gabriel."

The name caught in her throat. She was not sure she could, not when she remembered the way it had fallen so easily from Miss Bourne's lips.

He studied her hesitation, astute enough to know the cause. "Do not let another woman's ghost keep you from what is rightfully yours."

He spoke as if he belonged to her, not she to him.

Mrs Boswell's words echoed in her mind: to thrive she must learn to command. Olivia lifted her chin. "I'd like to show you what's in the valise, Gabriel. It makes no sense to me, and by your own admission, you enjoy a puzzle."

"No puzzle unsettles me more than you, my lady."

She met his gaze without wavering, though the weight of her new role pressed upon her shoulders. "Puzzles have a way of consuming a man."

"Perhaps being consumed by you is no bad fate."

She gave no answer, only a measured glance as they walked on. But the question pressing in her mind refused to wait.

"I'm told the main study is vast enough to impress visiting dignitaries, with a desk fit for a king and shelves that reach the cornice. Why keep to a few rooms when the house holds two hundred?"

He stiffened beside her, a shadow passing over his features. "For some, home is nothing more than walls to contain one's sorrow. Do you recall saying that?"

"Yes. It's been a long time since anywhere felt like home."

"I hate this house." The words fell between them, hard and echoing like footsteps on marble. "The past haunts these corridors like a malevolent spirit."

It seemed they were speaking of Miss Bourne and Justin Lovelace again. She might have quipped that anything was preferable to peacocks, but the sadness in his tone stilled her tongue.

"And now you have a new houseguest to contend with," she said gently.

His mouth curved, though without humour. "I want you to

feel at home, though this is the last place a person might find peace."

"Which is why you keep to a select few rooms?"

He surprised her with his answer. "Yes. Rooms my parents seldom entered."

She knew not to press him. That truth had not come easily.

They reached the east wing at last. He unlocked the door and held it for her. She moved past, close enough to feel the warmth of him, and the air seemed to tighten in the space between them.

The valise sat on the desk beside a dark glass bottle and two delicate stemmed glasses, yet it was not the promise of answers that drew her. The room itself held her gaze: dark wood panelling, gold damask curtains, shelves heavy with books, and above the mantel a vast painting of the Scottish Highlands, its sweeping landscape oddly peaceful.

His familiar scent lingered in the room, and hope rose in her chest, for she felt instantly at home.

He closed the door, locked it behind them, then shrugged out of his coat and draped it over the leather wing chair. "I took the liberty of opening a bottle of Madeira. A gift from the King. I've been waiting for a memorable time to uncork it."

"What's more memorable than one's wedding day?"

"Indeed."

She watched his hands as he poured, strong and elegant, the gold seal ring bearing the family crest: a dragon soaring above crossed swords, a fitting emblem for a man who lived in constant battle with his past. Her eyes traced the fine lawn of his shirt, pulled tight over powerful biceps. It was hard to believe this man was her husband.

"To answers," he said, handing her a drink.

"To fate and solving confounding puzzles." She raised hers and sipped. The taste was dark and mellow, as though summer fruit had been steeped in fire and sealed in glass. "Is there anything you want to ask me before we look inside the valise?"

He studied her over the rim of the glass. "What makes you think your father was a spy? To dare even mention it, you must have proof."

She took a fortifying sip of Madeira and set her glass on the desk. "My mother was killed in an arson attack on our home when I was fourteen." She spoke as if telling someone else's story, not as the daughter who had wept until no tears remained. "I remember my father sobbing, saying it was his fault, that he should never have joined the wretched fraternity."

His expression softened. "I'm sorry. No child should carry such a memory." He tossed back the Madeira in one swallow. "What fraternity?"

"I don't know. But we were given a house near Cambridge. Men visited often and spent hours in the study with my father."

"Do you know their names?"

"No. When the countess hosted her balls, I made a point of studying every guest, measuring their faces against my memory. Not one seemed familiar."

"Did they speak French?"

"No. Always English." Keen to prove her point, she added, "I peered through the keyhole once and saw maps spread across my father's desk. One man said they risked the noose if caught with them."

"What about accents?"

She shrugged. "It was years ago. My father spent more and more time away from home." One lie had followed another until she scarcely knew what was true. "He behaved like a man with secrets. Burning his clothes in the garden, saying he had spilt lamp oil on them. The cuts and bruises on his hands, he claimed, came from chopping wood."

He gave a cynical snort. "Better than being caught rutting the maid and claiming he tripped. But yes, it's often the ordinary things that rouse suspicion."

"He'd leave the house at odd hours, insisting it was parish business that couldn't wait, and stayed away for days."

He shifted his attention to the valise. "And you think the answer to the mystery lies in there?"

"I believe the answer to why he was killed lies inside the bag."

But there was something hidden within she hadn't understood before. Something that could shatter the fragile trust between her and her husband.

"Might I have another glass of Madeira before we begin?"

He determined why in two simple words. "You're afraid."

"My heart is beating so hard, it might burst from my chest."

He smiled, as though he found her weakness oddly charming. "Let it race. A quickened pulse means you're alive, and I intend to keep you that way."

He poured them each another measure. They drank in silence, eyes meeting over their glasses, tension humming between them.

Setting her glass aside, Olivia turned to the valise. Her hands trembled as she unfastened the clasp. "I shall reveal them at random. One at a time."

He gave a single nod, though a current of excitement

pulsed through the room. A powerful thrum that seemed to come from him.

She reached inside, letting fate decide the order. Her fingers closed around the wooden crucifix. Lord Rothley—Gabriel—didn't sigh or look disappointed. Intrigue burned in his eyes as she placed it in his hand.

"The wood is solid," she said as he examined it. "The body of Christ is silver, and the inscription on the back was carved by hand."

"Crude work," he murmured, tracing the letters with his thumb. "*In poems lie all life's answers.*" He looked up. "I can attest to that."

"Perhaps the message is to have faith."

"Indeed."

She withdrew the portrait miniature next. A man's face stared back, mid-forties, his grey eyes sharp beneath arched brows, his mouth fixed in a grim line. The brushwork was fine, though the paint had cracked with age, the background oddly clouded.

"It looks ordinary enough," she said, holding it to the light. "Yet the surface is uneven, as though another image lies beneath."

Gabriel leaned in to study the miniature, and she caught the warmth of his breath. "You might be right. Painters sometimes reused ivory. If the paint were thinned with spirits or lemon oil, whatever's beneath might appear."

Her pulse skipped. "I thought of finding a book on cleaning ivory but feared I might damage it and destroy any evidence."

"You were wise to show caution," he said, though the direction of his thoughts caught her off guard. "Is that why you spent so much time in the bookshop in Clerkenwell? Did your friend, the proprietor, not offer his help?"

She tilted her head. Was the Marquess of Rothley jealous or merely suspicious? "Yes. I used to watch my lodging house from the shop window while pretending to read. Mr Burke knew I feared burglars, though I would not call him a close friend."

"You lied to Mrs Hodge?"

"I didn't want her to worry."

He studied her for a long moment, something faintly questioning in his gaze. The calm in his voice did little to hide it. "What else is in the bag?"

There were two items left, one to feed his inquisitive nature, the other to rouse his distrust.

Nerves fluttered in her throat. Which to offer first?

He sensed her hesitation. "We don't keep secrets anymore, Olivia. Honesty is the price of my protection."

She felt the weight of the wedding band on her finger and rubbed it gently, as if it held some mystical power to show her the right path. "I know it's hard for you to trust me, but remember, I was preparing to leave London, to leave and never return."

He inhaled deeply through his nose. "I cannot imagine—"

A sharp knock rattled the study door, cutting through the charged air between them.

"Not now," he called, his tone strained. "I said no disturbances."

"My lord, you have a visitor," Mrs Boswell replied.

He marched to the door, unlocked it and flung it open. Doubtless he was about to remind his housekeeper to follow orders, but she was not alone.

The man in the doorway needed no introduction. Mr

Daventry, illegitimate son of a duke and favoured by the Home Secretary, was one of the most powerful men in London. His agents solved more crimes than the men at Bow Street. Handsome, dark-haired, and possessed of a calm authority that could unnerve the wicked, he was Lucifer with an angel's heart.

"Forgive the interruption." Mr Daventry's mouth quirked upon finding them together in a locked room, but he entered without hesitation. "I'm afraid the matter couldn't wait."

"Did your man report an intruder at World's End?"

"Not exactly an intruder."

Something in the remark surely unnerved Gabriel because he dismissed Mrs Boswell and abruptly closed the study door. "Explain."

Mr Daventry's gaze flicked past him to Olivia. "I'm here for Miss Woolf."

Her pulse lurched. "For me?"

"Lady Rothley," her husband corrected, the subtle note of possession impossible to miss. "We were married less than an hour ago."

The agent's dark eyes moved between them. "I see. That helps matters rather than complicates them. And can you confirm her whereabouts since she was last seen leaving her cottage?"

"I am here, sir," Olivia said, "and can speak for myself."

"Yes, but someone must vouch for your whereabouts, Lady Rothley. Someone willing to testify in court."

Her heart skipped a beat. "In court?" Had someone seen her with the valise and wished to accuse her of grave robbing?

Gabriel went still, the shift in his demeanour chilling the air. "What the devil do you mean? She took ill and has spent the last two days in bed. Gentry and Mrs Boswell will vouch for her."

"And there's no chance she might have left in the night and returned without your knowledge?"

The question struck the fear of God into her. This was what she'd dreaded. The fraternity had found a way to incriminate her for their crimes. It wouldn't matter what proof she uncovered in the valise. No one would believe an accused spy.

"Not unless she's a sprite," Gabriel snapped. "I've scarcely left her side, save to wash and change my clothes."

Yes, he had read to her by candlelight. It hadn't been a dream. The deep timbre of his voice had lulled her back to sleep.

Mr Daventry's sigh proved most unnerving. The man was known to be cool amid the gravest of challenges. "Even so, I'm obliged to escort Lady Rothley to Bow Street to take a statement."

"Like hell you will." Gabriel's nostrils flared. "You'll not haul my wife through the streets like a common criminal. I demand to know what she's accused of."

Spying. Stealing from a grave. Burglary of a tomb.

He drew a slow breath. "Murder."

"Murder?" She stumbled back, and Gabriel's hand shot out to steady her. Even so, she felt the tremor that betrayed him. "Who am I supposed to have killed?"

Mr Daventry paused. "Justin Lovelace."

Chapter Eight

The room tilted. The walls pressed close. For a heartbeat, Gabriel couldn't think, couldn't breathe. Then he shook his head, certain he'd misheard. There had to be some mistake.

He fixed Daventry with a stare that would give Medusa pause. "Explain yourself. And make it quick."

"The man found dead in the cottage at World's End carried a letter in his coat pocket addressed to Justin Lovelace." Daventry's tone was that of a barrister before the bench, though his gaze softened as it settled on Olivia. "The note's romantic tenor, and the fact it bears your given name, suggest an intimate connection."

She didn't gawp at Daventry but steadied herself against Gabriel's forearm, her frightened eyes meeting his. "I don't know Justin Lovelace. And I swear I have never been intimate with a man." The words rasped in her throat. "I haven't left this house since the night you rescued me from that fiend. This must be the work of the fraternity."

Gabriel looked into her angelic blue eyes and wanted to believe her. But she had already confessed that something hidden in the valise was a cause for doubt. Still, she was his wife. It was his duty to protect her.

"You couldn't have done this," he said, daring to trace the backs of his fingers along her porcelain cheek. He shouldn't have touched her, but he suspected he would regret it if he didn't. It was meant as reassurance, a gesture of friendship, yet her skin was so soft it roused feelings he struggled to master.

In the silence that followed, the world seemed to shrink around him.

Justin Lovelace.

Damn the man.

A decade lost to doubt and speculation, searching, cursing, hoping, yet he had always known the truth.

Justin had not died in Cambridge.

"Has there been a formal identification?" he asked, his tone iron-hard to mask the tremor beneath. Ten years of torment could not end with a scrap of paper and no explanation. "Or are you basing your accusation on a letter found in a dead man's pocket?"

"You know how these things are handled," Daventry said. "When a man is found dead under your roof, suspicion falls close to home."

Olivia pressed a hand to her brow, searching for sense in the confusion. "I returned the key to Mrs Hodge two days ago. She can testify to that. When the coroner confirms the time of death, surely my name will be cleared."

He saw the flicker of uncertainty in her eyes and hated that he could do nothing to ease it. "I'll accompany you to Bow Street. We'll see this matter settled and have you home before nightfall."

Home?

Studland Park was no one's sanctuary.

Indeed, his past felt like the devil at his heels. First Miss Bourne had sought to make amends. Now, if the corpse proved to be Justin, it meant his closest friend had not been the victim of a crime but the author of a lie.

Daventry moved to the door. "We must leave at once. I'll inform the magistrate that I'll stand surety and see that she's released into your custody. Then you'll visit my Hart Street office, and we'll try to make sense of this business together."

Gabriel would take any help offered, so long as Daventry didn't interfere. "I'll ride with you. My coachman can follow behind."

"Wait." Olivia caught his sleeve. "I will ride alone with Mr Daventry and explain on the way."

He tried to ignore the sharp sting of rejection. "I'm your husband. I made a vow, and I intend to keep it. You need my support, whether you want it or not."

"Gabriel, there's something you need to do without me. Look in the valise and examine the remaining two items. Decide then if you wish to follow."

Her calmness disarmed him more than any plea for mercy could. He saw only honesty in her eyes, the same quiet truth he'd glimpsed when she stood beneath the lamplight at The Jade reciting her own poem with unflinching grace.

He had wanted to own her then, had believed possession might still the restlessness in him. He had wanted to own her the moment he slipped his ring onto her finger. Except that claim had been born of hunger, not honour.

"Very well. I shall follow with Kincaid."

She turned to Mr Daventry. "I'm ready, and will have Mrs Boswell fetch my bonnet and pelisse."

At the threshold, she paused and looked back, her warm

gaze seeming to drink in the moment, as if this were farewell. "Regardless of what you decide, I shall never forget the kindness you've shown me. You're the most honourable man I have ever known."

She left him with that compliment, and his heart stumbled like a boy's at his first dance.

He reached for the bottle of Madeira on the desk and poured a measure, the amber liquid catching the light while something darker churned in his chest.

Damn fate for ruining his wedding day. Though he shouldn't be surprised. Happiness never lingered long in his grasp.

The valise drew his gaze. It sat upon the desk like a threat, and he dreaded what lay within. If only ignorance were bliss. But better the ugly truth than a beautiful lie.

He drank while he waited, wondering what destiny had in store. Then he gathered himself, settled into the chair, and reached for the valise.

He withdrew a brass pocket compass, its case dulled by age and the touch of countless seafaring hands. A common enough item, yet he owed it to his wife to examine it closely.

The metal was cool and solid as he turned it in his palm, the glass faintly smudged from use. Flicking open the lid, he watched the needle quiver before settling. The craftsmanship was fine, though unremarkable, nothing to explain why Olivia had guarded it so carefully.

There was no maker's mark, no telling inscription.

Tilting the compass towards the window, he tested it against his own sense of direction. Beyond the pane stretched manicured gardens and an elaborate fountain. North lay that way, yet the needle wavered, refusing to align.

A fault in the mechanism?

He took a silver letter opener from the desk drawer and worked the blade beneath the back plate until it lifted with a faint click. Inside, nestled beneath the inner workings, lay a small silver disc no larger than a shilling. He eased it free with the point of the knife. A swallow was engraved upon the metal, wings outstretched in flight.

"Interesting."

Swallows symbolised family and fidelity and were said to mate for life. Yet hidden inside the device, it became an emblem of distrust.

He slipped the disc into his waistcoat pocket, then reassembled the compass and returned it to the bag.

One item remained.

One that might alter the course of his fate.

He hesitated, though the pull of curiosity was stronger than caution, and he reached inside to remove a tiny oak box. Even with his vivid imagination, he had not expected this.

A single gold button.

Not any button; one nestled in red silk and bearing his family crest, a dragon. Beside it lay a sprig of pressed white heather, its petals faded to cream. A token of faith and hope. A folded slip of paper contained a handwritten note.

Judge not the hand that bears the mark,
for it guards thee unawares.

He froze. Chilled fingers closed around his heart. Miss Woolf—Miss Hawkins, or whatever the hell her name was—had deliberately sought him out. Their shared love of poetry meant nothing. His intelligence hadn't impressed her, nor his so-called masculine prowess. She had not heard destiny calling.

So that was the truth of it?

Her father had guided her to Gabriel's door.

And he had married her based on a lie.

Fury burned cold in his veins.

He wanted to hurl the button across the room and curse his rotten luck, but the impulse faded as quickly as it came. Anger was a fool's indulgence.

Indeed, the memory of their chaste kiss intruded. She had tasted soft and warm, like a lover, not a mere friend. In that fleeting moment, she had trusted him completely. And he could not bring himself to believe it had all been feigned.

He drew a slow breath, forcing his thoughts to order.

She had meant to run, leave London behind and take her troubles far from his door. Deceit had not been part of her plan, only survival. The move to World's End and her refusal to accept his help confirmed as much.

He rose abruptly, thumbing the dragon impressed into gold. Faith and hope were empty words, yet he clung to them like a lifeline.

He gathered the items and returned them to the valise. Daventry would want to examine everything. They needed a man with his knowledge of devious devils, one not so invested he might lose his damn mind.

In the corridor, he nearly collided with Mrs Boswell. Worry pinched her features, along with the pitying smile that said nothing in his life ever went to plan.

"I saw Lady Rothley leave with Mr Daventry," she whispered, glancing about to be sure they were alone. "I hear she's wanted for questioning at Bow Street."

Hellfire. Olivia must have told her. "Is this where you tell me I should have heeded your advice and waited before summoning the vicar?" he said curtly.

"No, my lord. It's where I say you were right to act in haste."

He blinked, surprised. "Because you believe the new Marchioness of Rothley is beyond reproach?" Indeed, grace came to her as easily as breathing.

"Because there's something between you. Something that feels like it was meant to be."

The comment slipped past his armour. "Like you, Mrs Boswell, perhaps she will prove to be a faithful friend."

"I sincerely hope so, my lord. Shall I have her things moved from the Peacock Room to the grand suite?"

"You seem quite certain I will bring my wife home."

Her smile held the assurance he had come to expect. "Once you set your mind to a task, the devil himself couldn't shift you."

"Then no. Lady Rothley will choose her own rooms when she returns." He checked his watch. "Inform Molière we will dine later, at nine. Tell him if he dares complain, I'll request toad-in-the-hole every night for a week."

"I expect the threat will leave him trembling. Shall I have the table laid in the dining room or your private quarters?"

"The dining room," he said at last. "Lady Rothley has a penchant for mausoleums."

While the soot-streaked facade of Bow Street's Magistrates' Office projected an air of authority, Gabriel saw only irony. The structure was sound. The morals of some who served within were not.

He climbed the steps, the valise light in his grasp, the blasted trinkets clattering like the questions that plagued him.

He hadn't meant to bring it, but leaving it unguarded had seemed the greater risk. Still, he had come to free his wife, not to seek answers.

The law had to tread carefully around a lady of rank, and he meant to use that to his advantage. The sooner this farce was over, the sooner he could take Olivia home. Yet as the thought formed, doubt gnawed at him. How many secrets could one woman carry before the scales tipped beyond reason?

Armed with his rapier tongue, he strode through the hall to a clerk hunched behind a crude oak table, quill scratching in a ledger while constables came and went.

"Lord Rothley to see Sir Basil Marden. He's expecting me."

The clerk's quill froze mid-stroke. He glanced up, eyes widening a fraction before he scrambled to his feet. "Yes, my lord. Sir Basil is in chambers. I'll inform him you're here."

He didn't wait to blot the ink but left his stool and disappeared through the door at the far end of the corridor. Murmurs rippled among the constables, the kind of wary silence that followed whenever a man of rank crossed their threshold.

Gabriel ignored the stares. He was used to such reactions.

But then the whispers faltered, their attention drawn elsewhere.

Aaron Chance, Earl of Berridge, strode into the office, his weeping countess at his side, and fixed Gabriel with a stare sharp enough to draw blood.

Cursed saints.

Joanna looked up as she dabbed her eyes and drew a shuddering breath. "Gabriel." She hurried to him, reaching for his hand as dear friends do. "Have you heard the dreadful news? You were right. You've been right all these years, and no one believed you."

He'd been called a madman and a murderer for being the last person to see Justin alive. Yet vindication brought no comfort, only the hollow sting of loss.

"Rothley." Her husband's measured tone spared Gabriel the trouble of reminding him he'd once saved his life. "We've just come from the watch-house in Chelsea. The coroner insisted on a formal—"

"Damnation. You let her identify the body?"

Berridge's jaw tightened, guilt flickering through his expression. "Trust me. I would have cut off my own hand to prevent it."

"I insisted." Joanna smoothed her palm over her abdomen, a futile attempt to steady herself, to draw strength from the child she carried. "He was my brother. I had to be certain."

Bile rose in Gabriel's throat. "Is it him?" He wouldn't believe it until he'd seen the evidence with his own eyes.

"Yes." She shivered, visibly shaken by the recollection. "He looks older than his years, but he has the same dimple in his chin, and the scar by his brow where he fell from a tree when he was ten." Her voice broke on the memory, the sound twisting something deep in him.

Questions crowded his mind. Did they know the body had been found in Olivia's cottage? Did they truly think her capable of murder?

"I'm so sorry, Gabriel." Joanna clutched his coat sleeve. "Instead of answers, we're left with more questions. How long had he been living in that miserable cottage in World's End?"

He drew them aside, considering his next comment carefully. "Do you trust me, Joanna? You both know what Justin's disappearance has cost me. I'll do everything in my power to find the truth, but you must keep an open mind, and permit me to explain."

A muscle in Berridge's cheek twitched. "You knew he was there?"

"No. But I rescued Miss Woolf from the same cottage three nights ago, where a masked man tried to kill her."

Stunned, Joanna frowned. "What are you saying? That my brother was living with Miss Woolf? In what capacity?" She caught her breath as another thought struck. "You knew where Olivia was, and said nothing? You know how worried I've been. I've not seen or heard from her in days."

"I was told of her whereabouts in confidence," Gabriel said, not wishing to mention his source, "and had to respect her privacy."

Berridge's mouth tightened. "Privacy is the least of her concerns now. If Justin was found in her cottage, the magistrate means to question her in connection with his death."

"Miss Woolf hasn't left Studland Park. I assure you, she isn't involved. The cottage was empty when we returned the key to the landlady. I checked the premises myself."

Rather than bring clarity, his words drew raised brows.

"Good heavens, Gabriel. You let her stay at your estate overnight? What were you thinking? She'll be ruined. You should have brought her to The Burnished Jade."

"She was preparing to flee London, fearing for her life. There's no place safer than Studland Park."

Joanna's gaze dropped to the valise in his hand, horror darkening her features. "You've brought her clothes? Tell me they're not taking her to Newgate?"

"I don't know. I've just arrived."

Berridge gave a dry scoff. "You didn't accompany her to Bow Street?"

"The ladies of The Jade follow their own rules."

Before Berridge could agree, the clerk reappeared, his earlier stiffness replaced by nervous deference. "Sir Basil will see you now, my lord. If you'll follow me."

"We're coming with you," Joanna said, striding ahead. "I won't wait out here while they question her."

The clerk hesitated, uncertain whether to object to the intrusion, but Gabriel's curt nod ended the debate. "Very well," the man murmured, turning to lead them down the corridor into Sir Basil's oak-panelled chamber.

The magistrate stood behind his cluttered desk, his heavy brows furrowed as he looked up from a stack of papers. Daventry occupied a leather chair to the right, his posture as composed as ever, though his eyes flicked briefly to Gabriel in silent warning.

Olivia sat in her modest wedding dress, grey a fitting shade, her face pale but composed. When she turned, her gaze met his with such fierce relief it struck him like a blow. She looked at him as though he were her saviour, and he would have sold his soul to trap that look in a jar, to study it unseen.

"Lord Rothley," Sir Basil said, offering a curt nod before turning to acknowledge the newcomers. His brows lifted a fraction. "Lord and Lady Berridge? I'm not quite ready for you yet. Perhaps you'd care to wait with my clerk. Perkins will fetch refreshment."

"We're all friends here," the countess said.

Olivia stiffened at the sound of her voice. "Lady Berridge." Her fingers tightened around her gloves. "I'm not sure you'll wish to stay once you know why I'm here."

Joanna's expression softened. "I know why you're here,

and I'm confident you didn't strangle a man with those dainty hands." She turned to the magistrate, her tone calm yet commanding. "You will, of course, release Miss Woolf into our custody until this matter is resolved and the true culprit is brought to justice."

Sir Basil cleared his throat and straightened the papers before him. "I've agreed with Daventry that she may return to Lord Rothley's care while we continue our investigations."

Joanna's eyes widened in alarm. "That's preposterous. Can you imagine the headline in the scandal sheet tomorrow?"

Sir Basil chuckled. "It's hardly a scandal to release a lady to her husband's care."

"Husband?" Joanna blinked and shook her head.

Gabriel answered before anyone else could. "We were married at Studland Park a few hours ago," he said, as if it were of no consequence, not an event that had shaken him to his core.

"You married Miss Woolf and didn't invite her friends?"

"Love has a way of catching a man unawares," he said for the magistrate's benefit.

Daventry came to the rescue, as he always did. "The only concern now is finding the person who tried to frame Lady Rothley for murder. I've agreed to look into your brother's disappearance, Lady Berridge, and to review the past evidence."

"You've made a formal identification, then?" the magistrate asked her delicately.

Joanna swallowed hard. "Yes."

"I'd also like to view my friend's body," Gabriel said, using the term loosely. "And I insist on seeing it tonight."

Joanna gasped. "You mean to visit the watch-house on

your wedding night? Will that be before or after your romantic dinner?"

He should have scoffed, but one glance at his wife brought a pang of regret. He pictured her cold and alone in the dark, while he hid in his own chambers at the far end of the house.

Devil be damned.

He was a fool to think this could ever work.

But his wife chose to prove him wrong.

"If my husband intends to seek the truth tonight, then so be it. There's ample time for an intimate wedding supper."

Sir Basil clapped his hands once. "Very well. I'll have a note drawn up for the watchman, granting you access." He reached for a sheet of foolscap, scrawled a few lines, then pressed his seal into the wax. "Present this and he'll admit you."

Gabriel accepted the folded paper with a curt nod.

He made no mention of the valise. It belonged to Olivia, and he would show Daventry only once he and Olivia had time to examine the contents more closely themselves.

"I suggest we all gather at my office tomorrow," Daventry said. "To examine all lines of enquiry."

"A few days would be better," Gabriel replied. "We've much to discuss before then." He hoped Olivia would read his mind and understand they needed time to weigh the possibilities before Daventry took command.

Daventry agreed. "It will give me time to send an agent to Cambridge to request the original inquest report."

Sir Basil nodded approvingly. "Very good. Report to me once your enquiries are under way, Daventry." He shifted his attention to Gabriel. "In the meantime, Lady Rothley is to remain at Studland Park. She is not to leave town without my permission. I trust that's understood."

Gabriel inclined his head. "Perfectly."

He would watch her like a hawk. To keep her safe. To guard his heart. For whatever truth lay buried in the past, he would uncover it before it destroyed them both.

Chapter Nine

"I must admit, I feared what the countess would say." Olivia studied Gabriel in the confines of his carriage, wondering how to raise the matter of the gold button and why he'd not mentioned it the second they left Bow Street. "I presumed she would hold me responsible."

He paused as if considering his reply. "Joanna was once suspected of killing a man. Like you, she was innocent. And she feels the sting of Justin's betrayal almost as deeply as I do."

He sat with easy confidence, legs spread wide, one arm resting along the seat. There was strength in the set of his shoulders, control in every measured breath, yet beneath the calm she sensed a gathering storm.

"Is that why you insist on seeing Justin's body tonight? So there can be no doubt?" She understood. He couldn't bear to spend the rest of his life looking over his shoulder.

He glanced out of the window as if it were a mirror to the past. Rain streaked the glass, dulling what remained of the daylight. "I'll not be played for a fool again. Not by him. Not by anyone."

"Is that why you've not asked about the gold button?"

He looked at her from beneath lowered lids, a faint air of mistrust curling between them like fading pipe smoke. "I see no point asking a question you cannot answer. You could have removed the button. Leaving it in the valise serves no purpose other than to prove your honesty."

"You're right. I don't know how my father came to own it. Perhaps you do. Perhaps I'm the fool, and you're part of this treachery too."

"If you believed that, you wouldn't have married me."

"I'm still waiting to wake up and realise it's all been a dream." Or for someone to pelt her with fruit from the theatre stalls, and she'd know it was part of some absurd play.

"A dream, not a nightmare? There's hope for us yet."

She smiled. "You have been a good friend to me. Based on the marriage you proposed, I'd say there's every chance of success."

The carriage rattled westward through the thinning streets, the bustle of the Strand fading behind them. Wheels splashed through puddles as they climbed towards Chelsea. Olivia wiped a misted patch from the window and glimpsed shuttered shops and the dark outline of a church beyond. A bell tolled nearby, deep and mournful, as they turned into a narrow lane.

"We're here." Gabriel shifted to the edge of the seat, unease evident in the tightness of his jaw and the brief hesitation before he reached for the handle. "Kincaid will wait with you. I won't be long. Under no circumstances are you to leave the vehicle."

Outside, a weather-stained board above the door read *St*

Luke's Parish Watch-House. Dread coiled in her chest, yet every instinct urged her to accompany him.

"I shall come too."

"It's no place for you." His voice softened. "The sight alone would rob you of sleep. Wait with Kincaid."

She weighed her options. They had married for friendship, and she would not fail him. "I'm coming with you because that's what friends do. They stand together in times of need." She gave a light laugh to ease the tension. "I won't swoon. You have my word."

"There's every chance I'll punch the wall and curse to high heaven. A husband should not appear weak in his wife's eyes."

Weak? Perhaps he'd not looked in the mirror of late.

"I disagree. We should be aware of each other's failings."

He regarded her with a glint of amusement. "You promised to obey me."

"And you promised to protect me, as every dutiful husband should. You can hardly manage that from inside the watch-house. I'd rather stay close to you."

"Close to me?" He leaned forward a fraction, a teasing smile tugging at his mouth. "Be careful, Olivia. These quiet provocations can heat a man's blood."

"Then I shall choose my words more carefully, my lord. We wouldn't want you overheating before we reach the door."

His gaze held hers, then dropped to her mouth. The shift was slight, deliberate, and enough to steal her breath. "Keep your wits. If you faint, I'll be the one forced to revive you. I'm sure the thought of a second kiss today would rouse you faster than any remedy."

A second kiss would be dangerous, blurring lines they'd

sworn to keep. Yet something in her thrilled at the idea of seeing the Marquess of Rothley undone.

"A second kiss, my lord, and you're likely to faint."

"If we're to continue discussing kisses, you had better call me Gabriel."

They should not be discussing kisses at all.

He stepped down to the wet cobbles and offered his hand, guiding her step. Coal smoke and the yeasty tang of brewing tainted the air, but something heavier beneath it made her scan the shadows.

"Stay alert, Kincaid, and keep your pistol cocked."

"Aye, my lord."

They crossed a narrow yard toward a small brick watchhouse, ivy climbing its corners and window ledges. It stood at the edge of the churchyard, half veiled by a thin river mist.

A stocky man in a black coat answered their knock, keys clinking at the belt barely visible beneath his paunch.

Gabriel drew the folded paper from his pocket and handed it over. "From Sir Basil," he said. "We have leave to see the body."

The watchman glanced at the seal, then nodded towards the dim interior. "There's a seat inside for the lady. You'll need to give the Reverend Clay a moment to finish his prayers."

Gabriel frowned. "The rector is with the deceased?"

Olivia looked at him. Twice he'd avoided using his friend's name. Was he still plagued by doubt, or fearful of what awaited him inside?

"Aye. When a man dies in tragic circumstances, the rector always says a few kind words to help the soul find peace."

Gabriel's snort said he'd lost his faith in the Lord long

ago. "I believe Mrs Hodge made the discovery." At the watchman's hesitation, he added, "Sir Basil sent us here to confirm the particulars. He'll expect a detailed report."

The tubby fellow nodded towards the road. "Mrs Hodge found him dead in his bed and ran straight to the rectory. Reverend Clay sent word to me, and I had a man ride to fetch the coroner. The poor fellow's to remain here till the matter's been looked into."

Not his bed. Her bed.

Not where someone had died. Where someone had put him.

"Is the rector in charge of all the burial grounds in the parish?" Olivia recalled Mrs Hodge saying the overgrown graveyard beside the cottage fell under his care.

"Aye, that's right," the watchman said. "From here to World's End, every patch of ground with a cross on it falls under Reverend Clay."

The rector emerged from the shadows, his black coat buttoned to the throat, white collar stark against his ruddy cheeks. He moved so quietly he caught them by surprise.

"I feel my ears burning, Barker."

"I was just explaining to the investigator that you've a job on your hands, sir, keeping all the burial grounds in order."

"It's a solemn duty, Barker. The Lord entrusts us to tend His flock, no matter how still they lie."

The rector introduced himself, his bushy brows lifting like angel wings as he studied Gabriel. A fool could see he did not work for a Bow Street magistrate. His scent carried a mix of spice and leather, his coat spoke of fine tailoring, his very presence a reminder that power could be as alluring as it was dangerous.

"Lord Rothley," Gabriel said, in the tone of a man with nothing to hide. One who dared the world to defy him.

The watchman's shoulders stiffened, and he tugged at his cap. "Begging your pardon, my lord. Had I known it was you, I'd have hurried things along."

The rector inclined his head with practiced grace. "Lord Rothley. An unexpected honour." His gaze shifted to Olivia, steady and measuring, as though he saw not a lady but Rahab the harlot, guilty of hiding spies in Jericho.

"Then you'll understand if we don't linger. I'll not keep my wife standing in the cold." Gabriel's declaration left no room for misconception. "I intend to have her home before nightfall."

Both men bowed, the rector with solemn precision, the watchman with hurried awkwardness. Yet something in Gabriel's possessive claim settled the unease twisting in her chest.

"Perhaps Lady Rothley would prefer to wait in the carriage," the rector said, his tone one of polite concern. "I can sit with her until you've concluded your business."

Gabriel put paid to the idea, gesturing for her to precede him. "My wife will accompany me. She's far more astute than I am, and I require her opinion."

His easy admission caught her off guard. Few men would have deferred to their wives, at least not in company.

She leaned closer as they stepped into the watch-house, where a narrow bench and worn desk served as the only furnishings. "Be careful, my lord. Such compliments can heat a lady's blood."

"Then perhaps it's as well you cannot read my mind."

Intrigue stirred. What did he think about when he watched

her so intently? Had those dark eyes conjured something indecent? The thought warmed her, and she was glad of it. The air inside the watch-house nipped her cheeks, the cold stone walls doing little to mask the stench of decay.

He paused before the barred door at the far end of the room. His hand lingered on the iron latch, the chill of the metal seeming to hold him still.

"You're sure you want to do this?" she asked quietly.

"I must." He drew a measured breath, pushed the door open, and stepped inside.

A rough wooden box rested on a trestle table, a shrouded form within. A lantern burned at the foot, casting a weak circle of light across the flagstones.

Olivia stood with her hands clasped, braced for Gabriel's reaction, not the sight of death.

He squared his shoulders, took hold of the muslin shroud, and hesitated for a heartbeat before drawing it back to reveal the dead man's face. He didn't move. Only the tightening of his jaw betrayed him.

She searched his face. All she found was doubt.

"Is it him?" She moved to stand beside him, resting her hand lightly against his back. "Is it Justin Lovelace?"

Forcing herself to look, she found a face pale and swollen, the features blurred but not beyond recognition. The skin had a waxen hue, the mouth drawn tight, caught somewhere between pain and peace.

He leaned closer, studying the jawline, the matted fair hair, the dark bruise at the throat. "It doesn't look like him." His voice faltered on the words.

"You've not seen him for a decade."

"No." Regret roughened his tone as he whipped off his

hat and raked a hand through his ebony hair. "Why the devil did he not confide in me? I would have given my life to protect him."

She didn't doubt it for a second.

"Because he's not the man you thought he was." Some people were conniving enough to hide behind a permanent mask.

The last thought brought a vision of her attacker. The beaked disguise, menacing in the dark. The exposed mouth beneath it. Smooth. Almost pretty. Just like the man in the box.

Shock sent her stumbling back. "Good Lord, it's him."

Gabriel's hand steadied her. "Him?"

"My attacker." Her pulse thundered in her ears. She remembered thinking how many women had mistaken that soft, delicate mouth for gentleness. "This is the fiend who fired at us on the lane."

Gabriel fell silent, studying the man who had evaded him for years. "What makes you so sure?"

She pointed to the perfect bow, the faint dimple beneath. "Few men have a mouth as delicate as his. And his front incisor was chipped." Strange, the things one remembered when fighting for breath.

Gabriel hesitated, then took a thin metal tool from the table and eased it beneath the cadaver's jaw. The lips parted just enough to reveal the broken tooth, a small flaw in an otherwise flawless smile. He drew back slowly, the truth settling heavy between them.

"When he fired, I doubt he recognised you," she said, seized by a sudden urge to ease his pain. "It was dark, and it all happened so quickly."

"He recognised me." The venom in his tone shocked her.

"He knew exactly who I was, and he meant to put a lead ball between my brows."

She turned to him. "So this is Justin Lovelace? You would swear upon it in court?"

Pain shadowed his eyes before his stare turned to flint. "No. I can't swear to it, and I'll be damned if I know why."

"It's all right. We'll find a way to prove it once and for all, so you might put this dreadful business behind you."

He tilted his head at her. "After what you've endured, most women would be weeping into a lace handkerchief or pacing a cell in Bedlam. Yet you wish to slay my demons?"

"They're our demons now. Our fates are bound by friendship." Yet despite her brave tone, she could not picture a happy future for them. "Let's begin by noting everything we observe here."

They turned their attention to the body.

He was half-dressed, his shirt open at the throat, no waistcoat, no shoes or boots, only a pair of black trousers. The linen was fine, the tailoring neat, hardly what one expected of a common intruder. Bruises marred his throat and shoulder, the remnants of a recent struggle. Someone strong had held him down.

"The letter was found in his coat," Gabriel said. "Where is it?"

"Perhaps with the coroner, or stored safely somewhere. I'm sure Mr Daventry will have that information."

Gabriel nodded. "Then we've accomplished all we can for now."

He led her into the main room, pausing at the crude desk where Mr Barker sat, his colleague slouched on the bench beside him, puffing on a pipe.

"Do you keep a record of those who've been to see the body?" Gabriel asked.

"Glad you mentioned it, my lord. I'll need you to sign the visitors' log." The watchman reached into a drawer and removed a black ledger, its edges frayed and stained with age.

As Gabriel took up the quill, he read the list of names before signing his own. "So besides the coroner, Reverend Clay, and the Earl and Countess of Berridge, no one else has entered the room?"

"No, my lord. Leastways, no one I've seen."

"Did the coroner store the victim's coat here?"

Mr Barker shook his head. "He took it with him, along with the gent's boots, watch, and purse."

Gabriel thanked him, left his calling card and asked to be informed should anyone else show an interest in the deceased. He pushed a few sovereigns across the desk, steel in his tone when he said, "If the resurrectionists take him, I shall hold you personally responsible."

The watchman blanched. "No one'll lay a hand on him, my lord."

Outside, a breath of cold air carried the river's chill. The haze had thickened, stealing the last of the daylight and casting the street into shadow.

The press of Gabriel's hand at her back did little to quell the sudden prickle of dread. The horses shifted and snorted, restless in the gloom. Fog was a friend to fiends and footpads. Having spent countless hours peering through a gap in the curtains, she knew that better than most.

"You sense it too?" Gabriel said, quickening his step and guiding her swiftly towards the muted glow of the carriage lamps.

"Yes. Where fog creeps, wickedness thrives."

Unease coiled in her belly as she gave voice to the fear.

A twig snapped somewhere behind them.

Something shifted in the dark.

Or perhaps it was only her nerves.

"Kincaid?" Gabriel said, his gaze fixed on the hulking figure atop the box.

"Aye, my lord. Best take care. There's movement in the kirkyard, and I'll warrant it's nae ghost."

A sharp click broke the silence—a pistol hammer drawn back. She prayed it was Mr Kincaid priming his weapon.

But Gabriel cursed. "Forgive me if I'm rough, but there's no time." He caught her by the waist and pressed her to the closed carriage door, his body a wall of heat and strength, the breadth of him blocking out the threat. She held her breath, her cheek grazing the coarse weave of his coat, the rapid thud of his heart close to her ear, his thighs anchoring her fast.

"If I'm injured, you run. You do not look back," he growled against her ear. "Daventry will help you."

Her heart lurched—a sudden ache at the thought of losing a man she barely knew. She clutched his waist. "Trust me. We'll be home within the hour."

She spoke too soon. A rustle from the shrubbery, a stranger's ragged breath, then: "Stand and deliver."

"Have a care, laddie," Mr Kincaid warned. "You'll be dead the moment yer finger twitches."

A shot rang out. Gabriel jerked against her, the impact driving her harder into the door. For a heartbeat she couldn't breathe. He'd been hit. She was certain.

"Gabriel!"

The acrid tang of gunpowder filled her nose. The crack had roused the watchmen. Mr Barker gave chase, shouting into the fog and whirling his rattle, but she barely registered it.

Gabriel was hurt.

He stepped back, but her trembling hands were already on him, smoothing over his waistcoat, his chest, the hard plane of his shoulders. Heat radiated through the fine wool, too alive for a dying man.

"Are you injured?" There had to be blood. Where was the blood?

His gaze locked on hers, breath unsteady as her touch searched for wounds that weren't there.

"Gabriel. Answer me. Where are you hurt?"

He caught her wrists, stilling her frantic exploration. The slow circle of his thumbs burned against her skin. "The fool missed. I heard the shot strike the carriage."

Relief hit hard. "Thank heavens." She should have stepped back, but couldn't. Her back was still pressed to the door, his hands still holding her, his thumbs tracing that maddening circle. "In the history of eventful wedding days, this must surely top the list."

"Yet the night is far from over."

She heard something in his voice—a note that belonged to candlelight, too much wine, and him reciting verse in that stirring vibrato. "Let's pray we reach home without further mishap."

He opened the carriage door and helped her inside, then took the plaid blanket and laid it across her lap. Stepping away, he spoke with the pipe-smoking watchman and a red-faced Mr Barker, who had returned without the villain.

Before climbing into the vehicle, he looked at Mr Kincaid. "Pick a man to accompany you on every journey until we know what the blazes we're dealing with. Someone with an excellent aim."

"Aye, my lord. I ken just the man for the job."

Two hours later, they sat at opposite ends of the long dining table in Studland Park, the fire banked high against the lingering chill, the distance between them as vast as a chasm.

"Are you warm enough?" he asked as the footman set down a plate of lamb cutlets à la Soubise, the rich scent of cream and butter making her mouth water.

"I beg your pardon?" She craned her neck to see him over the elaborate flower arrangement in the centre of a table that seemed half a mile long.

He spoke a few words to the footmen, and suddenly they were alone in a room fit for royalty. Gabriel took his plate and wine goblet and came to sit beside her.

"We don't need to dine formally," he said, returning for his cutlery and napkin. "Tonight was about cementing your place as my marchioness. The staff will know they're to obey your every word."

She surveyed the polished silver, the sparkling crystal, the mahogany table gleaming beneath the candlelight. "I'm sure this is the perfect place to entertain guests. Not the best place for an intimate conversation."

He regarded her as he leaned back in the chair and sipped his wine. "I'm in no mood to discuss the valise tonight. I've no taste for grim talk just now."

Beneath his calm tone, she sensed a lingering sadness. Not born of tonight's events, but of a grief that had waited a decade to be acknowledged.

"Perhaps we might retire to your private drawing room, and you can show me what you're reading." A means to shift his thoughts and lighten the mood.

His lips curved faintly. "You know what I'm reading."

"Do I?"

"The gift you gave me. To remind me that friendship can be found in the least likely places."

She remembered the look on his face when she'd given him the book of poems, like an urchin being handed his first pair of shoes. "But you've read Gray a hundred times."

"Not your copy."

She laughed. "It's the same as yours."

"It's not." He rose and came to her side, pulling back her chair. "Bring your food and wine, and I shall prove to you why mine is different."

Intrigued by the man and the notion, she gathered her plate while he wrapped their cutlery in napkins and slipped them into his coat pocket. He told one footman to clear the table and have the food sent to the sick in the parish; another carried her meal through the lofty halls.

In his private drawing room, firelight flickered across dark wood and burgundy furnishings, lending the space an unmistakably masculine air. She noticed the shift in him at once, the softer shoulders, the deeper smile, the whisper of relief.

The footman set a small table before the fire, arranged her plate and wine, then withdrew, leaving her alone with her husband.

How strange that a word, a title, a noun could create a sense of belonging, as if each syllable and vowel were invisible tethers.

She watched him cross the room to retrieve a volume from the narrow bookcase, allowing herself a moment to study his strapping physique. He had the strength and will to conquer the world, yet hid himself away in this quiet corner of the house.

He returned to the fire wearing a grin that said he knew he'd won the argument, then handed her the book bound in burgundy leather, open at one particular page.

"You've read it before?" he asked as their fingers brushed.

She tried to steady her heart. "Many times."

"Good. Read the final stanza, and tell me if your thoughts are the same."

While he settled in the adjacent chair, she read Gray's lament for innocence lost, for the bitter wisdom that comes with experience. The poet warned that knowledge brings sorrow, that it is better to remain ignorant than to face the truth.

Gabriel was right. The words conjured new images, of a man whose trust and heart had been broken long ago. Her throat tightened as she reached the line he had underscored in pencil.

And happiness too swiftly flies.

That's when she knew. He had studied the book she'd given him, noting every mark and crease on the page, the faint smudge where she'd gripped it too tightly, searching for truth in every leaf.

He was trying to strip her bare.

New images formed in her mind's eye. Not him delving into her psyche, but sliding her nightgown slowly from her shoulder, his warm mouth tracing her collarbone, his strong hands cupping her breasts.

"You wish to know more about me," she said, forcing away the erotic thought. "And believe my secrets are hidden within the pages of a book. Why not simply ask?"

He relaxed back, his legs wide, a picture of masculine dominance. "Because I doubt you'd have told me."

"Told you what?"

"That you linger on the pages where the poet speaks of love. That you wept as you read. That you believe yourself undeserving."

She might have snatched her wine and taken a gulp, anything to still the traitorous thud of her heart, but she refused to let him see her fingers tremble.

"Then what's baffling is why a man who seeks to solve every problem, a man whose heart has shrivelled and died, would marry a woman with an interest in love."

Something flickered in his eyes, perhaps surprise, but it was gone as swiftly as it came. "To prove that a marriage based on romantic love is folly."

"And how do you propose to do that?" There were flaws in his reasoning he had not considered. "Your view is biased. How can a woman who's never felt love or desire judge if it holds any merit?"

His fingers flexed against his thigh, a subtle tightening. "What are you saying, my lady? That you want your husband to give you a lesson in pleasure?"

"You should call me Olivia when we discuss pleasure." Just saying the words sent a delightful shiver down her spine. "I'm saying that without knowledge of it, I cannot agree with you."

"Desire is nothing more than a story conjured in the mind. The body reacts to a thought, nothing more."

And yet merely sitting beside him, every nerve alive, told her it had nothing to do with thought, and everything to do with feeling. "It's not a topic I can debate."

Silence settled, but his gaze remained dark, impenetrable.

The air seemed to hum with palpable tension. This was not the conversation he had intended.

They finished their meal and drank their wine, the space between them tight with expectation. Did she want to feel his hands on her body, to feel like a desirable woman on her wedding night?

She didn't know.

She knew one thing: Gabriel would not want to be found lacking. Better to leave before either was tempted to test the theory.

"It's late. The peacocks will be wondering what's kept me."

"You don't have to sleep there." He paused, catching himself. "There are fifty bedchambers in the house. I don't like you being so far away."

"You said the house is impenetrable." Almost as impenetrable as the master himself. "That I'm perfectly safe here."

He hesitated, long enough to unnerve her. "You are. Still, I shall walk you to your room."

"So I don't get lost?"

"So you can tell me how you like your desire best served."

"There's an option?" It didn't matter how it came so long as it came from him.

"Yes. You might like it tender, smooth on the palate." There was something undeniably seductive in his look. "Or hot, straight from the pan."

The air seemed to thin. Where did the kiss at the altar fit into his menu of temptations? An aperitif, perhaps, for the touch of his mouth had only whetted her appetite.

"You've studied me closely. What do you think I'd like best?"

"I imagine you'd want to savour every sensation. Tender might be the best place to start. But if your inquisitive mind insists on comparison,"—his mouth curved, a slow hint of amusement—"then I'll oblige you."

She steeled herself and rose. Something told her she might not get another chance to catch him so unguarded, and she refused to spend her life ignorant of her husband's charms. There was a reason women wanted him, and she had a strange compulsion to know why.

"Then I would like to sample the tender dish now."

Chapter Ten

The lesson should be simple. A taste of desire to sate her curiosity. But the moment she spoke, command in her voice and colour in her cheeks, Gabriel knew he was the fool in this arrangement.

The sooner he got it over with, the better. "Come here."

He stood rigid, determined to keep a firm hold on his control, to make this no more than a demonstration. But devil take it, his blood surged like a fast-flowing river, pounding against every barrier he'd built.

Temptation approached, teeth sinking into her plump lower lip, each hesitant step stirring that same maddening urge to play her knight-errant. "I shall follow your lead, as I did at the altar."

At the altar, he'd been one breath away from deepening the kiss, one step from wrapping his arms around her and summoning lust from its fathomless prison.

"A tender kiss should speak of restraint." He would hold the reins tight enough to leave no room for manoeuvre. "It's the promise, not the act, that kindles desire."

"The promise? The promise of what, exactly?"

He stifled a curse. "The promise of coitus."

"The prospect of making love?"

"Of indulging in carnal pleasure."

She tilted her head like a curious scholar. "There's a difference?"

He frowned. "Surely a woman as well-read as you understands the distinction between lust and love."

"Not necessarily. I've read about a pleasure-dome in Xanadu, but that doesn't mean I've been there."

The minx. Her wit was every bit as enticing as her mouth. "Then brace yourself. You're about to pay it a visit."

He didn't give her time to answer. One step closed the space between them, his hand rising to cradle her jaw as his mouth found hers. Her lips were warm and sweet, the nectar of the gods, and they stilled the storm within him.

Saints and sinners, he could do this every hour of the day: touch her, lose himself in her until nothing else existed. The thought alone was enough to make him break the kiss.

Their eyes met, and the faint disappointment in hers made him wish he'd plundered her lips like London's worst libertine.

Then she said the one thing guaranteed to wound his masculine pride. "The poets are known to exaggerate. Perhaps one must be addicted to opium to appreciate pleasure."

He wanted to remind her that friends did not mate with their mouths, but he knew the next time they crossed paths with Miss Bourne, his wife would look at her and wonder how things might have been different.

"Could we try again?" she asked softly. "The tender kiss,

but this time with me as a participant? After all, one needs flint and steel to create a spark."

The need to prove a point outweighed the need for caution, though he feared one more taste and he would combust.

"Certainly."

Before he drew a breath, she reached out, her hand gliding over the smooth silk of his waistcoat as if touching him was the most natural thing in the world.

"You're much warmer than you let people believe."

"You have a talent for melting frost."

The muscles of his chest tensed, hard beneath the lingering sweep of her fingers as they climbed to cradle his jaw. Heat tightened inside him, a deep, insistent pull that silenced reason. Their mouths met again, hunger rising from a place dark and long denied.

His restraint slipped the moment her breath mingled with his. When she rose on her toes to meet him fully, his control scattered like ash on the wind.

He traced the line from her cheekbone to the tender curve of her nape, fingers sinking into her hair. Silken strands caught around his knuckles as he drew her closer, coaxing her lips apart. She sighed into him, and that soft, helpless sound undid him more completely than desire ever could.

The lesson, the logic, the distance—none of it mattered. Only the heat of her, the taste of her, the sweetness that mocked his vow of indifference.

When she pulled away, breathless, he fought the sudden instinct to drag her back, to growl *you're mine*, and drink from her like a man parched.

She touched her lips with trembling fingers. "If every kiss

improves on the last, I can see why people become addicted to kissing."

He tried not to stare, but watching her rediscover her own mouth was its own form of torment. Another kiss and he'd be prowling the corridors at night, desperate for another dose.

"You prefer being an active participant?" His mind leapt to the promise he'd made, to let her sample him hot from the pan and hoped she liked her food sizzling.

"Undoubtedly. It makes me wonder if it's possible to have a marriage built on friendship and longing, while avoiding the other complications."

She didn't wait for his warning that passion was fickle and would wane, that when intimacy died, there was little left to salvage.

"Though you'll find that a troublesome idea, I'm sure."

Troublesome, and the most inviting prospect he'd ever encountered.

She smoothed her hands over her skirts, as if she'd dressed in a hurry after a fireside romp.

He stood rooted to the spot, a monument to contradiction. Bloody hell. He wanted to make love to his wife. In truth, he'd wanted to bed her the moment he'd placed that ring on her finger.

Perhaps she sensed his internal struggle. "There's no need to escort me upstairs. I can find my way. Doubtless, you consider these naive experiments tedious."

Logical Rothley would have seized the boon and quickly agreed, eager to put distance between them. The man before her had lost his wits somewhere between the chapel and the chancery.

"A husband should always honour his promises." But wanting to leave his wife mindless with passion had little to do with honour and everything to do with pride. "And in the name of education, it's better you understand the risks of indulging your impulses, so we may avoid them in future."

She pondered his reply. "I suppose desire is like analysing a poem. A meticulous study of our body's own lines and verses."

Oh, he would be meticulous. He pictured himself nestled between her thighs, his tongue paying homage, utterly absorbed in the taste of her arousal.

He cleared his throat. "Quite."

"Then *hot from the pan* implies urgency, surprise even."

Good Lord. He was fast discovering there were crueller forms of temptation than touch. She wielded curiosity like a blade, and he was bleeding from every careful word.

"Yes, and requires a different skill set entirely."

"But I'm a novice."

Hardly. She was passion disguised in muted grey. That clever mouth aroused him as surely as any kiss, and her curious mind promised she would be a spirited lover.

"Passion is the art of ignoring thought and yielding to feeling." He gestured towards the door. He needed to act before Mrs Boswell appeared to return his misplaced sanity. "Hence, I'll need two things from you as we walk to your room."

She led him into the corridor. "You'd rather I talked less?"

"No. I need your permission to touch you, to touch you until you tell me to stop." He just prayed she said the word with conviction.

"You have it. What else?"

He paused, not wishing to sound like a needy young buck infatuated with his maid. "For the experiment to work, I need to believe you want me. You must say arousing things you might ordinarily keep to yourself."

Would she blush and stammer?

Or approach the matter like a skilled academic?

"I see. I shall do my best."

He heard the nervous thread beneath her resolve.

"Shall I begin?" he said as they passed his mother's portrait. Those painted eyes would mock his lapse in restraint. Yet she would never understand the distinction. This was not indulgence but education. He would never permit another man to bed his wife.

"Please do."

He braced himself, expecting the truth to shock her. "When I shielded you from the shooter tonight, it wasn't death that set my pulse racing. It was your warmth, your softness, that made me hold you tightly against the carriage door."

He could still feel it now, the press of her body, the swell of her breasts beneath his hands. The danger had passed, but the memory remained.

The seconds of silence stretched before she said, "And I wasn't panting because I thought we might be shot. It was the feel of you, hard against me."

Bloody hell.

He should stop there, but his mind refused to obey.

"You have the most marvellous breasts, Olivia." He should know. He'd studied every curve during those poetry recitals. "I didn't pack your corset because I wanted to admire you without restriction."

The words had slipped out more boldly than intended, but there was no calling them back now. And he wasn't sorry. Not when her lips parted on a sigh.

A blush rose to her cheeks, but her voice held firm as they mounted the stairs. "And I find myself thinking about your chest, and wondering if you're just as magnificent beneath that towel."

Heat coiled in his abdomen. The image her words conjured—her eyes on him, her curiosity unguarded—struck like a blow. He'd been half-hard since the first kiss. Now, every step was an act of endurance.

"You should know your nightgown does little to protect your modesty when you're cold. And the shadow between your thighs is an exquisite kind of torture."

She inhaled sharply.

Perhaps he'd gone too far. Yet the sight of her flustered and breathless was its own reward.

"I've always longed for independence, yet the thought of your strong hands on my skin draws me perilously close to surrender."

Oh, she excelled at this game, as he'd known she would. It didn't feel like a game at all, but the first steps of lovers on their wedding night.

"Then know I mean to touch you without apology."

"That is what you promised."

He quickened his pace, the ache in his loins a siren's call luring him into dangerous waters. "And I'm a man of my word."

They stopped outside her bedchamber. Candlelight flickered over the carved panels, catching the copper in her hair. He reached to smooth a loose strand behind her ear, his fingers brushing porcelain skin.

"Your hair is extraordinary." It was the contradiction that fascinated him, her love of morbid verse at odds with the brightness within. "Like fire subdued, waiting for the right breath to wake it."

She looked up at him, her lips curving in a faint smile. "And there's something compelling about a man so dark he seems to carry the night with him."

"You make temptation sound poetic."

"Perhaps there's poetry in two people being honest for once."

It's an illusion, he wanted to say, yet every word he'd spoken rang true. "You have the allure of Aphrodite, a beauty that tempts a man to sin."

She held his gaze. "And you exude a power that draws me like the earth's magnetic pull."

He looked at her mouth. "Then what chance have we but to collide?"

He was on her in a heartbeat, kissing her open-mouthed, the woman he'd watched, wanted, and never meant to touch. Her lips were Spring itself, stirring what lay dormant, reminding him he was flesh and blood, every inch a virile man.

So much for being the tutor and this her lesson. Any hope of mastering his desire vanished when she twined her arms around his neck, arched into him and moaned into his mouth.

She wanted him.

And by God, he burned for her with equal madness. He needed her under him, against him, anywhere he could feel her.

The thought should have sobered him. So why the hell was he dragging his hands down her back, clutching her bottom, crushing her body to his? He needed her heat, her breath, the slick slide of her mouth beneath his. He craved the friction, the exquisite tension coiling between them. He wanted to see pleasure flare in her eyes, hear her whisper his name like a prayer.

Olivia, tell me to stop.

Damnation, say it now!

The plea echoed in his mind, but she didn't say stop. She tangled her fingers in his hair, tugging hard as she deepened the kiss, her need so fierce they stumbled into the door.

A guttural growl tore from his throat as he fought to ignore the throbbing ache straining in his trousers. Hell, this was pleasure and torment entwined. And he craved it like a drug.

If he didn't stop now, he would touch her. Slide his hand up her thigh. Find her slick and ready. Feel her pulse against his fingers. Make her shatter against the bedchamber door.

The Almighty, aware of his turmoil, sent someone to intervene. Not an angel, precisely, but a dutiful housekeeper who was so shocked upon finding them in a passionate clinch, she dropped the jug of water she carried.

"Good heavens. Forgive me." Mrs Boswell fell to her knees, dabbing frantically at the spill with a cotton handkerchief. "I came to bring her ladyship a fresh pitcher and didn't realise—"

"Leave it, Mrs Boswell." He released his grip on his wife's bottom and cleared his throat. "Give us a moment."

"Of course, my lord." She scrambled to her feet and scurried down the corridor as if there were a prize for the first to reach the stairs.

"So much for a private experiment," he said, staring after Mrs Boswell. If he looked at his wife now and found desire in her eyes, he doubted he'd have the strength to walk away.

"*Experiment* is the right word." Her breath caught, the husky edge confirming she was far from composed. "If desire were a lesson in chemistry, I'd have singed more than my eyebrows on the burner."

Trust her to make him laugh when he ought to repent.

"It did get rather heated for a moment." The air had cooled, yet the fire she'd kindled still burned beneath his skin. "Tell me, have you decided which you prefer? The tender or the urgent?"

She hesitated, and that silence was its own kind of invitation, forcing him to meet her gaze, to feel the ache of desire left unspent, to imagine what might follow if they carried the lesson a little further.

"Are we still saying things we should keep to ourselves?" she asked.

"I think we've passed the point of keeping secrets."

She swallowed. "As my friend, I'm grateful to you for taking a novice under your wing. And as for my preference, I like kissing you, Gabriel, regardless of the tempo."

The comment found a chink in his armour, and damn him if his heart didn't soften like iron in the forge.

"There are more than two ways to kiss." The words slipped from his mouth before his mind caught up. He was almost inviting her to enhance her studies. "Which is why desire is a dangerous game for two people bound by a pact of friendship."

Her understanding smile stung like salt to an open wound. "Yes, but we can use our wedding day as an excuse. Say it was a means to mark the occasion as memorable."

More than memorable. He would carry it with him for the rest of his days. "It's late. I shall bid you good night, Olivia." He placed a hand over his heart and bowed.

"Good night, Gabriel. I shall rise bright and early to begin our investigation. After all, that's the reason we find ourselves here."

It was undoubtedly the reason.

Except it wasn't.

Something else had driven him to World's End that night, the same reason he lingered at her door now, though he refused to name it.

He walked away. Behind him came the faint creak of the door, then the quiet click of the lock.

Mrs Boswell was waiting at the foot of the stairs, as silent as a priest at confession, her expression free of judgement.

"I know. I've inherited my parents' fondness for lewd antics in corridors." He adjusted his cuffs, feigning indifference, though the notion brought bile to his throat. "It seems I share their taste for coupling in public places."

Her brows rose, but her voice was gentle. "You're nothing like them, my lord. And kissing your wife on your wedding day is hardly considered debauchery."

He gave a mirthless laugh. "That depends on the intention behind the kiss, Mrs Boswell." His thoughts had been far from tame.

"Perhaps the intention was the first honest thing you've allowed yourself in years. I've never known you to act against your will."

"I fear I'm compelled by the same weaknesses as other men. That must be a dreadful disappointment."

"Or a blessing in disguise." Taking advantage of his mellow mood, she asked the question that had plagued her since his return from the watch-house. "Was it him? Mr Lovelace?"

"Probably." The image would haunt him tonight. "Possibly."

"You don't know?"

"I'll not commit unless I'm certain."

"Certain you're not being used to serve someone else's end?"

"You must admit there's something odd about the timing." Two friends lost a decade ago, both reappearing within days of each other. The question he had to answer was what it had to do with Olivia.

He saw a flash of fear in his housekeeper's eyes. "Perhaps you could take Lady Rothley and visit Eaton Chase. Let Mr Daventry and Lord Berridge handle things here."

"You're suggesting I run away, Mrs Boswell?" he mocked, though her concern touched him deeply. "My ancestor died protecting the crown on the field at Agincourt. I'll not be chased from my home by ghosts."

"Then I pray no one is wounded in the skirmish."

She'd watched him fight many battles, most with himself.

On that sobering note, he bid his housekeeper goodnight and returned to the sanctuary of his private chambers.

Except his rooms were no longer a refuge.

The drawing room still held her scent, roses laced with something indefinable, the same quiet mystery that surrounded the woman herself. Memories of their kiss crowded his mind, and he sat in her chair, savouring the thought because it was the closest he would come to living it again.

He lingered in his dressing room long after dismissing his valet, his gaze fixed on the concealed door to his private library, imagining her eyes on his bare chest, the memory brushing over him like an intimate caress.

His bed was cold.

Yet his body was as hot as a flame.

He fought the urge to take himself in hand, to end the ache while whispering her name. Bloody hell. Had he learnt nothing?

He stared at the ceiling, forcing his thoughts to still. Safe thoughts. Cold thoughts. Everyone lied in the end. Better to return to his old creed of solitude. The only defence a man could trust. The one that had never betrayed him.

Chapter Eleven

*Office of the Order
Hart Street, Covent Garden*

Three days later

Olivia sat on the plush damask sofa in the Order's drawing room, observing Gabriel as he explained what they'd discovered in the valise.

"The items hold nothing of interest, save for the metal token engraved with a swallow, and the phrase concealed beneath the painted miniature: *Beware the Ides of March.*"

While Mr Daventry listened like a man equally intrigued by puzzles, she studied her husband's mouth. Memories filled her mind, the heat, the intimacy, the skill in those tempting lips, but now they moved with careful precision, revealing nothing of the passion she remembered.

"And you think this quote relates to betrayal and your father's secretive dealings, Lady Rothley?"

Mr Daventry cleared his throat and repeated the question

while she sat staring at Gabriel like a bedlamite. Her husband was right. Awakened desire was like an ember that refused to die. The need to stoke the fire had become a quiet obsession.

"Lady Rothley?"

She started. "Forgive me. I'm not accustomed to hearing my new name. Yes, my father was trying to warn me about something."

"Or someone," the master of the Order added.

She thought of Justin Lovelace. Where had he been for the last ten years, and why try to kill a woman for a worthless trinket? Assuming the man in the watch-house was Gabriel's long-lost friend.

Mr Daventry must have read her mind. "I sent Gentry to examine the body found in the cottage. As a doctor, he understands how *rigor mortis* affects muscles and tissue. I asked that he compare the facial structure to the miniature owned by the countess."

Gabriel sat forward. "He went without me?"

"Yes. In a professional capacity. Gentry was also Justin's friend, and I didn't want the moment clouded by sentiment."

Gabriel's laugh rang with derision. "I don't have a sentimental bone in me."

She wondered if he knew that was a lie. Was the second chair he'd placed in his private library merely practical? What of the space he'd cleared for her small collection of books?

"I'm glad to hear it," Mr Daventry said, though his tone held no amusement. "Because resurrectionists stole the body."

Gabriel shot to his feet. "Stole it? When?"

"The night you visited the watch-house." Daventry drew a letter from his leather portfolio. "Barker admits the watch was lax. He said shots were fired as you left. The man must have returned to steal the body, though there are more holes in his statement than a cook's sieve. Barker spent the last two days searching for the culprit, hoping to have the corpse returned before the coroner discovered it missing."

While Gabriel cursed the watchman's incompetence, she felt a flood of conflicting emotions. Relief that the devil had met his due. Pity for the countess, who would have no closure. And sadness for Gabriel, who might never know peace.

"That's not all," Mr Daventry said, his tone grave.

"Let me guess." Gabriel returned to his seat, his irritation barely contained. "Your agent failed to find the original inquest report when he visited Cambridge."

"Apparently, it was lost some years ago."

A tense silence settled, along with the sense they were merely pawns in a game without rules.

"There's more." Mr Daventry met her gaze, and the knot in her stomach tightened. "Someone desecrated your father's grave. They left evidence to suggest they're from Whitechapel. And we're supposed to believe thieves journeyed sixty miles to disturb one plot."

A pang gripped her chest, sharp, disbelieving. Before she knew it, she reached across the sofa for Gabriel's hand. He took it without hesitation, their first touch since he'd torn his mouth from hers and broken lust's spell.

Her fingers clung to his. The room seemed to shrink, the air too thin.

She swallowed to loosen her throat. "They took him?"

"They took whoever was buried there and conveniently left a scrap of cloth with an undertaker's stamp. We can't be sure it was your father, just as we can't be sure what's been staged for our benefit."

Gabriel exhaled slowly. "Then we focus on what we do know, on what we can prove, in the hope of understanding what the blazes is going on here."

Mr Daventry agreed. "Can you recite the poem you mentioned during the drive to Bow Street? The one that led you to World's End and the mausoleum."

"I can do better than that." She released Gabriel's hand, yet the connection still simmered, the warmth of his touch refusing to fade. Reaching into her reticule, she withdrew a small scroll. "I wrote it out yesterday and made a copy. We spent the evening dissecting every line."

And sipping wine. Enjoying conversation. But no touches. No kissing. No teasing glances that might be misconstrued.

As Mr Daventry studied the verse, she wondered which lines captured his interest, and what he might see that they had missed.

"And you joined the ladies at The Burnished Jade because of the words in this poem?" he clarified.

"Yes, and because I longed for company of an evening. I feel as if I've been alone most of my life." Those nights at the countess's club had been among her happiest. It was where she'd first seen Gabriel, aloof and unreadable, yet under his gaze she'd never felt so alive.

"You had a maid," Gabriel said.

"Not when I first came to London." She had been more than capable of dressing herself and stoking the fire. "But a man followed me home when I lived in Clerkenwell. He spent an hour skulking in the doorway across the street."

After that, she'd hired a maid for protection, not propriety.

Mr Daventry glanced up from the poem. "That was before

the burglary, when the intruder stole your mother's jewellery box?"

"Yes, but the box didn't belong to my mother. I bought it for five shillings at the pawnbroker's, along with the paste brooch, comb and earrings, a distraction for a would-be thief. The man who attacked me at the mausoleum was the same one who broke into my home and stole the box."

"The same dead man found in the cottage," Gabriel stated.

Mr Daventry took up his notebook and pencil and copied several lines of the poem. "Where did you hire the maid?"

"The Servants' Registry in Bishopsgate."

"Near The Burnished Jade?"

"Yes." When Mr Daventry glanced at the poem again, she knew what he was thinking. "You believe my attacker knew I would visit The Jade?"

It was Gabriel who answered. "London is too vast for it to be a coincidence. The person expected you to visit the countess. Probably because Justin Lovelace was involved."

There were so many *probablys*, how were they ever to learn the truth? "The clues must be in the poem. That's what led me here. And something in the valise holds the answers we need."

"Or something in the mausoleum," Mr Daventry said. "The key was meant to lead you to the right place." He went on to recite a few lines of verse to prove his point.

> *This crypt, built to entomb the dead,*
> *Is now a prison for a living thought.*
> *A secret buried with a future dread,*

"It's poor prose," she said, "but the message is clear."

"I shall have an agent investigate those who are buried there."

She sensed Gabriel's frustration before he spoke. "We'll not sit idle. I suggest we question Mrs Hodge. She discovered the body and may have witnessed something important."

Mr Daventry consulted his notes. "She claims she worked for Sir Randall Ferguson. You should verify her account."

"I planned to call on him this afternoon."

Mr Daventry asked her to explain again what she'd witnessed while living at home with her father.

"So your mother died in the fire, but her body was never recovered," he said, making a brief notation. Then he stole the air from her lungs with a final question. "Might she have left, or been taken by this fraternity?"

Olivia sat with her thoughts, recalling the day with morbid clarity. If she'd known it was the last time she'd see her mother, she would have stayed longer. Said all the things that mattered. "My father called my absence a fortunate twist of fate." The lump in her throat made it hard to swallow. But lately, she'd begun to wonder. "What if it wasn't luck? What if it happened by design?"

"You were sent away," Mr Daventry stated, sounding certain.

"To run an errand that should have taken an hour."

"But there was an unexpected delay."

"Yes. When I took the basket to Mrs Jenkins in the next village, two of her children were ill. I fetched the doctor and stayed to cut linens and bring clean water."

"Your father was landed gentry." Mr Daventry, it seemed, had wasted no time gathering evidence. "Your childhood home in Lewes came with fifty acres, yet no servants died in the fire."

A small mercy no one questioned.

"He rented the land to local farmers, and we kept a small staff of three at my father's insistence. It was their half-day."

"Like your husband, perhaps he knew servants could be bought."

Gabriel shifted. "It's why I don't keep a butler. I've yet to meet one I can trust."

"You've yet to meet anyone you can trust," Mr Daventry quipped before returning to his original question. "Do the events of that day seem suspicious to you now, my lady?"

"Everything seems suspicious to me now."

"Then you and Rothley have much in common."

"Common ground is where all good friendships are built."

Mr Daventry glanced between them and gave a lopsided smirk. "My wife would agree. She's been my constant in a world of uncertainty."

Olivia managed a faint smile. Gabriel could never say that about her. The thought pressed heavily on her chest, an ache beneath her ribs, a reminder there was still something she hadn't told him.

Something he deserved to know.

Something that might change everything.

Perhaps it wasn't too late.

"You must understand that when your life is shrouded in lies and secrecy, it becomes difficult to trust your own thoughts." Her pulse drummed in her throat as both men fixed her with unnerving intensity. "There's something else. Something I've been afraid to mention. Two things, actually. One I'm fairly certain of. The other … less so."

Gabriel's weary sigh cut to the bone.

She braced herself, half expecting him to stand and walk out.

Instead, he surprised her. "I know how the mind plays tricks. How it recycles the same thoughts until you start doubting your own sanity."

"Yes." She smiled, hoping the warmth blooming in her chest reached her eyes. That he felt it. That he knew. "I prayed you'd understand."

"Still, I'll have your word this is the last time you'll keep secrets or fail to confide in me."

"I held my tongue to spare you the uncertainty, but I give you my word, there is nothing more." She gathered her courage, knowing what she said next might change everything. "I may have seen Justin Lovelace before. Two years ago, while peering through the keyhole of my father's study."

"You refer to the man taken from the watch-house?" Gabriel refused to confirm or deny they were speaking about his friend.

"Yes. And because something in the countess' expression when she's anxious reminds me of him." Anticipating their questions, she hurried on. "He'd come to collect a map. Whatever he planned to do with it, the risks were great, because he asked that those closest to him be protected."

Part of her wished she had remained abed and not been so inquisitive. But she'd crept to the study, determined to learn why her father disappeared at night.

"And you've no notion what was marked on the map?" Mr Daventry asked. "No names were mentioned."

"No. Only that he would receive the key from their contact at Shady Moor."

"Shady Moor? You mean Shadwell?" Mr Daventry said.

"No. It could have been Shadymere. They spoke in hushed voices."

"Shadowmere?"

"Yes, that may be it." She frowned, the name stirring a faint unease. "The other man called it a place of ill repute, and said it would be the only time he was expected to participate."

Mr Daventry's dark gaze shifted to Gabriel. "It makes sense they'd use Hawke's licentious gatherings to pass information, the noise and chaos would mask any exchange. But you know what this means."

"Yes. The spies hold positions in society." There was something in Gabriel's tone, a quiet thrill, as if he would enjoy holding them to account. "Faces I may even remember from my parents' wild parties."

"We'll visit Dominic Hawke once we've gathered more information." Mr Daventry gave a mocking snort. "Before we march into Shadowmere, we'd better be certain of the facts."

A knock on the door announced the cheerful housekeeper, Mrs Gunning, balancing a laden tea tray, the smell of freshly baked lemon cake filling the room.

"I thought you might fancy a little something to keep the hunger pangs at bay," she said, smiling as she set down the tray. She poured the tea, bobbed a curtsy, and retreated as swiftly as she came.

Olivia's gaze slid to Gabriel. The remark had been innocent, yet lemon cake would not satisfy the hunger that had taken root inside her.

Gabriel reached for a slice and took a bite, licking a few crumbs from the corner of his mouth. "You mentioned two things," he said. "One you were more certain of."

"Yes." She paused, considering whether she could trust these men, and decided she must. "I was told to take a note to a carriage waiting a mile down the lane and give it to the coachman. At the time, it felt like an errand, but now I believe I'm implicated in an event that happened a month later."

She remembered the fear in her father's eyes. How he'd hesitated before handing her the lantern. How his voice caught as he told her to be quick, to keep to the edge of the road.

"You read the note?" Gabriel asked.

"It wasn't sealed. I believe that was deliberate."

"Do you recall what it said?"

"Almost word for word. I have a memory for these things." She took a sip of tea and set down her cup, the clatter of china belying her nerves.

Gather in St Giles, dusk, 7th May.
Signal: three lanterns in window of The Mason's Arms.
Target the polling booths at Westminster and Guildhall.
Wheels and barrels for barricade at Holborn.
Burn goods at Shadwell if pursuit begins.
Pay ringleaders five shillings apiece.

Gabriel's expression darkened as she finished. A brief silence followed while he and Mr Daventry exchanged a guarded glance.

"That sounds like instructions for the planned riot during the Days of May," Mr Daventry said.

"When the country teetered on the edge of revolution," Gabriel murmured. "One spark, and London might have burned."

Mr Daventry sighed. "Then perhaps we're not dealing with spies at all, but revolutionaries."

"And the coachman could testify that I was the one who delivered the rioters' instructions." She wore the weight of her actions like iron shackles. "I could be hanged for treason."

A shadow crossed Gabriel's face, as if he'd glimpsed a premonition. A vision of the tragic end that awaited them both. "They'll have to kill me first."

He spoke in earnest. He never said anything he didn't mean. He could have bought her a gilded carriage, a team of muscled Arabians, or a palace grander than Versailles, and it still wouldn't have touched her as deeply as that fierce declaration.

Sweet mercy. If he meant for her to fall slowly in love with him, he was going about it the right way.

"The few rioters caught were transported," Mr Daventry said. "I'll have an agent gather their names and see if there's a connection between them. But the unrest didn't begin with the Days of May. Men have been plotting to overthrow the government since before King William took the throne."

"Yes, for more than a decade," Gabriel added, before mentioning Justin Lovelace. "Did the coroner find anything in the dead man's pockets?"

"Nothing but a few coins in his purse."

A silence followed. Talk of riots and treason had Gabriel shifting in his seat, the drum of his fingers on the armrest betraying the urge to move, to act, to chase the truth wherever it led.

"There's one question that demands an answer," he said, turning to Olivia. "Sir Randall is a generous man, but how did Mrs Hodge come to own two cottages in World's End?"

"Her sister left her a small inheritance." Mrs Hodge had made a point of saying she'd bought the properties for a bargain price. "Few people want to live beside a graveyard."

He frowned. "How did you come to hear of the property?"

"The poem mentioned World's End and a graveyard, so I visited every burial ground along that road, believing the key would open a crypt. When I found the cottage standing empty, Mrs Hodge appeared, and we got talking. She offered to let it for a modest sum. Living there gave me more time to search the burial grounds."

She had gone seeking the poem's meaning and found only her own folly. Mrs Hodge's appearance could not have been chance. Had the woman warned her attacker?

A chill threaded through her thoughts. Time was against them. They were missing a vital piece of the puzzle, and someone was willing to kill them to find it.

Conduit Street
Mayfair

Olivia glanced at the elegant facade of Sir Randall Ferguson's townhouse and dared to make the suggestion she knew Gabriel would dismiss before she'd uttered the last syllable.

"After what you learnt this afternoon, I think it best you introduce me as one of Mr Daventry's enquiry agents."

Gabriel arched a brow as he helped her down from the carriage. "You're my wife. No foolish errand for your father will change that."

"But I committed a criminal act," she whispered, mindful of passers-by. "I could be transported if the truth came to light."

Though her feet were planted firmly on the pavement, he didn't release her hand but drew her close, impossibly close.

"We're all one step away from breaking the law. I'd hurt any man who threatened you. Besides, no one can prove you gave the coachman the letter without implicating themselves. The act served one purpose. To buy your father's silence."

It seemed he'd considered the matter carefully.

"You're not disappointed you married a fool?"

He tutted softly. "A fool wouldn't have read the letter and memorised its contents. A fool would be walking around blindly, not searching for answers."

"Is there anything I could say to make you regret marrying me?" Every moment spent with him only reinforced that she had made the right decision.

His tepid smile said there was. "Don't ever profess to love me and disappear the same night."

A vision of the incomparable Miss Bourne entered her mind, and she dismissed it at once. How did one prove one's loyalty?

"Give me your thumb." While she relished his baffled expression, she took the pin from her bonnet, removed her glove, and stabbed the pad of her own thumb. A scarlet drop formed. It might be the only part of herself she would ever give to him. "Let us make another pact. On my oath, I will never leave Studland Park without discussing it with you first."

Mildly amused, he took the pin and pricked his own thumb. "You broke the pact of friendship when you kissed me. What's to say you won't break this one?"

"We broke the pact of friendship to test the boundaries." She pressed her thumb to his, their blood mingling, warm and binding.

His eyes darkened to inky pools as he stared at the

crimson stain. "I believe that's the most erotic thing a woman has ever done to me, and in the street, no less."

"With a harem at home, I find that surprising. And it's hard to comment when my list of erotic experiences is limited."

"Permit me to rectify that." He held her captive with his gaze as he drew her thumb into his mouth and sucked it clean.

Desire unfurled in her belly. The need to feel the glide of his mouth over every inch of her body made it hard to breathe.

"Remember," he said, removing his handkerchief and wiping blood from his thumb, "I keep a harem of one, and she has a penchant for poetry and peacocks."

Despite claiming he had a heart of stone, Gabriel knew how to make a woman feel special. "I thought the point of a harem was to choose a partner to suit one's mood. Does one not limit your options?"

"Not if she surprises me at every turn."

"I don't do it on purpose."

"I know. That's what makes you unique."

He offered his arm, and she took it without thinking. One firm rap of the polished brass knocker brought the butler, an efficient man too handsome for his own good. The mere mention of their titles saw them swiftly ushered into the hall.

Sir Randall came to greet them, his white hair and faint Scottish brogue lending him a jovial air. "Did I hear correctly?" His gaze moved from Gabriel to Olivia. "My butler announced you as Lord and Lady Rothley. Are congratulations in order, or has the man made an embarrassing mistake?"

"Your butler was correct," Gabriel said, his hand settling at Olivia's back. "Sir Randall, my wife, Lady Rothley."

"Then allow me to offer my felicitations." He inclined his head. "May your union bring you every happiness."

Gabriel's hand slid lower, a fraction too low. "I'm confident it will."

Sir Randall clapped his hands together. "Excellent. Now, to what do I owe the pleasure?"

"We're here to enquire after your former housekeeper, Mrs Hodge," Gabriel said as they were shown into the baronet's musty study, though they chose to stand. "She claims to have worked at Canfield Manor. We need to clarify a few facts."

"Facts?" Sir Randall's cheeks puffed. "Are you hiring her? You make it sound as though she's given false references."

"She's a witness in a criminal case," Gabriel said, omitting to mention that his wife was a suspect, "and claims to have been in your employ for fifteen years."

His eyes narrowed. "Footpads operating in World's End again? Aye, it'll only get worse when the nights draw in. Why she'd want to live out there is beyond me. But if Mrs Hodge described the bandits, you may depend on it being right."

"You were satisfied with her work?" Olivia asked.

"Aye, my lady. Her work was exemplary. My sister Martha had a great fondness for her. Truth be told, I'd have been lost without Mrs Hodge in those last few months."

Olivia offered her condolences. "Mrs Hodge said she knew it was time to retire when your sister sadly passed."

Sir Randall glanced at the door before stepping closer. "It helped that Martha left her a small annuity, and a diamond brooch she insisted Mrs Hodge sell. I helped her use the money to buy that cottage out in the back of beyond."

"Mrs Hodge owns two cottages in World's End," Gabriel said.

The man raised his chin. "Aye. She mentioned buying the one next door, but I've nae heard from her since she settled there."

"Do you know what made her choose that area?" He masked the hint of suspicion in his tone with a note of amusement. "Few people would live on a road frequented by thieves or beside a graveyard."

"I suggested one in Brompton, but she was eager to do the Lord's work and made the acquaintance of Reverend Clay when he came to take tea with Martha."

Olivia was a little confused. "She met the rector in town, or did he visit Canfield Manor?"

Sir Randall's expression grew sombre. "Though the country was the best place for her, Martha insisted on spending her last months in town. Mrs Hodge left her post to act as nurse and paid companion."

During a brief silence, Sir Randall dabbed a tear from his eye.

"If I may say, you make it sound as though Mrs Hodge is the footpad, nae the witness."

Olivia wondered how Gabriel would explain their prying, but he carried that quiet air of authority she found so attractive.

"She came across the victim. As the last person to see him alive, naturally, that makes her a person of interest."

Sir Randall seemed appeased. "Is Daventry so short of agents he's taken to leaning on friends now?"

"It's in all our interests to keep the streets safe," Gabriel replied, an almost predatory look in his eyes. "And there's a certain thrill that comes with engaging in dangerous pursuits. My crest bears a dragon for a reason."

It sounded like a veiled warning.

Perhaps he'd noticed the same curious object on the desk, and had begun to doubt Sir Randall's sincerity. Either way, she felt compelled to offer a similar caution.

"Ridding London of scoundrels is to be our new pastime." She slipped her fingers around Gabriel's arm, feeling the solid strength beneath the fine cloth. "Someone must make a stand, and we cannot leave it to politicians."

Sir Randall hesitated, shifting his weight before saying, "True enough. Useless lot, and nae a backbone between them."

Her gaze drifted to the desk, to the marble heart resting atop a stack of papers, its polished surface faintly veined with grey. "What a beautiful paperweight."

Sir Randall smiled. "Aye. Martha had a fondness for the thing, and I cannae bear to part with it. Her late husband gave it to her on their wedding day, said it was a symbol that love is timeless."

"What a romantic thought."

He gave a small shrug. "Sentimental nonsense, but she always kept it close."

Gabriel exhaled. "Some men know how to touch a woman's heart. The rest of us are left wandering blindly in the dark."

Sir Randall laughed. "Ye've done something right, my lord. It's nae every day a man's wife takes his arm while merely standing in a study."

She felt the muscle in Gabriel's arm tense beneath her fingers, and he covered her hand with his own. "Perhaps strength in a marriage lies not in gifts, but in finding someone you can depend on."

The baronet chortled. "'Tis easier on the purse, too."

Keen to leave, Gabriel thanked the man for his time.

She waited until they were settled inside the carriage before sharing her observations. "Do you know why I asked about the heart?"

"Because it's a line in your father's poem."

"*My secret slumbers in this marble heart*," she quoted. "It's likely just a coincidence. A symbolic reference."

"A coincidence?" Gabriel raised a brow. "That its owner died the same time as your father? That Mrs Hodge owns a cottage beside the mausoleum, and you have the only key? That I've never seen a marble heart before, and her former employer just happens to possess one?"

"You're right. It does sound odd."

She expected they'd drive to World's End to question Mrs Hodge, but Gabriel gave the order for home.

"Home? You don't think we should question Mrs Hodge about the man she found dead in her cottage?"

"Not today. Whoever orchestrated the attack on you could have a man watching Sir Randall's house. I'd rather not risk it."

"You're being cautious, my lord. Almost as if you can't bear to lose me." A teasing smile touched her lips, though the image of his body shielding hers as shots rang out stirred a thrill she ought not to feel.

"Lose the best thing that's happened to me in years?" He almost smiled, and she suspected the confession had cost him dearly. "As a husband, I may stumble in the dark, but even I know the value of a gift."

Chapter Twelve

Something was off, and it wasn't the sole meunière. The clink of silver on Sèvres porcelain grated, as did the blank stares of the liveried footmen and the incessant ticking of the mantel clock. Though she sat beside Gabriel at the head of the table, his mood had cooled since his confession in the carriage.

His sighs deepened with each mouthful of sautéed green beans. Twice, she caught him studying her over the rim of his wine glass, his gaze travelling over her as if she wore a silk chemise rather than a simple grey dress.

She scoured her mind, replaying her reply.

Then I hope you never tire of your gift.

Was he wondering how they might live together when kissing lost its charm? Or which one of them would feel regret first? Was that what troubled him now?

"You seem preoccupied tonight," she said, determined to uphold their oath and be honest. "I'm surprised we're dining here, and not in your private chambers."

His gaze flicked to the footmen, and they left without a whisper. Then he took a long drink of his claret. "Do you know why the gossips think I keep a secret harem in a hidden cellar?"

The question caught her off guard, though the answer came easily. "Because you're an exceptionally handsome man who avoids female company, especially the ladies of the *ton*?"

He seemed to find that amusing.

"Because my parents held wild parties here. They spent their whole married life breaking their vows, degrading their union, disappointing one another."

She wondered why he was telling her now.

"Is that why you don't believe in love?"

He stared at his plate, wincing as though the sight of food sickened him. "Love is a weapon. A means to inflict pain. I learnt that long before Miss Bourne took my father's bribe. She was the final lesson."

What does it have to do with me? she wanted to say.

"You're not your father, and I'm not Miss Bourne."

"No. You're not." He met her gaze, his fingers tightening around the glass, the corners of his eyes creasing. "But I've broken my vow to you, and you cannot know how much that pains me."

She was quick to correct him. "Forgive me. I'm struggling to see how. You promised friendship, and you've proven you're the person I can trust most. You swore to protect me and have saved my life twice."

"I think you know what I'm referring to."

"If it's the *experiment*, then I fail to see the problem."

"It's not the experiment."

"What then?"

"It's how easily you undo me."

The words stole her breath.

This strong, self-possessed man, undone by her lips? Perhaps it wasn't her, but the years spent denying himself affection.

She reached for her wine and took a fortifying sip. "And so you're rebuilding your fortress and scouring the kingdom for the strongest armour, in a bid to lock me out?"

"That's all I know," he confessed.

Her heart softened, though she battled two instincts: one to reach out and take his hand, the other to protect herself, for she feared Gabriel would be all too easy to love.

"It doesn't help that we're working so closely on the case," she said. He made her feel like his equal, and she would always admire him for that. Yet for all his talk of restraint, he touched her as often as she touched him. Perhaps she should be the one wearing a chest plate of steel. "We might need to limit the time we spend together at home. See each other less."

Would that appease him?

Ease his guilt for passionately kissing a friend?

The furrows between his brow said not.

Still, he needed to draw his own conclusions. Solitude, not sympathy, was the best course. A man skilled at deciphering poetry would, in time, make sense of his own tangled emotions.

She dabbed her mouth with her napkin and rose. "It's been a long day, and I've no appetite. A little time apart might help you see you've done nothing wrong other than test the natural boundaries." Before he could reply, she added, "Goodnight, Gabriel."

He murmured her name, a plea, an apology, who knew? But she pretended not to hear and left the room. She didn't linger but hurried upstairs and dressed for bed. Still, she paced, wondering if he'd drink until he drowned in regret.

Mrs Boswell came to turn down the bed, explaining that the maids always took supper when the master dined, but word had already reached below stairs that Olivia had left before finishing her meal.

"Once you're settled, we should sit down and discuss your expectations, ma'am." Mrs Boswell folded back the coverlet and placed a sprig of dried lavender on the pillow.

"You mean I shouldn't expect too much of him?"

"I mean, discuss the maids' routine, the menus, and which room you'd like for your private office, where you might deal with correspondence. There'll be letters from charitable foundations and invitations to balls, though not before you've been presented at court. We'll need to hire a modiste to design your wardrobe. The countess can recommend someone suitable."

"Oh. I see." It all sounded rather daunting. And to think she'd imagined spending her days walking the grounds with him, discussing poetry. "Forgive me, I've been so intent on solving a mystery, I've not given it any thought."

"The mystery of who killed Mr Lovelace and why someone might wish to blame you?"

"That, and how best to help my husband manage his feelings, though the latter is rather more complex, I fear."

Mrs Boswell gave a knowing smile. "May I speak freely, my lady?"

"Of course." She was out of her depth in every regard.

"Shall I tell you how many ladies his lordship has invited into this house since his father passed nine years ago?"

"Please do." Jealousy slithered through her chest like a serpent in the grass. In truth, she would rather not know.

"None." Mrs Boswell paused, letting Olivia feel the weight of her answer. "And shall I tell you how many ladies have occupied space in his mind?"

"I suspect you're going to."

"None but you, ma'am."

That wasn't entirely true. "His preoccupation with Miss Bourne is common knowledge. He refers to her often."

"Then I ought to have spoken more wisely," Mrs Boswell said, inclining her head, "and said how many ladies he's thought of with any real feeling. The Marquess of Rothley does not kiss in corridors, nor does he keep a particular poetry book at his bedside. He lets no one into his carefully constructed world."

"What are you saying, Mrs Boswell?"

"I'm saying he hasn't been the same since he met you, my lady. And now he's gone and broken his word, and nothing unsettles him more."

"We merely kissed." Which was entirely her fault. "He's not really broken a vow."

"You can be sure he has in thought, if not in deed, ma'am."

Her mind raced. What had he imagined them doing? Doubtless something so passionate it had driven him to this moment of self-flagellation.

"And this obsession with honour stems from his parents' raucous parties?" Small wonder the gossips never let him forget.

Mrs Boswell paled, her shoulders curling inward. "No child should see the things he did. I was barely a woman myself then, but it shocked me to the core."

Olivia studied her, struck by the depth of her distress. It

explained his hatred of the house. A place more like a mausoleum than a home.

"Then why stay here? Why torment himself with painful memories when he has a grand property in town?"

Mrs Boswell moved to the door, peered into the corridor, then returned and lowered her voice. "He's afraid she'll return."

"Miss Bourne?"

"His mother."

Olivia pressed a hand to her throat. "I assumed she passed years ago, before the incident with Miss Bourne."

"She left after his father died, when he needed her most. The butler went with her. When his lordship inherited, he dismissed her lover and forbade her friends from calling at the house."

Olivia's heart sank. He had comforted her while carrying his own sorrow alone. And she'd never even thought to ask.

"He stopped her from taking the Rothley jewels, but she left regardless. It's said she perished with her lover in some hellhole in France. But, like everything in his life, it's shadowed by uncertainty."

She absorbed the words, a glimmer of understanding and pity stirring in her chest. It explained his obsession with betrayal.

"I cannot thank you enough for trusting me, Mrs Boswell, though I doubt I'll sleep a wink tonight." Had she known this half an hour ago, she might have stayed downstairs. Might have kept Gabriel company.

"I've just the remedy for restless thoughts, ma'am."

It wasn't merely restless thoughts. Her body craved his touch, the slow burn of it, the ache that bloomed after. But he was right. Friendship shouldn't feel like this. Every hour in his presence blurred the lines a little more.

"I'll not take laudanum."

"I was thinking of a peaceful walk, my lady. His lordship's grandmother designed the sensory garden that leads to the fountain. It's still light. I can show you the way. I'll just fetch your half boots and a wrapper."

The need to escape the house, and to still the pulse that quickened whenever she thought of him, had her agreeing. While she tied the belt of her muslin wrapper, Mrs Boswell insisted on brushing out her hair.

They took the servants' stairs and met no one en route.

"I'm told her ladyship always began in the herb garden, with the gentle scent of lemon thyme," Mrs Boswell said as they stepped out into the warm night air. "The path will take you through the ornamental gardens. Keep to the gravel, and when you pass the statue of Psyche, follow the roses until you reach the grand fountain."

Olivia touched her arm. Mrs Boswell's motherly manner was something to be treasured; she made everything feel less daunting.

"You're welcome to accompany me."

"Thank you, ma'am, but the sensory garden is meant to be enjoyed alone."

A breeze stirred the herbs, releasing a crisp, calming note.

Then she startled Olivia by pressing a small pocket pistol into her hand, folding her fingers around the cool metal. "Take this as a precaution. It's served me well in darker days. His lordship would have my guts for garters if I let you wander about unarmed."

"Perhaps I should stay inside."

"You're perfectly safe, ma'am. Still, I'll let his lordship

know where you are. Now, take your walk. The night air works wonders for a troubled mind."

The thought of pacing her chamber all evening held little appeal. She slipped the pistol into her pocket and nodded. "Very well. I shall be but half an hour."

The last of the daylight lingered on the horizon, bathing the garden in hues of lilac and gold. She followed the path past banks of rosemary and lavender, the air growing sweeter as it wound between clusters of roses and night-blooming jasmine.

It was beautiful here, but Gabriel saw only the pain of the past. She thought of the night he had come to the cottage. How different things might have been had he arrived a minute too late.

She ran her hand through the lavender and thought of every kiss they had shared, the tender press of his lips, the deep sweep of his tongue, the fever of passion they could never quite suppress.

But even beauty had its shadows.

Only time would tell whether fate was a blessing or a curse. The weight of the pistol in her pocket was a sober reminder that danger was never far from her door.

Gabriel held the poetry book in his hands, but the words on the page swam before his eyes, blurred by thought and his lack of interest in anything but the woman he had married.

He reached for his brandy, then decided against it. He considered changing the book, but nothing would distract him tonight—not a hard ride across open fields, not a brawl with the king of rogues in the basement of Fortune's

Den, not the answers to every damn question that plagued him.

Nothing. Except her.

He should have stopped her from leaving the dining room. Given her the key to his fortress and invited her to come and go whenever the hell she pleased.

What the blazes was wrong with him? He shot to his feet. So what if the saintly Lord Rothley had broken a vow? He hadn't done so alone.

Hypocrite. The word hissed through his head. He'd promised to love and cherish her, all while expecting to do neither. Why not admit he'd married her because he wanted her, not out of some noble act of benevolence?

He turned on his heel and strode out of the library only to meet a breathless Mrs Boswell hurrying along the corridor.

"If you've come to tell me Molière is in a temper, you'll find I've no sympathy to spare."

"No, my lord, though he has locked himself in the pantry with a dish of peaches à la Condé. I came to inform you that her ladyship has left—"

"Left!" He froze. She'd broken their blood oath already?

"To walk in the garden. I only mention it because, with talk of secrets and dead men, I insisted her ladyship take a pocket pistol."

Suspicion flared, an old pattern he couldn't break. "Did she take her coat and bonnet? Are her clothes still in the armoire? For heaven's sake, Mrs Boswell, did she pack a valise?"

His mind raced through possibilities, none of them good. The image of her alone on the road, unprotected, twisted his gut.

"She's taking the sensory walk in her nightgown and

wrapper. It was my suggestion. I thought time alone might ease her mind." Mrs Boswell hesitated. "She should still be in the garden. If you're quick, you might see her from the window."

Mrs Boswell hurried away before he could call her back.

He didn't wait to argue. He was already moving, taking the back stairs two at a time. The room at the end of the upper corridor, once his grandfather's beloved art room, offered the best view of the gardens.

The fountain stood beyond the glass, a monument to past debauchery, and he forced himself to banish the memory of naked revellers cavorting during the summer solstice.

Instead, he searched the paths for her—his wife—for the soft billow of muslin, the glint of copper hair, movement among the roses.

His breath caught when she stepped into view, her wrapper drawn close, her hair a glowing cascade that brushed the pale curve of her neck.

Something tightened low in his chest. He told himself it was concern, the need to ensure her safety. But the truth settled like heat beneath his skin, a fire crawling through every inch of him.

She bent to smell the lavender, and the sight near undid him. The delicate grace of her hand. The sensual flare of her hips. Hell, he had no right to want her. Yet his body had ceased to care about rights or reason.

He pressed his palm to the glass, the chill doing little to temper these confounding urges. Lust was a devil.

Then movement beyond the topiary caught his eye, a lone figure approaching the fountain, just as his wife stepped into the clearing, blissfully unaware she was being watched.

Or was she?

Was this all a ruse?

A planned arrangement?

Had he been played for a fool from the very beginning?

He pushed away from the window and strode for the door. The corridors blurred as he descended, his boots striking hard against the marble floor.

Something made him run.

He avoided the gravel path and cut across the grass, the truth the only lure now.

The murmur of voices near the fountain made him slow and slip behind the tall topiary hedge. He recognised the woman speaking to his wife, for arrogance coated every word.

"It's obvious Gabriel is using you to hurt me," Miss Bourne said, her tone sharp with spite. "You should visit the vicarage and speak to the vicar. There's every chance the marriage is a sham. I heard a rumour the register was faked. A prop for appearance's sake."

Gabriel was about to march into the clearing and put the woman in her place, but Olivia proved she could hold her own.

"And yet Gabriel proposed before you returned to Islington. I went with him to fetch the licence. It was my name he called in the throes of passion last night."

Miss Bourne's light chuckle made his stomach roil.

"You don't need to pretend," she said. "You sleep in separate rooms. You with the peacocks, him in his hideaway."

Damnation. Who the devil told her?

He had a traitor in his midst again.

"That just goes to show how little you know about the man you betrayed." Olivia sounded confident, as if born to trap deceivers, yet went on to tell a convincing lie of her own.

"We made love in the library. And in his private drawing room. With two hundred rooms to choose from, we'll be occupied for months. Not that it's any of your concern."

Miss Bourne was undeterred. "Soon, I shall be the mistress of Wynbury Hall. Gabriel will be free to visit whenever he pleases."

"The disillusioned mistress of Wynbury Hall," Olivia returned. "Do remember, I am the Marchioness of Rothley. You'll be expected to curtsy every time we meet."

He smiled, suspecting Miss Bourne's nostrils were flaring. He would give his wife her moment of glory before he intervened.

"Enjoy it while you can, *my lady*. Gabriel has spent ten years struggling to forget me. How long before he tires of playing the dutiful husband and seeks excitement elsewhere?"

"Oh, I don't know. He seems rather smitten to me."

"Is that why you wear a pauper's band instead of the Rothley diamonds? Even a maid deserves better."

Guilt surfaced. Perhaps he should have bought her something grand and ostentatious, something befitting her position in society. And yet he prayed she'd read the symbolism in its simplicity.

"The ring is a statement, Miss Bourne. My husband knows I cannot be bought. He alludes to Donne's poem, that love, like metal beaten thin, needs no embellishment to endure." Olivia paused. "What looks plain to you is something I will always treasure."

He stepped away from the hedge, his heart stirring, because she was the only woman in the world who truly understood him. He returned to the path and called, "Olivia? Olivia, my love." He'd be damned if Kate Bourne destroyed his life a second time.

"Here, Gabriel!" Olivia's voice carried across the garden. He started towards the fountain as she addressed Miss Bourne. "You're trespassing. Leave now. Don't force me to draw my pocket pistol. It's perfectly lawful to shoot poachers."

The rustle of verdure and a sly comment signalled Miss Bourne's swift departure. But when he entered the clearing and saw his wife—a cascade of copper hair and lips soft as a sigh—he took her hand and drew her close.

"You should have told me you wanted to walk in the garden." He bent his head and kissed her without hesitation, certain Miss Bourne still watched from the shadows beyond the shrubs.

Her breath caught, the faintest tremor passing through her fingers where they rested in his.

He told himself it was theatre, a lesson in appearances. Yet when Olivia's lips parted beneath his, he was lost to need, to hunger, to the sudden truth that she was all he wanted.

He deepened the kiss, coaxing rather than taking, tasting rather than claiming. The world slipped away. There was only her warmth, the steady thrum of her heart, and the ruinous tug of lust.

She broke the kiss but didn't step back. Her breath came quick, her fingers still tangled with his. He'd forgotten how to breathe altogether.

"Come," she said softly. "Let's walk back to the house. We might find a little privacy there. I'm quite certain we need it."

Neither spoke.

Her hand remained in his, small and certain, guiding him along the path and into the house. They walked through the dim corridors, the brush of her wrapper against his thigh a prelude to seduction.

She paused by an open doorway. Moonlight spilled across the floor. "Here," she murmured, and he didn't ask why.

The room lay in shadow, the furniture shrouded beneath dust sheets, shapes touched by the faint silver sheen seeping through the curtains. Olivia closed the door. The soft click sent a thrill through him—part anticipation, part danger, all desire.

She faced him, meeting his gaze with unflinching defiance. "Don't ever do that to me again," came her terse warning, not the rampant coupling he longed for. "Don't use me to make her jealous. The moment you called out to me, it was obvious you knew she was there. That kiss was staged to prove a point."

It took him a moment to gather his wits. "I wanted her to know she's not the woman who keeps me awake at night."

"Why? Why is her opinion so important?"

"It's not. It's your opinion that matters most." Frustration —and the throbbing ache in his trousers—drove him to close the gap between them. "Did you not hear what I said during dinner? Do you not see what you do to me?"

She raised her chin. "Explain it again. You seem to change your mind as often as the weather."

He reached for the belt of her wrapper, untying it slowly. "I lied when I offered a marriage built on friendship. I simply didn't know it was a lie at the time."

She inhaled sharply as the garment fell open, his hand finding the curve of her hip. "Then you agree we might have a marriage based on physical needs as well as friendship?"

He almost laughed. Presently, the righteous Lord Rothley would say anything to join her in bed. "Let's just say it's no longer my opinions that are rigid. And the feeling I have when I kiss you is the only honest thing I've felt in thirty years."

A hint of a smile graced her lips. "And if we tire of each other? What then, Gabriel?"

He slid his hand higher, his thumb coming to rest an inch below her breast. "I'm not sure we will. We're matched mentally, the attraction is undeniable, and we're sensible enough not to have grand expectations."

She considered the proposal. "Why the change of heart?"

"It's not a change of heart. I'm merely accepting the inevitable." His gaze dropped to where his hand rested. "May I touch you, Olivia?"

She swallowed, the rapid rise and fall of her chest stealing his attention. "Tell me first why you gave me a plain band as a token of our marriage. Be honest. Did it belong to a family member?"

He knew the answer would surprise her.

"No. I had it made in town while you were sleeping." He'd paid the goldsmith a small fortune to have it ready the same day. "I measured your finger and had him engrave the inside. You deserved something more personal than diamonds."

Her brows lifted slightly. "There's an inscription? What does it say?"

He hesitated, his thumb tracing the outer curve of her breast. "You must discover it for yourself. Look when the time is right. When our troubles are behind us." He hoped it was soon. "Now, will you permit me to ease this restlessness that exists between us?"

Her gaze softened, her lips parting on a breath as she

arched into him and mouthed, "Yes. Touch me. You never need ask again."

It took him a moment to master his lust, not to pin her to the wall and ravish her until her knees gave way. But he wanted to watch her. To witness the heady haze of desire light her eyes. To know he'd put it there.

He cupped her breast, soft, full, heavy in his palm, her nipple hardening against the gentle stroke of his thumb.

Her eyelids fluttered, her sweet moan an arousing aphrodisiac.

"Look at me, Olivia. Let me watch."

She met his gaze. "Watch?"

"Watch you lose yourself to pleasure." His voice was rough, a testament to restraint. "I'll not rest until every part of you smells of me."

Her breath caught. "You mean to make love here?"

"Not tonight." His thumb traced a slow circle over her nipple. "You need to decide if you like what happens between us when I touch you intimately."

"I'm confident I will."

"Shall we find out?"

He kissed her deeply, intoxicated from the first touch, steeped in everything he had ever wanted to say to her.

You're mine.

I knew it the moment we met.

I feel it every time I touch you.

And I'll be damned before I deny myself again.

He wanted to taste every inch of her, to etch the memory into his soul, to banish every doubt that fate would one day steal this fragile hope from him.

The thought drove the kiss harder, rougher, urgency laced through every desperate stroke of their tongues. His body throbbed with need, hard and aching for her, but this was her awakening, not his. He wanted her to feel it. To know her power. To understand the hunger she could stir in him with a single sigh.

He broke the kiss to trail his mouth along her jaw, down the smooth line of her throat. The womanly scent of her was intoxicating. His hand slipped beneath the thin fabric of her nightgown, tracing the length of her thigh, his breath a warm whisper against her flushed skin.

"Part your legs for me, love."

She yielded to him, a silent plea for something more intimate.

"Say the word, and I'll stop," he reassured her.

She cupped his cheek, closed her eyes, and kissed him with such fervour he nearly hauled her against the wall, desperate to be inside her.

Her moan vibrated against his mouth, and he drank it in, his hand gliding up the silken inside of her thigh.

"You're sure about this?"

"Yes," she panted. "Don't stop, Gabriel."

Her skin quivered beneath his touch, heat meeting heat, and for a moment the world shrank to the slow slide of his fingers and the sound of their unsteady breaths.

God, she was sweet. Sweet and wet and his for the taking.

"Do you know how long I've wanted to touch you?" His voice was almost feral as he circled the tight bud, finding the right rhythm. "Since that first night in the music room at The Burnished Jade. Long before I dared admit it to myself."

She gripped his shoulder, her fingers sinking into the fine wool as he slipped two fingers into her wetness, his thumb teasing the centre of her need.

"Gabriel," came her plea.

"That's it, love. Let it take you." He watched her, a sliver of moonlight catching her parted lips and the rise of her breasts as she came undone.

Desire clawed at his control.

Hell, he was ready to spend in his trousers.

Her head fell back, her mouth parting on a moan—the most beautiful sound he'd ever heard. He held her as her body shuddered through the exquisite sensations. It took Herculean strength not to lower her to the bare boards and lose himself completely.

They stood, gazes locked, their breathing gradually steadying.

"That was … that was—"

He kissed the words from her lips. "Don't say it now. Think about what it means to have me in your bed. Take all the time you need." Because he feared that once he had her, his heart might never recover.

She nodded. "Have you and Miss—"

"I've never touched her the way I've touched you."

He straightened her nightgown and tied the belt of her wrapper.

"Allow me to escort you back to your bedchamber. We can discuss the pleasures of married life tomorrow."

She smiled now the urge to make love had ebbed, yet something else thrummed in the air between them.

Something powerful.

Something he couldn't name.

Chapter Thirteen

Morning brought no peace.

Olivia had slept as if in a dream, only to wake with her body still thrumming from Gabriel's touch. His cologne lingered on her nightgown. The faint ache between her thighs stirred memories of his voice, his hands, the hunger in his eyes when he brought her to completion.

He'd been right to urge caution.

Such intimacy did more than blur boundaries. It left her tethered to him in ways she couldn't explain. She felt him still, as if he lived beneath her skin. As she dressed, the whisper of fabric over her thighs made her catch her breath, as though he were there, touching her again.

When he appeared at breakfast, immaculate in his dark blue coat, their eyes met and her heart stuttered. Heat unfurled in her belly, a want she dared not indulge.

He came to her, his fingers finding hers as he brushed a chaste kiss across her knuckles. The fleeting contact, the charged awareness between them, had her clenching her thighs beneath the table.

"I thought I'd come down to find you finishing your coffee," she said, conscious of his gaze on her body.

"It took me a while to settle after I left you last night."

Oh, she was back there in a heartbeat, her shoulders pressed to the wall, moonlight softening his features but doing nothing to tame the rough sound in his throat as he pushed into her.

A blush warmed her cheeks. "Troubling thoughts about the case?"

"A man's mind wanders in the small hours. It's difficult to rest when one is plagued by *hard* problems."

"Let's pray Mrs Hodge can tell us something useful today." She didn't hold out much hope. There was every chance she had been used as a pawn in this game too. "It's impossible to know who to trust."

"Indeed." He took his seat at the head of the table, dismissing the footmen before they poured his coffee. "I don't care for gossip, and someone in this house has a loose tongue."

"You refer to Miss Bourne and her knowledge of our sleeping arrangements?" The woman wormed her way into every conversation. Would it always be this way? "She obviously feels comfortable enough to come and go as she pleases."

"We'll visit her aunt on our return from World's End. Ensure Miss Bourne knows she's not welcome without an invitation."

Olivia glanced at her plain grey dress and almost groaned. "I can't call on a neighbour looking like the newly hired governess."

Her husband leaned back in the chair, his thumb brushing his lip in languid appraisal. Anyone would think she wore nothing but Chantilly lace and silk stockings.

"You look like passion wrapped in mystery. I doubt any man would find a more tempting combination."

Her composure faltered for a heartbeat. For someone who claimed to live behind stone walls, he said the most beautiful things. She touched the gold band on her finger, wondering what he had inscribed inside.

"Commanding a room is about presence, not clothing," he added. "You put Miss Bourne in her place last night while wearing a nightgown."

"I did have a pistol in my pocket."

He smiled. "Then carry it with you today. Your secret weapon."

He was her secret weapon. But she did as he suggested, tucking the pistol into her reticule before they set out for World's End. They had barely reached the gravel drive when Gabriel spotted Mr Kincaid's new assistant and swore.

"I told you to bring someone with an excellent aim, not a twelve-year-old boy from the stables."

Poor Alfie, who'd been sitting proudly atop the box, slumped in his seat. "On my oath, milord, I can shoot better than any man here. Ask Mr Kincaid. I split a bottle top from ten yards."

"I feel uneasy about bringing the lad too," Mr Kincaid said, nudging the boy and offering an encouraging smile, "but he reckons he's got a debt to pay and a point to prove. And he's a better shot than me, I'll give him that."

"I won't have a child in the line of fire. What the devil were you thinking?"

"That he'd nae forgive me if I left him behind, my lord." Mr Kincaid gave a discreet jerk of his head towards the boy. "'Tis important to feel at home. Every soul needs a hearth to belong to, else he's naught but smoke on the wind."

Alfie dragged off his cap, his freckled face earnest. "I swear I'll be no trouble, milord."

"But can you swear you'll stay alive?"

"Happen the point is to make sure you and Lady Rothley come to no harm, but I'll do me best."

Gabriel sighed. "Very well. But it will be Kincaid's neck on the block if anything happens to you."

They set out for World's End.

Gabriel sat opposite, composed as ever while the countryside rolled past in a blur of green and grey. Olivia tried to focus on the view, not the man. Yet her gaze wandered of its own accord, tracing the long lines of his body, the strong hands resting on his knees.

For one dangerous moment, she imagined herself straddling his lap, skirts to her thighs, her husband moving inside her, each—

"Rein in your imagination, my lady, at least until tonight," he said in that velvet voice she loved. "As much as I want you, I won't indulge in reckless behaviour with Alfie aboard."

She laughed to hide her mild embarrassment. "You sound so sure of yourself, my lord. I was merely daydreaming about—"

"Having me, Olivia. Your tongue brushes your bottom lip when you're thinking about the things we do together."

Forced to admit it, she said, "Isn't that what you intended? To introduce me to the sensual art of seduction. To make me want you."

He didn't have to try too hard.

"You need to want me when I've done nothing to deserve it."

"Then I shall bear that in mind."

By the time they reached World's End, the windows had fogged, and Olivia had counted every beat between his glances and hers. Not once had he looked away first.

Mrs Hodge's red-brick cottage stood silent, its shutters drawn. Weeds choked the path, and the garden had run wild. An eerie stillness had Olivia glancing back at the coach, wishing they'd left Alfie behind.

Gabriel rapped twice on the weathered door and waited.

No answer.

"She should be home from the market by now." A prickle of unease raised the hair at her nape. What if Mrs Hodge had been dealt with too? "Mr Harper always gives her a ride in his cart."

Gabriel tried the door and found it locked, then opened the shutters, cupping his hands to the glass as he peered through the grimy pane.

"She's not inside," he said, stepping back from the window. "But it appears she had visitors last night. There are cups on the table, two chairs drawn to the fire, and signs she left in haste this morning."

Strange. In the weeks Olivia had rented the cottage, she had never known Mrs Hodge entertain.

"While Mrs Hodge is away, perhaps we should visit the mausoleum." Standing idle would do little to stem her nerves or the feeling they were being watched from the trees. "I brought the key, and it's safer in the daylight."

"Agreed. And it may be worth checking the cottage next door. Mrs Hodge, or the careless watch, may have left it unlocked."

He told Kincaid to keep his eyes peeled and decided Alfie would be better off waiting in the carriage. "You can catch any bandits by surprise and give us an advantage."

The doors to Olivia's old cottage were locked, yet Gabriel stared at the narrow path that ran from the back garden to the graveyard. He crouched, his trousers pulling taut over his powerful thighs, and touched the ruts too deep to have been washed away by rain.

"The man found dead in your cottage was killed in the graveyard and dragged through the gate, not carried," he said.

She came to stand beside him and studied the deep grooves in the earth, marks left by the heels of a man's boots. One person had killed Mr Lovelace and staged the scene.

"I'm not strong enough to drag a man through the garden and up the stairs."

"But why blame you?" He stood and brushed the soil from his hands. "They must believe you have something that could expose them. Seeing you in Newgate achieves two goals. It keeps you from running, and gives them the chance to bribe a guard to beat the truth from you."

A shiver traced her spine. The logic was sound. Too sound.

"Then why try to kill me?"

"I doubt killing you was the plan." He looked about, wary as a wolf on the scent. "More likely, he meant to frighten you into giving him what he wanted."

The words dragged her back to that night, the cold press of stone, the scrape of boots behind her. Her stomach tightened. She forced the images away, clinging instead to the memory of Gabriel's commanding voice.

He'd not abandoned her.
He'd come back.

"I'm just so grateful you came when you did."

His eyes found hers. "I knew you needed me."

Perhaps he needed her too, though she didn't say it aloud. "Then we must believe fate is on our side."

That thought stayed with her as they walked past crooked headstones, overgrown grass peppered with wild violets, and a rotting wooden bench slick with algae. When they reached the steps of the mausoleum, they found the door ajar.

"Someone has prised the damn thing open." Gabriel stepped forward, forcing her to remain behind him as he pushed the door wider and glanced cautiously inside.

She caught hold of his coat. "Well?"

"Everything is as we left it."

She exhaled, not realising she'd been holding her breath. She'd expected to find... who knew what. "Mr Daventry believes the answers lie here, but it's hard to know what we're looking for. Why not just hide a list of names? Why the complex puzzle?"

"It had to be cryptic. Hidden from everyone but you. Your father knew they'd kill you once they had it. If only we knew what *it* was."

They stood in silence, reading the epitaphs on the two stone tombs, but decided against moving the lid of the wooden coffin on the floor.

"There's every chance that's what made you ill," he said.

"What if the clue is inside the casket?"

He seemed unwilling to accept the possibility. "A man who cared for you wouldn't ask you to examine a corpse."

"My father wouldn't expect me to move a stone slab, either."

"Then the clue is hidden in plain sight."

They spent a few minutes in the cramped chamber, testing

whether the flagstones were loose and shifting the casket to see if anything was written beneath. She ran her hand over the Roman numerals, pressing them, half expecting a hidden catch—all to no avail.

"We're wasting our time." She cursed her father for placing her in this predicament. "We have nothing but a bag of useless trinkets and a key to this pointless crypt."

Gabriel stared at the floor, lost in thought. "And we have a poem. Did your father know of your fondness for the Graveyard poets?"

"Yes." He'd given her Gray's *Elegy* on the day of her mother's funeral. "I've been drawn to the soul's search for peace ever since my mother died."

A subtle smile touched his lips. "I understand. Peace is fragile where absence lingers."

How astute he was. She laid her hand on his coat sleeve, the wool soft beneath her fingers, though she knew the strength that lay beneath. "I'm here to listen, if you ever wish to talk."

"You have a gift for putting stubborn men at ease."

"And for thawing frost."

His gaze deepened, something almost reverent in the way he looked at her. "Yes. You have the power to chase away winter's chill."

The moment hung between them, full of things left unsaid.

Then he seemed to remember himself, his expression turning thoughtful. "We must look for the symbolic meaning in everything. The items in the valise, the key, the poem are all relevant."

She'd tried, but this man occupied most of her thoughts lately. "Let's consider the items in the valise. If the compass points west instead of north, it could signify many things: my father being led astray, false leads, deception. In Ancient Egypt, west was the direction of the netherworld."

His gaze snapped to hers. "Who told you that?"

"My father."

"He did direct you to a graveyard."

"Then perhaps the mausoleum is the centre, and the clue lies west of here, away from London and towards the Thames bend."

They left the mausoleum and returned to the graves.

"Did you say you covered all the burial grounds on this road?" Gabriel asked, surveying the tilting headstones. "How many lie between the church and the cottage?"

"Three. Aside from houses, the only significant place west of here is the rectory. Mrs Hodge said Reverend Clay prefers to live away from St Luke's."

The rector had been left alone with Mr Lovelace at the watch-house, and had inspired Mrs Hodge's move to World's End, yet neither seemed capable of plotting the fall of the government.

"Perhaps we should call on the rector," Gabriel said, like a barrister certain of a defendant's guilt. "To express concern over the theft of a body in his parish."

"You mean the theft of Justin Lovelace?" Why would he not say his name? "It is him. The man who visited my father."

"I'm sure you're right."

"What makes you so unsure?"

The strain behind his eyes deepened the lines on his brow. "Because that would be too simple. And because I would know it, in my heart."

"The heart you claim is made of stone?"

The heart she knew was anything but.

His lips quirked. "Yes, that one."

"The countess confirmed his identity." Joanna was strong and intelligent, not prone to sentiment. "She would have said if she had doubts."

"We've not seen him in a decade. Her focus is on her own family. I suspect part of her seeks closure." He paused, the silence heavy with uncertainty. "Besides, the man I knew would never hurt a woman."

She touched her throat, recalling the strength and determination in her attacker's ironclad grip. "People change. Not always for the better."

How had a loving father become a revolutionary? A man who betrayed his family only to betray his comrades. She was certain he'd left evidence that exposed them. They simply needed to find it.

As if the Lord had heard her request, the sudden murmur of voices and soft tread of footsteps drifted on a breeze. Anticipating danger, Gabriel circled her waist, drawing her behind the shelter of the mausoleum.

"It may be mourners come to pay their respects." She clung to him for no reason other than it brought peace.

He peered around the stone building, squinting against a ray of sunlight. "It's not mourners. It's Mrs Hodge and Reverend Clay. They're examining the headstones and making notes. He's kneeling beside a mortstone, searching through the weeds and grass."

"Having seen the carriage on the road, I'm surprised they aren't looking for us."

"Kincaid would have given a bird call had they come through the main gate. There must be another entrance."

"Yes, a path adjoining the field."

"Well, we won't find answers hiding here." He took her hand and placed it in the crook of his arm. "They must believe we trust them. It will buy us time."

"Assuming either of them is guilty."

"In this case, they're guilty until we prove them innocent."

They stepped out, her confident stride belying the hollow pit in her stomach, and made no attempt to disguise their approach.

Mrs Hodge looked up first, her face blanching as if she'd seen ghosts. She tapped the rector's arm, drawing his attention from the notes he was scribbling in his book.

The clergyman looked equally startled. He snapped the book shut and tucked it under his arm. "Lord and Lady Rothley, good day to you."

Mrs Hodge's mouth fell open, yet she masked her surprise with a curtsy. As she rose, she held Olivia's gaze but said nothing.

"What brings you to such a desolate part of Chelsea?" the rector asked, then winced as his memory caught up with his tongue. "Oh dear, you must still be looking for that poor man's body. Dreadful turn of events. Quite dreadful."

"Yes, we're searching all the burial grounds in the area," Gabriel said with the aristocratic air that made lesser men uneasy, "looking for signs of a disturbance. The magistrate believes a show of authority might appease the restless parishioners."

"We wondered if you were doing something similar," Olivia said, "as we saw you making notes in your book."

Mrs Hodge was quick to answer on his behalf. "We're taking down names in the hope we can persuade family members to tend the overgrown graves. With crime on the rise, there are too many places for footpads and robbers to hide."

Olivia frowned. Grave-tending was the sexton's duty, not the rector's. Since when did clergy concern themselves with weeds?

"And that awful murder, right on our doorstep, will have folk moving further out to Fulham." The rector glanced heavenward. "Let us pray that a generous benefactor donates the funds to hire another gardener."

She thought Gabriel might contribute or offer to send his own man, but giving money to a suspected revolutionary could implicate him in their crimes.

"Have you thought of approaching Sir Randall?" Olivia wanted Mrs Hodge to know they had spoken to her former employer. "His sister thought highly of you. He did nothing but sing your praises when we met yesterday."

The woman shifted, as though a pebble had found its way into her shoe. "I wouldn't want him to feel obliged. He took her passing badly, and I'd not wish to stir painful memories."

"He keeps her marble paperweight on his desk, and seemed quite eager to talk about her."

"All the same, I'll not ask for his charity."

"I'm sure the Lord will provide a solution." Gabriel returned to the subject of his murdered friend. "Before we leave you to your work, there are a few questions we must ask on the magistrate's behalf. Concerning the body found in the cottage."

"By all means," the rector said, "though I presume the suspect has reached Brighton by now. I believe the lady who rented the cottage has an aunt there."

Olivia's chest constricted. She counted the seconds until

Mrs Hodge revealed her secret, that she was Miss Woolf, the missing suspect.

"I told the constable all I know," Mrs Hodge said curtly.

"If you wouldn't mind confirming the facts." Gabriel fixed her with that penetrating gaze one dared not refuse. "It might help us understand why the resurrectionists took a body that was two days old, when the surgeons pay more for fresher specimens."

Mrs Hodge hesitated, fingers picking at the edge of her coat as if buying time.

The rector gave a genial smile. "Go ahead, Mrs Hodge. His lordship is merely seeking answers."

After stuttering over the first words, she said, "I came to clean the cottage after the tenant left and found the poor gentleman dead in the bed."

Olivia shivered, imagining Mr Lovelace lying lifeless in her old bed, and some devil planting evidence to incriminate her.

And why had Mrs Hodge been so vague? Referring only to 'the tenant' and not Miss Woolf? Perhaps she was afraid of Gabriel. Or perhaps she hoped the constables would waste time chasing shadows because someone had helped her murder Mr Lovelace.

"Was there any sign of forced entry?" Gabriel asked.

"The back door was ajar, as though someone had opened it with a key. But I had the only key, so whoever it was must have had a spare or used tools to pick the lock."

While dragging a body from the graveyard through the garden? "Were there muddy footprints on the floor?" Olivia asked. "Might you have noticed the size or shape?"

"How intuitive, Lady Rothley," Reverend Clay said.

"No, ma'am. There was no sign anything was amiss until I went upstairs and came across the horrid scene."

She wondered if her thoughts and Gabriel's were aligned? Had he noticed the lack of empathy? The calm detachment of a woman who had seen such horrors before?

"What was he wearing?" Gabriel said.

"Dark trousers, an open shirt. His black jacket hung over the chair, his boots placed neatly beneath." Mrs Hodge clasped her chest, remembering she was supposed to be shocked. "I ran to the rectory." She turned, pointing west of the mausoleum. "Reverend Clay fetched the watchman and dealt with things from there."

"So you didn't find the letter?"

"The letter?" the rector repeated.

"There was one in the man's pocket."

Mrs Hodge kept her expression neutral, the sort that would appease any jury. "Once I confirmed he was dead, I left the house and haven't been back since."

"And you've not seen the man before?" Gabriel's tone held the subtle desperation of one seeking the truth.

Mrs Hodge faltered and glanced at Olivia before replying. "I can't be sure. I may have seen him on the road."

Gabriel stiffened beside her. No wonder. Mrs Hodge had looked at her like a woman who entertained secret visitors.

He spoke again. "And the man's boots? You're certain you saw them?"

Mrs Hodge blinked. "Yes. They were under the chair."

"They were clean?"

"Yes."

Olivia heard the edge of defensiveness in her tone. Perhaps it was shock. Or simply exhaustion. But something in Mrs Hodge's manner set her on edge.

"If we have any further questions, we'll be in touch." Gabriel thanked them before capturing her elbow, suddenly eager to leave. "One last thing. Someone has forced the mausoleum door. Do you happen to know if there's a relative responsible for the plot?"

The rector seemed unconcerned. "Probably a vagrant. I can check the parish and sexton's registers. If the family purchased the plot, it should be noted there. Though in truth, records are often hard to find once the grave is sealed."

"Will the sexton not know?"

"Nesbit?" The rector spoke the name as if it were the bane of his existence. "He's new, my lord, hired after his predecessor passed. I'm happy to question him when I find him. The man has a habit of wandering."

Mrs Hodge stepped forward. "You've enough to attend to, sir. I can speak to Nesbit and check the burial book while I'm searching for the other relatives." She gave a polite smile that didn't quite reach her eyes.

"Good, good," the rector said. "Rest assured, we'll have this place looking respectable in no time."

They left them to their work, though Olivia felt Mrs Hodge's gaze burn between her shoulder blades as they walked away. A cold weight settled in her chest. Something had shifted. The air, the truth, perhaps even Gabriel's faith in her.

She glanced at him, searching his face. "If you're wondering. If you're doubting. Gabriel, I've only seen Mr Lovelace when he visited our house, and when he attacked me in the graveyard. Whatever impression Mrs Hodge gave, you must know—"

"That Mrs Hodge is a liar." He placed a steady hand at her

back. "And she knows a damn sight more than she dares admit."

Chapter Fourteen

Wynbury Hall
Islington

"Do you know what ails Mrs Culpepper?" Olivia asked as they waited in the fusty hall of the old Elizabethan manor house. "None of the servants at Studland Park seem to know."

Gabriel was almost grateful for the diversion. He hadn't set foot in the house for ten years. Not since the day he pounded the door, demanding to know what had happened to Miss Bourne. The memory brought the sharp sting of bile to his throat. Some mistakes deserved to haunt him.

"Gentry spoke to her physician, who mentioned a heart complaint, offered no further explanation, and declined his offer of assistance."

Olivia lifted her chin and sniffed the air. "They're treating her with herbs and opiate tinctures. The scent cuts through the stale stench of neglect." She studied him as if seeing the man behind the mask. "But that's not what's troubling you. You're thinking about the last time you were here."

"Yes." Shame pressed close, unwelcome yet all too familiar. It had been his greatest moment of weakness. "A clueless fool searching for answers."

"You're not a fool, Gabriel." She stepped closer, her calm presence settling his pulse. "A fool would punish every woman for the sins of one. An intelligent man punishes himself. A wise one learns it's all part of a greater design. Isn't that why you find solace in graveyard poems?"

"Lately, I read them and think only of you." He wished they were home in bed—her heat, her breath, her closeness replacing the chill of this centuries-old mausoleum and its ghostly echoes.

She smiled like she wanted to believe him, but he saw her silent misgivings and hoped time would erase them.

The butler reappeared, a middle-aged man Gabriel barely knew. "Mrs Culpepper has agreed to see you, my lord. But only for a few minutes. I'm afraid her strength is slowly ebbing."

"We'll be mindful of her frailty," he said.

"We?" The butler hesitated. "Mrs Culpepper will see only you."

Gabriel stiffened. The woman sought to control everyone and bore some blame for Miss Bourne accepting the bribe. Once, he might have cursed her to Hades. Now he felt like kneeling at her bedside and offering a prayer of thanks.

"I insist my wife accompany me."

"My mistress was quite adamant, my lord."

Olivia touched his arm. "I'll wait in the carriage. It's important you speak to her, to ensure there are no misunderstandings."

He covered her hand with his, reluctant to release her. "Not without you."

"We need to put the past behind us. Speak to her. Make your intentions clear. Let there be no more confusion."

Despite his grumble of frustration, he knew she was right. He escorted her to the carriage before returning to the house and following the butler's trudge upstairs.

"Is Miss Bourne at home?" he asked, not because he gave a damn, but because it was odd she hadn't swept into the hall and made a grand entrance.

"Not at present, my lord."

He was led into Mrs Culpepper's dark, curtained chamber, the air laced with the cloying scent of sickness and medicine. The sixty-year-old woman sat propped against a snowy mound of pillows, some spotted with blood, her grey hair tucked beneath an ugly yellow turban.

She raised a gaunt hand, beckoning him to the foot of the poster bed. "Come closer. It's my heart that's failing, not my lungs. You'll not catch scarlet fever." She waved the butler away. "Close the door on your way out, Jenkins."

After a brief coughing fit that had Gabriel reaching for the glass of herbal infusion on the nightstand, Mrs Culpepper sipped and found her voice again.

"Well? Is it true? Did you marry the chit?"

He ground his teeth so hard he might chip one. "I did, and you'll speak of my wife with more respect."

Mrs Culpepper's weak sneer was barely audible. "Why? You married her to spite Katherine, to prove you've not been pining for her all these years."

"Pining?" He scoffed. "All I've ever wanted are answers." An end to the constant questions. An explanation for all the lies.

"Who told you my niece had returned to England?"

"No one. I made the discovery when she called at Studland Park." A wraith in the night, so confident she would earn his forgiveness. "And I married for many reasons, none as petty as spite."

Mrs Culpepper drew a stained handkerchief from her sleeve and dabbed at her lips. "There's talk you married a wanted felon."

"That's a lie. I'm her alibi." Someone had betrayed them. In his own damned house. "As for my visit, tell your niece I'll have her hauled before the assizes for trespass if I so much as see her shadow on my land again."

Mrs Culpepper's mocking snort dissolved into a cough. When she finally spoke, she lifted her chin, her tone clipped and sour.

"Perhaps you've forgotten the night I caught you kissing her in the garden. I've never seen a man so besotted. Such love cannot be supplanted. How long before you send your wife to live at Eaton Chase, so you may court the woman you truly desire?"

The words should have cut deep.

They should have stirred an old ache.

They did neither.

What he'd felt then was infatuation. What he felt for Olivia ran deeper. It was desire, yes, but anchored in devotion. She was everything the girl in the garden had only pretended to be.

He met her gaze. "I'm in love with my wife."

He pitched the words to land hard, but even as he spoke, something shifted inside him, as though saying it aloud carved it deeper into his soul.

"Some rumours about me are true. I'd die to protect what

is mine. If your niece is seen sneaking about my estate again, there'll be hell to pay."

"My niece is the devil. Surely you've realised that."

Though he laughed, fear sliced through him. For the first time in his life, he had something he couldn't bear to lose. "Be assured, she has met her match."

"It's because you're her match that she'll need your help running Wynbury Hall when I'm gone." Mrs Culpepper tried to stifle another cough and failed, doubling forward as a harsh retch tore from her. Gabriel steadied her with a hand. "And as for your wife," she croaked, clutching his coat sleeve, "if you married for love, why have you not spent a night in her bed?"

Damnation. He'd string his loose-tongued servant up by the ballocks.

He stepped away from the bed. "I don't know which of my servants is spreading lies, but I have made love to my wife." At least in thought, if not in deed. "There'll be no annulment."

"No, I'll give the chit her due. She was clever enough to snare you, but I doubt she's clever enough to keep you. Not now Katherine has come home."

His temper flared. He turned for the door before he lost the last shred of his patience. "Rest, madam. If you survive another day, you'll need your strength to meddle."

He marched from the room and descended the stairs, resisting the urge to sprint to the carriage and take Olivia far from this accursed place.

She seemed surprised he was back so soon.

"What happened? Was Mrs Culpepper too ill to speak?"

"Take us home, Kincaid." He closed the carriage door with a weary sigh. "Miss Bourne responds to bribery. When her aunt is dead, I shall purchase the house for an extortionate sum and ensure she can trouble us no more."

"I see." Her voice was calm, but she lowered her gaze. The meaning beneath was clear. She thought he wished to be rid of temptation, not trouble.

"Protecting you is my only concern," he said.

"Of course."

"You don't believe me?"

"I believe you want to think so, but something Mrs Culpepper said has clearly left you unsettled."

As the carriage rattled down the drive, he repeated the exchange so she could be under no illusion. "What concerns me most is who's been feeding the gossip mill. The bitter take comfort in making others suffer. I'll not permit Miss Bourne to hurt you to spite me."

He took her hand and held it in his lap, threading his fingers through hers. Yet it felt as if they teetered on a precipice, and she was slowly slipping from his grasp.

"I suspect Mrs Culpepper believes her niece is incapable of managing the estate," Olivia said, staring at the passing scenery, "and assumed you would welcome her back with open arms."

"Then she was sorely mistaken." The future seemed remarkably clear to him now. "All I want is peace. And you, Olivia. I want you, not some boyish fantasy that turned into a blasted nightmare."

"It's hard to think amid these wicked machinations." She looked at him then, but her light had dimmed. "Things seem so simple when we're alone together, when no one interferes."

His stomach flipped. What was she trying to say? "Because we're open and honest and can speak freely." Still, he couldn't tell her that she made him feel alive, that his heart had never beaten so fast, that every thought revolved around her.

"They're the makings of an excellent friendship," she said.

Friends? Like hell that was all they'd ever be. A woman didn't kiss the way she did unless she wanted a man for her lover.

"But what I feel for you is no mere friendship, Olivia. I want you. In every way a man can want a woman." He wanted her to feel the depth of his devotion, even if she couldn't yet trust his words. "Don't answer now. Wait until this wretched business is behind us. But if you want me, you know where to find me. Just ... don't come to my bed out of obligation."

After a pause, she said, "It may be hard to believe, but everything I've done with you, I've done because I wanted to."

The tension in his shoulders eased. "Shall I remove your hatpin, so we might make another blood oath?"

"There's no need. We must learn to trust each other."

Her words stayed with him as he dressed for dinner. Trust. That was the real oath, and far harder to offer than blood. It led him to consider the note left with his gold button:

*Judge not the hand that bears the mark,
for it guards thee unawares.*

Her father knew his poem would lead her to The Burnished Jade. That Gabriel would be there, and her love of poetry would draw his notice. That a man who had been wounded would seek a woman who understood the nature of betrayal.

There was only one way he could have known Gabriel's story. He must have heard it from Justin Lovelace. He'd known to include white heather, a symbol of faith and a sign of hope.

Gabriel had never felt more hopeful than when Olivia approached the dining room, dressed in a midnight-blue gown that hugged her figure to perfection.

"A new dress?" he said, his throat tight, scarcely able to look away. In grey, her strength of character shone through. In this, she exuded a soft, feminine allure that made him wonder how easy it was to remove.

"The countess sent a chest of clothes. I can keep them until I have a proper wardrobe of my own."

"She certainly knows what suits you." His stomach growled, not from a longing for turtle soup, but from the ache of wanting his wife. It promised to be another long, excruciating night. How long before they found him dead, scratch marks on the door?

"Then you approve?" Her smile could have lit the stars. "I thought you might think she was interfering."

Approve? One slip in his restraint and he'd be drooling. "On the contrary, I can see you appreciate the gesture. We'll invite her to dine with us when our troubles are over."

"Dine here? In this house?"

"I'm more than willing to accommodate trusted friends," he said, leading her into the dining room. Their meal was already laid, and not a footman in sight. "We'll serve ourselves tonight. I've no appetite for servants who sell their souls for a few shillings."

"Did you discuss the problem with Mrs Boswell?" she asked as he pulled out her chair.

He let his gaze drift over her nape, where fine wisps of copper hair trailed against her skin. "Yes, but it will take time to lure the fox from its den. Gossip passes so freely, it's hard to trace the source."

"Mr Daventry says it's always the person you least expect."

"It's not Mrs Boswell." His tone brooked no argument. He took his seat at the head of the table, steadfast in his conviction.

"I've never heard you speak about anyone with such certainty. Though Mrs Boswell is the last person I would suspect, too."

He poured the wine and served her first. The simple act was strangely intimate, as though every movement declared what he could not say aloud. He'd underestimated how it felt to care for a woman, to serve and yet feel masterful, to find peace in her contentment.

"Tell me a secret you've never shared." She leaned back, the rim of her glass touching her lips, mischief lighting her eyes.

Her playful tone made it impossible to refuse her. "Recently, I tossed a halfpenny into a pond and made a wish. You'll be the first to know if it comes true."

"That doesn't qualify unless you tell me what you wished for."

"If I do, it may not come true." Nothing was more important than that one wish now. "Then let me give you another." He paused, wanting to share something honest. "You make this house feel like a home. I need you to chase the ghosts from every room." He raised his glass in salute. "Your turn,

Olivia."

She didn't sit trawling through memories but seemed to know exactly what she would say. "When my father died, I swore I'd never depend on a man again. It's a vow I'm slowly breaking."

He drew a deep breath, her quiet faith hitting him square in the chest.

"Tell me what you're thinking," she said.

"That if we'd been intimate many times, I'd sit you on the table and show you how dependable I am."

Colour rose in her cheeks as her fingers toyed with the edge of her neckline. "I suppose the first time shouldn't be a hurried coupling on the dining table."

Hellfire. The image alone was enough to make him hard. "No, it should be somewhere comfortable, where you can relax." In bed, he could take his time with her, learn her responses, pleasure her until she forgot her own name. "These things can't be rushed."

He savoured those final words like a rare vintage. Heaven knew how he would sleep tonight. It was absurd. The man who prided himself on control, undone by his own wife.

"Before this conversation strays beyond redemption, perhaps we should discuss something that doesn't involve me removing your new dress."

She nodded, tried to hide a smile. "We've made some progress today. We know Mrs Hodge is acting strangely, and that the rectory lies west of the mausoleum."

"Daventry's man reported she goes nowhere but home, the rectory and church. Perhaps we should attend Sunday service at St Luke's."

"She visits the market most mornings," Olivia added.

"Perhaps she's in cahoots with the fishmonger. At this

point, I wouldn't be surprised if half of London were part of the conspiracy. I'd wager a crate of mackerel she has no intention of checking the burial records."

"We can call at St Luke's and check them ourselves. We need something constructive to do tomorrow."

Tomorrow? Surviving the night would be challenge enough.

They continued eating, though he was a man with a fever, delirious enough to watch every morsel that passed her lips. For two hours, they spoke of Kincaid's Scottish heritage, the families in the parish, his grandmother's sensory garden, about everything but the slow burn of desire between them.

They retired to his private drawing room, drank wine and debated whether the poets should focus on traditional faith or question it. The intelligent conversation was nowhere near as satisfying as the curve of her smile when he conceded a point.

"I'll walk you to your room." He rose, not quite ready to say goodnight.

Along the way, he paused before various paintings, naming ancestors and recounting family tales. At one portrait, he smiled. "Cecil wore his doublet so tight people wondered how he drew breath."

He ignored the likeness of his mother. He'd need to be three sheets to the wind to pass comment.

They stopped outside the Peacock Room.

Invite me in, Olivia.

But it wasn't what they'd agreed.

"I've had a lovely evening. Thank you for explaining your family history, though I doubt I'll remember all the names." She hesitated, the moment turning faintly awkward. "Good night, Gabriel."

She rose on her toes, her mouth an inch from his.

One more breath, and he would stop pretending he could resist her. He saw the invitation in her eyes, felt his restraint snap, bent his head and kissed her.

The kiss was urgent, desperate, all heat and hunger, too fierce to retract. He wanted her now, tonight, of that there was no doubt. He'd be fit for Bedlam if he waited another hour, let alone a day.

But a gentleman never went back on his word.

He broke the kiss, the devil on his shoulder prodding him with its pitchfork, begging him to crush her to his chest and feast like a beast.

"Forgive me. I didn't mean for—"

Her finger touched his lips. "I'm your wife. No apology is needed. We both crave companionship. But I shall abide by your request and come to you when I'm ready. How will we ever trust each other if we cannot keep our word?"

He stepped back. The distance failed to dampen his ardour. How could it, when he'd tasted heaven and longed to wallow in it?

"Good night, Olivia. I trust you'll sleep well."

He'd spend the night pacing like a caged lion.

"Good night, Gabriel."

"Lock your door."

Her hand was already on the handle. "I will."

Refusing to linger like a love-sick buck, he strode away, scanning the shadows for the servant with a tongue as loose as a bawd's drawers. If only this were Fortune's Den and he hosted boxing bouts in his cellar. A good fight might be the only cure for such restless energy.

As he undressed, he reminded his valet what it meant to betray his master. "What happens in this house stays in this house. There's nothing more despicable than a man who sells secrets." Other than a father who endures his wife's infidelity and tups the maid in revenge.

He'd been in bed an hour, reading the same damn page of morbid poetry, when a light knock sounded at the door. He lowered the book and peered around the burgundy hangings.

"Enter."

He held his breath. Time stilled. The faintest hope stirred. If it was the valet, he'd hurl the book at his head.

But it wasn't his valet.

It was his wife.

She opened the door a fraction. "May I come in?"

"Of course." Merciful Lord. His blood was already pooling low, and all she'd done was close the door. "You need never ask."

She stepped closer to the bed, the firelight painting her in amber, its glow tracing the soft lines beneath her silk nightgown. A gift from the countess, no doubt. Not that it mattered. It would soon be a pile on the floor.

"Have you come to borrow a book?"

He watched the pulse at her throat, the way it worked as she drew a breath, her gaze brushing his bare chest, lingering a beat too long.

"No. I couldn't sleep and wondered if I might lie beside you."

Heat gathered beneath his skin. He forced his hands to stay still, though every instinct urged him to reach for her. "I'm naked, Olivia. You're welcome to stay, though I can't promise to behave."

"What can you promise?"

Her hair glowed like burnished copper, loose about her shoulders and tumbling down her back. The courage it took to come to his chamber, intent on seduction, was perhaps the most beautiful thing he'd ever witnessed.

"I can promise hours of untold pleasure," he said, almost humming at the prospect. "And that the warmth of my body will chase away the chill. I can promise you won't regret a single moment."

She worried her lower lip. "Even though I'm afraid?"

"Never be afraid of me." The next words surprised even him. "I'll wear nightclothes. We don't need to do anything. I'd be glad of your company." He shrugged a shoulder, though his heart hammered. "I can read to you."

He wasn't sure what he'd said to make her draw that deep breath, what word had her unbuttoning the pearl fastenings of her nightgown, what impulse made her lift the hem and pull the garment over her head.

As he drank her in—the swell of her breasts and the curve of her hips—thought deserted him.

"Make love to me, Gabriel."

Those words would be etched into his mind until the end of days.

He pulled back the sheets, letting her see what he'd kept hidden beneath the towel, giving her a moment, just one, to change her mind.

She didn't.

She climbed into bed, her hand trembling only slightly as she brushed a lock of hair from his brow. "You're the only man I'd want to share this moment with."

Chapter Fifteen

The moment Olivia's body settled against his, her breath caught. She'd never felt so exposed, or so certain she'd done the right thing. She hadn't known what to expect, but his warmth surrounded her, and the last of her doubts slipped away.

When he drew the sheets over her, she was grateful for the gesture. She still couldn't believe she'd found the courage to bare herself, but the look in his eyes, part awe, part disbelief, had been worth every trembling second.

He propped himself on one elbow. "What made you come to my chamber tonight?" He took a lock of her hair and let it slip through his fingers. "What gave you the strength to be bold?"

Even wrapped in confidence, there was something cautious in his voice, a need to know she had chosen this for herself.

"It was when you mentioned your grandmother's motto. While showing me her portrait."

She remembered the subtle tremor in his voice, the

longing he hadn't meant her to hear. It stayed with her, refusing to fade. And when he'd kissed her afterwards, and it almost hurt to let go, she'd realised how desperately she wanted this man.

"That the precious things aren't made of diamonds?"

"That life is fleeting, and not to waste another second."

He brushed the backs of his fingers across her cheek, his breath a sensual sigh. "That's the only reason? The wise words of a woman who saw the joy in everything?"

She dropped her gaze, but he caught her chin, urging her to look at him, to let him hear her confession.

"You want the truth?"

"Always."

Her mouth was dry, but she owed him this.

"I can't think when I'm with you. I just need to feel, feel your mouth on mine, your hands on my skin. The fire that burns through every thought until there's nothing left but us."

She had never felt more alive than in those passionate moments.

"But I'm afraid, Gabriel."

"Afraid?" His voice gentled. "I told you, I'll be mindful—"

"Not about making love." She touched his chest, trailing her fingers through the dark hair there. He was remarkable in every regard. The strength beneath her hand was tempered by absolute control, every muscle honed, every breath measured. "I know you'll be kind and gentle."

"Then what? You fear the men hunting your father's secrets?"

"No. I'm afraid I'll wake in the morning and realise this was all a wonderful dream." Worse than that. "Or that you'll wake and think this—us—was a dreadful mistake."

His hand skimmed the curve of her hip, drawing her against him. "Let me prove every part of this is real. Let me show you why it could never be a mistake."

The first kiss was slow. Tentative.

Their breath mingled, lips brushing, as if neither dared move too fast. He deepened it by degrees, and the warmth between them bloomed. Her moan spilled into him as he crushed her closer, their bodies pressing tight, the kiss turning fierce. What began as hesitation unfurled into hunger, mouths parting, thoughts dissolving, until breathless pants became a wordless plea.

"God, woman," he growled, fisting her hair and holding her mouth to his. "You don't know what you do to me."

Arousal slid through her, potent as a drug. He couldn't kiss her deeply enough. Each long sweep of his tongue tightened her belly, the pull sharpening until her breasts felt heavy and tender, desperate for his touch.

They were so in tune he seemed to read her mind. He rolled her onto her back, pressing her into the mattress, every hard plane of him moulded to hers.

"I do nothing by halves, Olivia." His smooth baritone sent tingles down her spine. "Not when it comes to you. I have to touch you, every part of you, with my hands, my mouth. If it's too much, if I'm too much, you must tell me."

She looked up at him, the candlelight carving shadows over his chest and shoulders. He was all power and purpose, dark hair falling over his brow, tension rippling beneath every muscle. He smelled of spice and wood and something wilder, of distant forests and midnight rain. A peaceful place. Her place.

But it wasn't his strength that held her still. It was his eyes, dark as obsidian, dangerous to most yet heaven to her.

"You could never be too much." She cupped his cheek. He would never hurt her, she knew, and that frightened her all the more. Because to trust him was to risk loving him.

"But do you want me? All of me?"

All of him? The notion proved a little startling. "I thought that was obvious. Do you know the strength it took to come to your room?"

He nudged her legs gently apart with his knee. "Do you know the effort it's taking not to forget everything except the need to be inside you? How the thought of it has driven me half-mad."

"Then don't wait."

"And forgo the chance to pleasure you?" His grin carried a trace of arrogance. "To show you what it means when a man makes love to his wife, when I make love to you, Olivia?"

"Then show me, Gabriel."

"It would be my pleasure."

If she'd had to list the places a man might kiss a woman, she would have fallen dreadfully short. He pressed his lips to her forehead, her cheek, her jaw, her mouth. Each kiss led him lower—the hollow of her throat, the languid brush along her collarbone, the curve of her breast.

He looked up at her through lowered lashes before tracing her nipple with the tip of his tongue and drawing it softly between his lips.

She moaned quietly, barely moving until the sensation sent flutters through her belly. Need overcame hesitation. She slid her fingers into his hair and arched her back, pressing herself deeper into his mouth.

"Gabriel, please." The sound of her own voice surprised her, so desperate, so needy, driven by every teasing suck and the hard ridge of him hot against her thigh. "Don't stop."

He moved to worship the other breast, then continued lower, slowing as he trailed kisses down her body before settling between her thighs. "You wanted to know what I could promise?"

If his vow was to make her feel wanted, to leave her aroused beyond reason, he had already fulfilled it.

"I mean to taste you. And I promise you'll crave more of me when I do."

He parted her legs and lowered his mouth to her most intimate place. The first stroke of his tongue stole her breath. With it came the realisation she had made a shocking error of judgement. With others, Gabriel was staid. Principled. But with her, he was a man ruled by need, by hunger, by a reckless desire to possess.

Yes, you're so different with me.

She smiled, the thought oddly pleasing.

No one had ever touched her like this. As if he meant to learn every inch of her, to claim her, brand her, undo her until there was no part of her that didn't belong to him.

"Let me show you how it feels to be mine," he murmured against her skin, his tongue tracing slow, torturous patterns until she could no longer stay still.

She could no longer think. Only feel.

Every flick of his tongue wound her tighter, until pleasure coiled and broke in one breathless rush.

Release took her, swift and shattering. The world fell away until there was nothing but him.

The man who'd saved her. The man who held her. The man she feared had claimed her heart.

The pleasure was fierce, but it was the connection that left her shaken.

"Gabriel ... yes. Oh, sweet heaven."

She panted his name, the sound a plea, a prayer.

He rose over her, a fire in his eyes, his tongue skimming his lips as though he'd tasted Molière's peaches à la crème. One hand closed around himself, a shudder running through him as he stroked, deliberately.

"Do you want more, Olivia?"

She looked at him, at the hard, pulsing length of him, and dismissed her concern. "I want it all." A vision flashed through her mind: a real marriage, a real family, a love that might last a lifetime. "You promised to leave no part untouched. I mean to hold you to that vow."

"And I always keep my word."

He pressed against her, thick and insistent, sending a ripple of tension through her body. Then his eyes found hers, searching, waiting for permission. She gave it with a trembling nod.

He hesitated, the moment a tense beat between them.

"If we do this, there's no going back."

"I know." Her hands smoothed over his taut arms, urging him not to wait. "Everything about this feels right."

Surely fate couldn't fool her again.

Nothing prepared her for the moment he entered her.

He was tender, careful, as if she were something precious.

She tensed at the unfamiliar pressure.

His hand slipped into hers, grounding her. "Tell me you're all right."

"Yes, are you?"

He bent his head and kissed her. "Never better. But I can't promise this won't hurt."

"Nothing you do could hurt me, Gabriel."

She wanted all of him, with a longing that bordered on desperation.

He filled her slowly, and she felt it all, the stretch, the sweetness, the sense that her body had been made to welcome him. Every inch of him seemed to claim a piece of her heart, binding them together in a way words could never undo.

He withdrew with a groan, then thrust deeper.

Her breath caught on a gasp.

"Olivia?"

"I'm all right," she whispered, her fingers finding his shoulders. "Don't stop."

Not now. Not ever.

He froze, just long enough to look into her eyes.

Then he moved again, each stroke measured.

"God," he breathed, the sound rough with wonder. "You're mine now. And you feel like heaven."

Her heartbeat thundered at the husky command in his voice. She wrapped her thighs tighter around him. This felt like heaven too.

He moved inside her, deeper, then faster, until the rhythm found them both. The bed creaked beneath them, the headboard knocking softly against the wall.

Every thrust drew a sound from him she'd never heard before. The plea for more from a man who never begged. The incoherent growls from one who took pride in his eloquence.

He pinned her wrists above her head with one hand, the other gripping her hip, holding her steady as he kept the promise to leave no part untouched.

Pleasure surged through her, curling her toes, lifting her spine from the bed.

He kissed her deeply, recklessly, a taste of everything

they'd denied themselves, a need so fierce it threatened to undo them both.

Desire licked along her body like flame, each stroke fanning the heat higher. She clung to him, nails digging into his back as his body drove into hers in a hard, desperate rhythm.

Oh, the things he did to her. The way he made her feel.

There was no thought now. No restraint. Only sensation, skin to skin, breath to breath, his voice shuddering against her name.

They moved as one. The world narrowed to the wild beat of their hearts and the hush of whispered pleas.

The pleasure came swift and shattering, stealing every sense until she was lost in him.

Just before release claimed him, he withdrew, groaning as he spilled over her belly, his breath ragged, his muscles taut from the strain.

For a moment, he hovered, chest heaving, head bowed. Then he gathered her close, one hand at the nape of her neck, the other cradling her hip, grounding them both in the stillness that followed.

His mouth found hers in a kiss that was all devotion and disbelief.

When it ended, he stayed close, forehead pressed to hers.

Neither spoke.

There were no words.

Only the slow return to breath, to the shape of his body wrapped around hers. And the quiet certainty that she belonged there.

Chapter Sixteen

St Luke's, Chelsea

Some men stepped into church and came out reborn.

Gabriel's rebirth came with the trust and tenderness in Olivia's eyes last night, in her thighs tightening around him, drawing him deeper, welcoming him in a way that awakened something he thought long dead.

He loved her.

He'd held her for an hour as she slept, trying to pinpoint when that truth had taken hold. He would die for her. He had known it since the night he sensed her distress and tore back to World's End, since the fear of losing her had slashed through him and stolen his breath.

With her, he saw a future. Something bound them together, something no mortal man could sever. And woe betide the fool who tried.

He'd wanted her again the moment dawn touched the room, but she'd slept so deeply in his arms he hadn't had the heart to wake her. After all she'd endured, she deserved rest. She deserved peace.

And yet fear clung to him, a vagrant begging for a penny he did not have to give. No matter how he tried to shake it, the wretched thing followed at his heels, whispering of dangers he could not name, of shadows waiting to steal what he held most dear.

Even the hush of St Luke's and the holy presence did little to calm his restless spirit. Not when the devil lingered at his door.

"You're certain the rector won't be here?" Olivia observed the empty pews, her gaze lifting to the lofty nave and majestic stained window. "With our luck, he'll have misplaced the records, and we'll never know who owns that wretched plot."

"I believe the rector is giving a sermon at the Ladies' Benevolent Society on the Christian duty of justice." Gabriel approved of the old maxim, *an eye for an eye*, and intended to punish everyone who'd conspired against them. "It includes luncheon."

"How do you know?"

He gestured to the vestibule. "It's on the noticeboard outside."

She turned to him and smiled. "I must have missed it. The late night has left me fatigued this morning. Thankfully, little escapes your notice."

"Other than the mysteries surrounding your father's riddle and the childhood friend who may or may not be dead."

He suspected the answers to both were a clue away.

It was imperative they found it quickly.

"On a more important note," he said, his thoughts

narrowing to nothing but her. "I wondered if you might care to lose an hour's sleep tonight."

She didn't play coy or feign flirtation. "If you're inviting me to your bed, Gabriel, just say so."

"It is an invitation, but not necessarily to a bed."

Her tongue swept lightly across her bottom lip.

God help him—she was remembering it too: their bodies moving as one, every delicious tremor, the way he'd wrung every last whimper from her, broken her breath into ragged little gasps he still heard in his head.

Oh, Gabriel ... Gabriel.

His cock stirred at the memory.

If she touched him now, they'd be arrested for indecent conduct.

"If not in bed, where then? How will you divert my mind from our current predicament?"

Oh, he could think of a hundred ways.

None of them fit for church.

He chose the most likely to please a woman with a passionate heart and an inquisitive mind. "*Julius Caesar* is playing at the King's Theatre tonight, and I have a private box. It's time we were seen together in public, and the tragedy may shed light on your father's warning. *Beware the Ides of March*."

Excitement lit her eyes, and he would never be the reason it faded.

"It will give me a chance to wear one of the gowns the countess sent, and there has to be some connection to the play. Why else would my father take such pains to hide the clue?"

"It is a play about murder and political ambition." The image hidden in the miniature was warning enough: unrest, conspiracy, danger closing in. "Which is why I must insist you sleep in my room until we identify the traitor in the house."

Before she could respond, footsteps echoed along the aisle.

"Hello? May I help you? Are you here to see Reverend Clay?"

Gabriel turned to find a short, tubby fellow in a black cassock approaching. "And you are?"

"Mr Plunket, sir. The verger here at St Luke's. I'm afraid the rector is away for most of the day, giving a sermon at—"

"The Ladies' Benevolent Society, I know. We're here at the magistrate's behest to search the burial records and the sexton's books, if they're kept here."

Gabriel presented his calling card.

Plunket accepted it. The instant he read the name, his hand gave a sharp tremor. "My lord ... my lady." He dipped into a hurried bow, nearly dropping the card in his haste. "Forgive me. Perhaps I might be of service."

"Good. We welcome your assistance, Mr Plunket."

The man would likely prove more helpful than the Reverend Clay, whose word could not be trusted.

"Of course, my lord." His manner changed at once. "This way." He hurried ahead, cassock swaying about his ankles, and gestured to a narrow door beside the vestry as he led them down the nave. "The burial registers are kept in the clerk's office. We maintain records going back near a century."

Gabriel held the door for Olivia, the scent of old paper and damp cloth drifting out to greet them.

Plunket bustled to a tall oak cupboard and produced a ring of keys. "Which records did you wish to see, my lord? We've the churchyard registers, the new ground, and there's an older set for the plots out east of the rectory."

"Yes, the old burial ground," Gabriel said.

Plunket paused mid-motion, a flicker of something crossing his face, then nodded. He selected a long, leather-bound volume from the shelf. Dust motes spiralled as he carried it to the clerk's desk.

"Folk rarely ask to see these, my lord." He placed the register down, the heavy leather thumping against the wood. "Not unless there's been a dispute over a plot—families arguing over who owns which corner, who was buried where, that sort of thing." He flipped the cover open, but seemed possessed of a need to keep talking. "Or if there's confusion about dates. What year did you say you were searching for?"

Gabriel looked at Olivia, hoping she remembered.

She frowned slightly. "The inscription gave the year in Roman numerals … MDCCCXIII. I believe that's 1813." Almost as an afterthought, she said, "Yes, the fifteenth of March, 1813."

Gabriel stilled. Plunket seemed unaware of the importance as he turned another brittle page and sneezed into his handkerchief.

"The fifteenth of March," Gabriel echoed. "The Ides of March. When Caesar was struck down in the senate."

Olivia's eyes widened, but Plunket appeared none the wiser.

This conversation was best kept for the privacy of their carriage.

"Our search relates to the Roman-style mausoleum," she said. "We need Mr Hathaway's last known abode and the name of the officiant who performed the ceremony."

The verger found the relevant month and flipped back and

forth through the pages. He drew a magnifying glass from the desk drawer and ran his gaze down the list of names. "Hathaway, you said, my lady? Any chance there might be an error with the name?"

"No, I'm quite certain." She flinched, just a fleeting tremor only a man who couldn't take his eyes off her might notice. Something had caught her attention. "There's no mistake."

The verger looked at her, almost embarrassed to continue. "There's no one listed by that name in the whole month of March. Nor in April."

Had it been any other date, Gabriel would have returned to the mausoleum to check their facts. But this date? Its absence sharpened his suspicions.

"You do have the sexton's records here?"

"Yes, yes, my lord." Plunket practically shook with the need to please. "They're in the parish chest." He gestured to an oak trunk tucked away in an alcove.

"Someone would have recorded a tomb of that scale."

They waited while the verger knelt beside the chest and rummaged through the musty contents. For a good ten minutes, he sifted among the disorganised tomes, muttering and blowing dust from their covers, until at last he unearthed the correct volume. He opened it, turned a few brittle pages—

—and found nothing.

No Hathaways.

No purchase of a mausoleum of that grandeur.

Not so much as a passing reference.

Plunket blinked down at the page, confusion knitting his brow. "That's ... most irregular. A structure of that size would require a record of fees paid." He rubbed a thumb along the margin as if a name might magically appear. "You may wish to speak to Reverend Clay, my lord. Though he's only been the rector here these past ten years."

Ten years. A bloody decade.

The word ought to be struck from every page in every book.

Plunket closed the tome with a soft thud. "I'm afraid the previous rector can't help, my lord. Poor soul retired to the coast and perished not long after. Slipped on the coastal steps during a storm, or so I was told."

Or pushed to silence him.

"Where will I find the new sexton?" Gabriel asked, keeping his tone even. "And surely there are Hathaways living in the parish."

"None that I recall, my lord." Plunket cast a glance towards the door. "Mr Nesbit should be in the churchyard tending the graves. If he's not there, I suggest trying The Bear Tavern. But you didn't hear that from me."

Armed with a description of the sexton, they left the church and crossed directly into the adjoining graveyard.

Order reigned here. The stones stood mostly straight, some worn to a soft blur of names, others newer and unmarked by time. Flower posies rested at a few graves, and an elderly couple gathered by a headstone, speaking in hushed tones. The paths were swept, the grass trimmed.

"It's hard to believe the same sexton tends both graveyards," Olivia said. "It's clear where he spends his efforts."

Gabriel stopped a gardener busy clipping back the long summer grass. "Might you tell me where I'll find Mr Nesbit?"

The man paused, shears idle in his hand and doffed his cap. "He's gone to look in on a burial plot out by the rectory, sir."

That was a lie. There were no empty burial plots at the rectory. "Then perhaps you'll direct us to The Bear Tavern."

The gardener nodded towards the far boundary wall. "First left off Sydney Street, though it's popular with gravediggers, and no place for a lady."

They left the churchyard, but Gabriel paused at the gate.

"Perhaps you'd prefer to wait with Kincaid and his intrepid companion."

"We agreed we'd remain close." She held his gaze, the spark behind her eyes a forbidden promise. The same spark that had undone him once already. "And I'll not miss another chance for you to play knight-errant."

Temptation stirred. "I admit, I am rather partial to the role."

"I could always start a commotion, so you can carry me out."

"There are places I'd rather carry you." His voice dropped a shade lower. "Rooms in our house no one else will ever enter."

She slipped her hand into the crook of his arm, the gesture so natural it felt like a prelude. "Then perhaps we might explore them on our return home from the theatre tonight."

He pictured the possibilities, never more grateful for the cavernous house. His mind lingered on shadowed corridors, the hush of hidden rooms, all the places he might have her to himself. Want simmered beneath the surface, but he kept his composure and instructed Kincaid to follow.

They entered The Bear to the scrape of chairs and the murmur of voices. Ale soured the air. A few labourers sat hunched over tankards, caps pushed low, eyes lifting just long enough to mark the newcomers before turning back to their drink.

The sexton was easy to spot: too idle to be a mourner, too clean to be a gravedigger, too glassy-eyed to be sober.

"Nesbit." Gabriel strode up to him, refusing to waste another minute. "A private word, unless you'd rather the rector discover how you've spent your morning." He silently counted to three, jaw clenched. "Now, Nesbit, before I drag you out. Don't make me raise my voice again, not in the presence of my wife."

The fellow turned too quickly and nearly slid from his chair. He blinked at Olivia through bloodshot eyes and slurred, "What's this about?"

"It's about missing records, a magistrate expecting answers, and finding you here, drunk, instead of doing your duty."

The mention of the magistrate had Nesbit lurching to his feet, though he swayed as he walked to the door. Outside, he was quick to make a host of excuses for his presence in The Bear.

"I was only resting my legs. A man needs a moment to wet his whistle." He wiped his brow, looking anywhere but at Gabriel. "I only stayed because the landlord said he'd got a message for me."

"You're neglecting your duties. You've not visited the burial ground near the rectory for months." It was too odd to ignore. Why leave that plot in such disrepair when it lay so close to the rectory? "I demand to know why."

Nesbit shifted his feet. "You wouldn't believe me if I told you."

Gabriel didn't blink. "Try me."

"There's ghosts out there."

"Ghosts?"

"Aye. Some of the men say they've seen things. Shapes

moving between the headstones. Strange groans at night. And the rector, he's worried about footpads and the like, causing trouble."

"I lived in the cottage next door for a time and saw no criminals working in the area," Olivia said. "And certainly no ghosts."

Perhaps they'd seen the man in the beaked mask.

The sexton opened his mouth, then thought better of it.

Gabriel removed gold coins from his pocket and held them stacked between his thumb and finger. "Five sovereigns if you tell the truth. If not, you'll be taken in as an accessory to grave robbing. Someone broke into the mausoleum."

"It ain't a mausoleum," Nesbit muttered, glancing over his shoulder. "It's where men meet, not mourners. Mostly after dark. I'd wager there are no bodies in that tomb."

Gabriel let two sovereigns fall into the man's palm. "Why do you say that?"

Nesbit pressed his lips together and cast another glance towards the tavern.

Gabriel eyed the remaining coins. "There are three more if your story is worth hearing."

A moment passed before Nesbit nodded. "Something the old sexton said. He was told not to tend the graves. And he saw men meeting there at night, bringing things and hiding them beneath false gravestones."

Gabriel's pulse stirred. At last, something that resembled honesty. Or a tale a half-sotted man might conjure for coin. Whether fact or invention, it was more than they'd had an hour ago.

"What about the lady who lives there, Mrs Hodge?" Olivia said. "She assured me it was safe. Just stories, she said. And no cause for alarm."

"She would say that. Some of them go into her cottage and don't leave till morning."

So that explained the cups on her table, Gabriel thought. No wonder she'd insisted on speaking to Nesbit herself.

"If you ask me," the sexton said, lowering his voice, "they're footpads, using the graveyard to stash stolen goods. Happen the rector is afraid to confront them and turns a blind eye. That said, I've not seen anyone there these last few weeks."

As he rambled about the rector and the overgrown graves, several things struck Gabriel. Nesbit was remarkably free with his information. And footpads did not keep records, gather at night by appointment, or use mausoleums.

Hang a few thieves and no one asked questions. A convenient excuse, should the fraternity need to allay suspicion.

"That's all for now." Gabriel had heard enough. "For your sake, I trust you've told the truth."

"I've told you what I've seen and heard," Nesbit muttered. "Make of it what you will."

Gabriel let the remaining coins fall into Nesbit's palm, not as a kindness but a warning. "Return to your duties. I may have further questions, and I've no wish to scour taverns looking for you."

He waited until Nesbit had slouched off towards the church, then handed Olivia into the waiting carriage and instructed Kincaid to head for Covent Garden.

"You don't believe a word Mr Nesbit said, do you?" Olivia straightened her skirts and held the strap as the carriage lurched forward. "If it's footpads they fear, why did the rector pretend he needed to trace the families of those buried there?"

"He may have been searching for the stolen goods,"

Gabriel said, "but we both know there's more to this than thieves hiding their bounty."

"Are Reverend Clay and Mrs Hodge being paid for their silence," she said, "or accomplices in something larger?"

"We'll ask Daventry to have his men watch them. They might lead us to something useful." He studied her, briefly wondering what he used to think about before her—before them. "On the subject of clues, you changed when the verger asked if there might be a mistake with the name."

She tilted her head. "You noticed?"

"I notice everything about you."

"What else have you noticed?"

That she spoke his name like a breath when she wanted more of him. That when he'd moved inside her, she had looked at him with longing, not shyness or fear.

"You're more relaxed around me. More tactile since we were intimate last night." Her fingers hadn't simply rested in the crook of his arm on the way to the tavern; they had drifted over his bicep.

"And you, Gabriel," she said softly, "I've lost count of how many times you've touched my back. Or how often you've looked at my mouth today."

"You are ... difficult to ignore."

He'd been studying her for months, through crowded rooms and entire recitals, seeing nothing but her. Answering a call he couldn't quite explain.

"And you've always had a way of drawing my attention. It seems neither of us is particularly good at hiding how we feel." The subtle purr in her voice stirred the hair at his nape. "Perhaps this is what happens when lonely people seek companionship."

It was a damn sight more than easing loneliness.

Or was he imagining she felt the same?

He was fluent in suspicion, not sentiment.

He could read a man's lies, but not a woman's heart.

Was he alone on this journey? Expecting too much from someone who had practically been forced to marry him?

It was a sobering thought. One that sat heavy in his chest. One he didn't wish to explore. Not yet.

And so he turned the conversation back to the case. "What was it that piqued your interest at the church?"

She wasn't surprised by the change of topic. "Hathaway. The surname of the couple. Shakespeare's wife was Anne Hathaway. The link to Julius Caesar. It can't be a coincidence."

Lord above. He'd been too busy watching her to see what was right in front of him. "It's certainly not a common name, so perhaps it's a sign we're meant to follow."

Daventry agreed when they put the theory to him in his Hart Street office. "You're right to visit the theatre tonight. There's every chance your father planned this before his death."

Gabriel nodded. It certainly had the makings of a Shakespearean plot. "But he couldn't have known I'd agree to help his daughter, that she'd find the mausoleum, or have the foresight to search for the hidden clue behind the miniature."

"*Beware the Ides of March*," Daventry muttered. "I'm sure you have a copy of *Julius Caesar* at home, likely a rare edition. Have you looked there?"

Gabriel inwardly grumbled. Daventry could make an intelligent man feel like an imbecile. "Before today, we had only one reference to the play. Besides, her father never visited my house."

A pang of doubt struck him. Many men had visited the

house in the past. The rooms were rarely empty. Justin Lovelace had been a frequent guest, free to roam as he pleased.

"We'll search the libraries upon our return home," Olivia said.

He liked the way she said *home*, as if it were a comfort, not a burden.

His parents had called it The Park.

Their guests, Sodom and Gomorrah.

He had always thought of it as hell.

"We hoped you'd post a man at the graveyard, sir, and have him watch the cottages. Maybe even the rectory."

"I've had a man patrolling the area for the past two days. On the surface, the only offence Mrs Hodge seems guilty of is being a snoop. Three times in one night, she took a lantern and a swordstick and walked the cemetery grounds."

Olivia sat forward. "Alone?"

"Yes. Always alone."

"And the rector?" Gabriel asked.

"Makes regular house calls as you'd expect, and often stays late at St Luke's. A man with a cart collects him and takes him home. And he never leaves the rectory at night."

Gabriel exhaled, his patience wearing thin. "Did you have any luck with the undertaker's cloth? Any news of the body stolen from the watch-house?"

Daventry sat back, drawing a hand through his thick, ebony hair. "I can tell you this. Those involved operate at the highest level. The absence of credible information says more than any report ever could."

"Then you have nothing to tell us?" Gabriel hoped the agent felt as useless as he did.

"The cloth found at the grave was deliberately placed.

Undertakers haven't used fabric of that kind for years. There's no record of Mrs Hodge owning the cottages. And my men have"—he paused, choosing the polite phrasing—"used every lawful method to persuade the known resurrectionists to confess to the crime at the watch-house. All to no avail."

"Who does own the cottages?" Olivia asked.

"I don't know. There's no paperwork."

In his dealings with Daventry, Gabriel had never seen the man stumped. It did not bode well.

"I checked the maid you hired from the registry, and there's nothing suspicious there." Daventry hesitated before offering a redeeming detail. "There is one thing. A woman matching Mrs Hodge's description frequented the bookshop opposite your old address in Clerkenwell."

Gabriel muttered a curse. "She's been watching you for some time." He felt it then—the cold calculation of it. While he'd been listening to Olivia recite verse, Mrs Hodge had been gathering information. "Can we not confront her?"

"With what?" Daventry said, sounding a damn sight calmer than Gabriel. "Visiting a bookshop? Taking a late-night walk?"

After a shared exhale, Gabriel said, "There is something strange we should consider."

"I'm listening," Daventry replied.

"The fact that I knew exactly where to find Olivia." He paused. Breaking a confidence didn't sit well with him. "But I imagine Gentry will accept that patient confidentiality doesn't apply here."

Daventry frowned. "What are you saying? Gentry told you Miss Woolf had moved to Chelsea?"

"He was far more specific. Mrs Hodge is one of his recent

patients and happened to mention her new neighbour. Details that would mean something to me personally. Her love of graveside poetry. Her distinctive red hair. And a habit of dressing in grey to avoid attention."

Olivia drew a sharp breath. "Then she knew who I was. She meant to expose me. She sent you to World's End so the villain could dispose of us both."

"Still, without proof of intent, Gentry's statement is merely gossip," Daventry replied. "That said, she found the body in the cottage. We could use that as an excuse to question her again. I'll have her brought to Bow Street tomorrow. Sir Basil will support the decision."

"I cannot help but think she is the key to this." If she was not the architect, she was at least the messenger.

They moved on to Nesbit and what he'd revealed.

"Never underestimate the power of money when a man has none," Daventry said. "The only way to know if he's lying is to visit the mausoleum and check the tombs. Let's meet there tomorrow. There's no need to seek permission."

Olivia shifted nervously. "Still, would it not be wiser to inform the magistrate? There is doubt over my involvement, and I would rather Sir Basil hear it from us."

"You have nothing to fear." He'd drag the magistrate to hell and back before letting him put her behind bars. "I won't see you spend a night in gaol."

"The fewer people who know of our movements, the better," Daventry said. "Constables and men of the watch are easily bought."

Olivia's lips thinned. "Does it not frustrate you, sir, this fight for justice when half the world is corrupt?"

Daventry pondered the question. "It's not justice we're dealing with. It's politics. And on the bright side, if we uncover a plot to destabilise the government, the King will grant you favour."

"Favour?" Olivia sounded half shocked, half amused.

"He may see that you married for necessity," Daventry said, "and consent to an annulment."

Chapter Seventeen

The King's Theatre
Charles Street, Haymarket

Gabriel hadn't mentioned Daventry's ridiculous suggestion.

Neither had Olivia.

Not on the way home from the Order's office.

Not while searching the library.

Not in the carriage to the theatre, nor over an intimate supper in the private room adjoining his box.

Silence did not mean ignorance. It simply meant neither dared test the boundaries of what was changing between them. Perhaps because neither was sure how the other truly felt.

Since when had honesty become so complex?

Since the outcome truly mattered.

They settled into plush velvet seats, the eyes of the *ton* fixed on them, not the stage, not the orchestra, not even Lord Morton and his scandalous mistress.

"They're probably wondering why you married a

nobody," Olivia whispered, gazing at the crowd through a long-handled lorgnette.

She was mistaken. Who would look at her and see a nobody?

She possessed a quiet elegance, the kind that drew notice. No one would deem her anything less than remarkable.

"It's not you," he said, hearing admiration in his own voice. *It could never be you.* "I suspect they're wondering why a man who despises deceit would want to watch *The Tragedy of Julius Caesar*."

"Let them wonder." She turned from the audience and looked at him, her gaze an unexpected shield. "They don't know you as I do. How could they when you hide your true self behind a forbidding facade?"

"Do I detect a compliment, Olivia?"

"Gabriel, you're the finest man I know."

His chest tightened. He was used to harsh opinions, not honest praise. Even so, it meant more coming from her.

"I doubt you know many."

"You're the finest I've ever known."

The words breached his armour.

She saw him. No one ever had.

"Yours is the only opinion that matters."

The lights dimmed. In the pit below, the orchestra raised their instruments and launched into a rousing overture. The curtains parted, and the play began, the *Ides of March* mentioned three times in the second scene.

While she listened to every word spoken on stage, he kept hearing hers. It was all he could do to keep his mind on the play, not the woman beside him, her praise an echo he couldn't silence. Nothing in his life had ever landed so quietly, yet struck so deep.

They sat in silence as the actors spoke of omens and unrest, of fire raining from the sky, of a lion seen prowling near the Capitol, of men claiming they had walked in flames and felt no harm. Olivia leant forward slightly, her gloved hand resting lightly on Gabriel's leg, not entirely by accident but enough to draw his attention.

She did not move it.

Nor did he.

Thunder cracked from the stage, part of the storm in *Act II*, yet the sound tore through his composure as though it were real.

In an instant, he was no longer in the theatre. He was ten years old, hearing his parents argue in the drawing room against the call of distant thunder.

"Someone has forced the lock on my desk drawer," his father had said, suspicion coating every syllable.

"I suppose you think it was me," his mother replied, her voice colder than a winter's chill.

"Who else skulks about in the dark, scheming against me?"

"You really are quite pathetic."

"Leave if you cannot abide my company."

"And abandon my son?"

"You don't give a damn about the boy. He's nothing more than a pawn to you. A weapon to use against me."

"To you, he's merely an heir."

Distrust had poisoned the house long before it destroyed it.

Years later, during a raging storm, he had confronted his mother in the great hall. His father had already been in the ground for six months, taking Gabriel's respect with him. She had glared at him, giving her usual list of demands.

"You must choose, Mother. Your son or your lover." He'd known the answer before the words left his lips. "Your position or your disreputable friends."

She left that night. No word. No warning.

Thunder rumbled again from the stage, the theatrical clash of cymbals echoing through the auditorium. Olivia's hand remained on his leg, a gentle pressure that anchored him to the present. She turned, just enough to let him know she saw him. Not the marquess. The man. Her man.

"What is it?" she said. "Every muscle is tense."

He swallowed, unsettled by the thought of how easily things could change. "I've never been comfortable with storms. They always herald something tragic."

She was perceptive enough to know what he was thinking. "You're afraid this won't end well? The case, not the play."

"I've come to expect disappointment."

God help him, but he needed this to be different.

She must have sensed something in his silence, for her hand slipped a little higher, her fingers brushing along the muscle of his thigh. Not a bold touch, but a gentle, deliberate caress meant to soothe him.

He drew a deep breath.

Then it faltered.

His eyes closed.

There had never been comfort like this. The kind meant to settle a storm. The kind meant to unravel a man and see him undone. Soft. Feminine. A call to the soul.

"Let me help you forget," she whispered.

He couldn't refuse even if he'd wanted to. Her fingers grazed his growing arousal, and it took all his strength not to groan aloud in a theatre full of people.

"Olivia." Her name left his lips, but he didn't clasp her hand to stop it roaming over the placket of his trousers. "Do you know how easily you undo me?"

God help him, his body had already betrayed him. She must have felt him, hot and hard against her palm, yet she didn't pull away.

"I have some idea." A coy smile touched her lips. "You don't exactly hide it well."

"Hide it? You're about to bring the Marquess of Rothley to his knees before the whole auditorium."

No one else had ever wielded such power over him.

"Let me do this for you, Gabriel. Watch the play."

He tried to focus. But the next line from the stage—*Let us be satisfied!*—was devilishly ill-timed.

His wife sat perfectly composed beside him, face angled toward the stage, the picture of decorum. But he felt her deftly slipping the buttons on his trousers, the action hidden from every eye but his.

"Do you mean to test the limits of my control?"

"I mean to ensure betrayal is the last thing on your mind tonight."

"What I'm thinking now isn't fit for respectable company."

"And yet I need to hear it."

She slipped her hand beneath the placket, a slow, tentative touch. Not practised. Not polished. But it stole the breath from his lungs and scattered reason like leaves in a gale.

"You want to know what I'm thinking?"

"Yes."

"That I'd rather be alone with you. Doing something far more satisfying than watching this play."

Her tongue skimmed her bottom lip, that maddening

gesture he'd come to recognise. Her gloved hand slowly circled him. Silk on skin. Torment and paradise in one forbidden touch.

"What would you rather do?"

"You know the answer."

"Tell me."

"If we were alone, you wouldn't be touching me like this. You'd be under me, panting my name, urging me deeper, begging me not to stop."

He felt the gentle tremor in her hand. Heard the hitch in her breath that proved she wanted him. His body was already hers. One more stroke and he'd spend in her hand like a schoolboy.

"And if we were alone," she murmured, "you'd find just how ready I am for you, Gabriel."

He hissed through his teeth. "Are you deliberately trying to make me climax in a theatre box?"

"What? Is the staid Marquess of Rothley about to lose control?"

"Damn right I am."

God help him, it wasn't just desire. It was the dawning realisation that restraint would soon become impossible. That with her, he lost all semblance of sanity. Yet he welcomed the freedom it brought.

"Our private parlour is mere feet away. When this play ends, I intend to close the door, lift your skirts, and show you precisely what you've awakened."

Applause broke out, sharp and sudden. The curtain fell on the third act. All around them, people stood, the hum of chatter swelling as the familiar rush to the refreshment room began.

He rose, turning towards the curtain that shielded the rear

door. With measured movements, he restored his composure and everything her hand had undone.

Then, as though their entire exchange had been nothing more than polite conversation, he turned back to her. His coat lay smooth, his cravat immaculate, yet the truth surely burned in his eyes. Want. Hunger. The aching need to claim her.

He extended his hand. "Shall we?"

She took it without a word. The sultry curve of her smile confirmed she knew precisely what to expect as he led her into their private room.

He drew the curtains. Turned the key in the lock.

He held her gaze while shrugging out of his coat and laying it over the leather chair. "Tell me you feel it too. That you can't wait until we're home to have me."

That you've never wanted anything quite so badly.

"Surely the answer is obvious."

Her eyes settled on the velvet settee, and he knew, with sudden certainty, she meant to ruin him for any other woman.

He stepped closer, his gaze dipping to the same red sofa. "If we make love here, I'll insist we attend the theatre weekly."

"Then we should always arrive an hour before supper." She eased off her slippers, an act of silent surrender. "We'll have to go home after this and miss the end of the play."

He sat on the settee, bracing his hands on his thighs to settle his pulse. "I know every line. I doubt we'll learn anything here, other than how to please each other."

He parted his legs, then unfastened the fall of his trousers, daring her to watch. There was no mistaking what strained beneath. He made no effort to hide it. Not when she stood in her stocking feet, her slippers abandoned like a promise on the carpet.

"Do you see how restraint is a foreign word when I'm alone with you?"

Her breath caught. Her eyes widened, enough for him to know she understood precisely what was about to happen.

"Come here." It wasn't a command, not quite a plea, but something ruinously close to both. "If you want me"—he paused, letting the air stretch, tighten—"come and take your place on my lap."

Watching her was his favourite sin.

He would not take her over the arm of a chair. He wanted her here. Facing him. Seeing his desire unmasked.

She didn't speak. She didn't blush. She simply gathered her skirts and crossed the space between them like a woman who had already made her choice.

"Show me."

He looked up at her, heat pulsing through every vein.

"I need you now, Olivia. While you're standing here like this. Wanting me."

He reached for her, his hands skimming the silk at her hips before sliding upward, gathering the fabric until he touched the warmth of her thighs.

"You've only yourself to blame," he said, voice deepening, his thumbs tracing the bare skin above her stockings. "For looking at me the way you do. For touching me. For making me forget everything but having you."

For saving me without ever meaning to.

She raised her skirts, revealing the barest glimpse of thigh and the soft shadow between. Then came the tangle, silk and petticoats and limbs, before she settled astride him, pressed tight to his body, driving the air from his lungs.

Sweet mercy.

His hands found her hips, rougher than he intended, his

control hanging by a thread. "Yes. There. Exactly where I need you."

He felt her, flush to him, slick, hot, the pressure exquisite. Her soft moan told him she felt it too. He tightened his grip, moving her slowly, rhythmically, over every throbbing inch.

"This is what you do. You strip me bare. You get past every defence ... and touch me like no one else ever has."

She arched her back, every subtle shift of her body drawing a rough sound from his throat.

"I'm not sure how or why I have that effect on you," she murmured, "but you leave me near mindless, too."

She quickened the pace, rubbing against him.

"That's it. Take what you need. You can come like this."

Their breath turned ragged, lost amid the hum in the auditorium. The world outside seemed to fall away. No stage. No audience. Only the shocking truth of how badly he needed her.

"Gabriel ... please. I need you inside me."

He gave her what she wanted—what he craved—easing into her in one slow, measured stroke. Saints preserve him, the way she yielded. Enveloped him. Drew him deeper. A groan escaped before he could stop it.

"Do you feel that?" He held her closer, rocking her slowly, the world narrowing to the heat of her, the way her breath caught every time he moved. "Feel how hard I am for you? Feel the power you wield?"

"I feel it," she whispered, a silk tendril slipping free of its pins and brushing her cheek. "All of you, and still ache for more."

"Then take more."

Her mouth found his in a rush. There was nothing careful

in it. She kissed him like she meant to take every breath he had, and he gave it willingly.

His thoughts scattered.

He kissed her back, open-mouthed, tasting her, answering every shift of her body with his own.

She moved with him, the rhythm deepening, growing frantic, her fingers tightening on his shoulders as her composure unravelled. He watched it—felt it—each tremor of her body building like a storm behind her eyes, until it tore through her with a cry she didn't try to silence.

Pleasure broke over her like something startled into existence, too real to be contained. She didn't hide from it. And he knew she could not lie. Not in this.

But now was not the moment for thoughts. His body rebelled, needing its own reckoning. He buried his face against her neck, gripping her as he drove into her, hard and deep, until the last of his control gave way.

"Olivia ..." His voice broke as the moment overtook him.

She understood, softening against him, trusting him even now.

He barely withdrew in time, release catching him mid-motion, hot and breathless as he spilled over her thigh. He had never known a release that felt so little like pleasure, and so much like surrender.

Neither of them moved.

Then she kissed him softly. "Is it always like this?"

Not until you.

He brushed a lock from her cheek. "You mean so intense?"

"So beautiful I'm at a loss for words."

He wasn't at a loss. He should speak the truth, tell her he

was in love—but he held them back instead of trusting his instincts. Theirs was no polite marriage of friendship. It was a love affair. In time, she would come to that conclusion too.

She smiled. "Who knew that when we discussed morbid poetry we'd be making love like this?"

He'd known.

Somehow, he'd always known.

But she sounded like a woman bathing in the afterglow of lust, and despite the ache in his chest, he wore his usual confident smile.

Now wasn't the time to say what burned behind his ribs. But it was coming. Sooner than he was ready for.

"The circumstances we found ourselves in were rather unusual." He drew his handkerchief from his pocket and wiped her thigh. "Who knew I'd be tending to you while Rome mourns Caesar on stage?"

"I feel terrible about missing the second half of the play."

He laughed. "I don't. The idea that we might find our villain disguised as a plebeian carrying a placard was always fanciful."

"Perhaps we've let imagination get the better of us."

"It's our imaginations that put us here." He brushed his thumb along the line of her jaw, arousal quietly thrumming beneath his skin. "You're still astride me, and I'm in no rush for the play to end."

She brushed an errant lock from his brow. "Clothes are cumbersome, and I'd prefer we were at home in bed."

"Then I revise my earlier statement. Let's leave now before—"

He didn't finish.

The paintings on the far wall caught his attention. Six

small prints of ancient amphitheatres, collected by his father on his Grand Tour. Rome, Verona, Athens, to name a few.

Olivia followed his gaze. "What is it? What have you seen?"

"It's probably nothing." He lifted her gently off his lap, buttoned his trousers, and helped her straighten her clothing. He caught her hand and pressed a kiss to her knuckles, a small promise of what awaited her later. "We'll continue this at home."

But his gaze had already returned to the wall.

He didn't move at first. Then something, a vague remark made years ago, drew him forward.

Olivia moved with him, silent, yet equally curious.

He stopped before one print. Not the Colosseum, nor Verona's arena, nor a theatre in Athens.

The fourth. The smallest. The Theatre of Pompey. A ruin barely recognisable as anything grand, columns half-buried, a portico of broken stone.

His father had once held the print and called it a *hive for traitors.* The comment had meant little to Gabriel then. Now it sounded like a prophecy.

"You've seen something," Olivia whispered.

"Caesar died at the foot of Pompey's statue. Not in the Senate House as Shakespeare depicted or people like to claim."

She bent her head and read the faded inscription. "*Theatrum Pompeii—Campus Martius.*"

The words chilled him, reducing him, briefly, to the boy who had crept from his bed to watch a play. Not in a theatre but in the ballroom at Studland Park, where the lighting was low, and the dancers moved like shadows. Shadows that wore no clothes.

He coughed, his throat tight.

His parents had entertained with satire and spectacle, rewriting classical plays for their own pleasure. Lace, ribbons, painted lips and sin masquerading as art.

He had not thought of it in years.

He had no wish to now.

"We were never meant to watch *Julius Caesar*." He touched the gilt edge, lifted the print from its hook, and turned it over, pulse ticking at his temple. "Perhaps we were meant to find this instead."

A small square of folded paper was fixed to the wood with a single dab of sealing wax.

Olivia inhaled sharply. "It wasn't placed here recently. The paper is foxed with age. Have you always rented this box?"

"My grandfather helped pay for the restoration after the last fire, over forty years ago. This box was his recompense, secured under a contract that would span a hundred years."

"When was the room last refurbished?"

"Three years ago, maybe four. But the prints were my father's. They've always been here."

They both stared at the rough-edged scrap, the silence thickening between them, before he tugged it free of the wax.

It wasn't a letter.

Not a note.

Not co-ordinates to buried treasure.

Just a torn scrap, creased and dulled with age, bearing a faint wash of pale blue ink. Wings. The outline of swallows in flight.

No words.

Not one.

She leaned closer. "What does it mean?"

"I don't know." Yet he suspected he did. It was familiar, and he wasn't sure why. "The image is like the one on the disc found in the compass. Though I can't help but think I've seen it before."

She held out her hand. "May I see?"

"Of course."

She smoothed her fingers over the worn surface, her brows drawn. "It feels like wallpaper. A pretty wallpaper, were it not so faded. Swallows instead of peacocks." She paused. "Since the prints belonged to your father, might there be a similar design at Studland Park?"

He shook his head. "I'll have to ask Mrs Boswell."

"You don't know?"

"No."

He might have said the past was behind him, covered in dust sheets like everything else in that house. But it wasn't. It lingered in every room, a quiet ghost. Just like it clung to his heart.

"There's a reason my father carried a button bearing your crest," she said quietly. "And why he left the white heather as a sign I could trust you. He knew it would lead me to you. Somehow there's a link."

The thought brought no comfort.

It wasn't fate that drew them together.

It wasn't a blinding attraction they couldn't fight.

It was planned. Orchestrated.

And yet he'd fallen in love.

He stared at the swallows in her hand, wings extended mid-flight. So much pointed to the past, to things hidden, arranged, manipulated.

But she was here. Real. Warm.

Wanting him.

If there was truth in anything, it was in the way she touched him. In the way he lost himself inside her, silencing every doubt that threatened to rise.

Chapter Eighteen

Olivia stood near the fire in the Peacock Room, not to warm her hands after the long carriage ride home, but to study the painted birds. She'd told Gabriel she would change and come to his chamber within the half hour. Instead, she had spent ten minutes opening doors along the corridor, searching for swallow wallpaper.

The young maid moved quietly about, drawing the curtains, turning down the counterpane, filling the washbowl, laying out a fresh nightgown.

Olivia watched her, the question an irritating echo in her mind: *Where might I find a room full of swallows?* But she held it back. If Mrs Boswell caught wind of it, she'd have half the household on the hunt instead of settling her weary bones into bed.

They had agreed to face it tomorrow, when rest might bring clarity, when desire no longer blurred reason. But his invitation to join him in bed, the parting kiss that scattered her thoughts and left her knees weak, was the only temptation tonight.

The maid cleared her throat politely. "Would you like help undressing, my lady?"

She could manage, but it was important to act like the lady of the house, not a guest. "If you could help me out of this dress and brush out my hair, I'd be grateful."

The maid bobbed a curtsy and moved to unfasten the tiny hooks along the back of Olivia's gown. The stiff bodice loosened. Cool air kissed her skin. Stockings, stays, and petticoats followed, and the maid helped her into a nightgown and silk wrapper before guiding her to the stool at the dressing table.

She began removing the pins, placing each one carefully in the silver dish. "Half these pins are loose, ma'am, and it's a wonder you didn't lose the sapphire comb. Shall I mention it to Jane?"

"No, that won't be necessary. It's entirely my fault."

As the brush moved gently through her hair, her mind drifted, not to wallpaper, or hidden secrets, or even the threat of danger. But to the way Gabriel had looked at her as they made love in the dim theatre light.

She was in love with him.

It frightened her just how much.

How much she stood to lose.

But the words had gathered on her tongue. Reckless words. The kind friends and lovers rarely spoke. She had been full of them, overflowing, the confession beating against her lips.

Oh, I'm so in love with you, Gabriel.

But she had kissed him instead, and her heart had answered for her. In her wildest dreams, she'd never believed it possible. Only weeks ago, she'd been planning a lonely life abroad. An escape, not a future. And now, nothing could tear her away from—

A snag at her scalp made her wince, dragging her from her reverie.

"Oh, forgive me, ma'am. I've more practice with broom bristles than hairbrushes."

"It's all right." Shame rose in her chest. She didn't even know the girl's name. "We're all still finding our way. It will be easier for us both in time."

The maid sighed softly. "Mrs Boswell said you'd be kind. Said if anyone was meant to be a marchioness, it's you, ma'am."

Yet she felt like a trespasser in someone else's life, trying on a title that didn't quite fit. "I'm sure it's all been rather unsettling for you." It had been unsettling for all of them.

"Mrs Boswell said—" She stopped herself. "Forgive me, ma'am. My tongue runs away with me, and I've no wish to speak out of turn."

"You may speak freely here." The house held too many secrets. And the girl was trembling, poor thing. "Forgive me. I don't know your name."

"Daisy, ma'am. After the flower, not my father's heifer."

Olivia smiled. "A pretty name. I'll be sure to remember it."

Daisy relaxed a little, then prattled on about household matters, even mentioning Cook's tendency for tantrums. "He's taken to locking himself in the pantry more often of late. But we all know it's best to leave him there."

"He'll be too busy to hide in the pantry. We plan to spend more time here."

For a moment, she let herself imagine it. Gabriel at her side, the house alive with laughter, the staff settled, the ghosts of the past laid to rest. Perhaps when all this was over, life might truly begin.

Daisy's eyes widened. "Oh, we'll all be glad of it, ma'am. Mrs Boswell always said things would work out in the end. Said some things are just meant to be. Better than if he'd married the countess."

Olivia frowned. The poor girl was at sixes and sevens. Weren't they all? Everyone's thoughts were muddled these days.

"The countess? If you're referring to Lady Berridge, she's married to Aaron Chance."

"Before that, ma'am, when she was facing the noose, and his lordship knew marrying her was the only way to save her neck."

The words landed like a brick in a well.

Gabriel had offered to marry the countess?

To save her from the threat of death?

To ease the pain of the past, no doubt.

Surely he would have told her. Not let her discover it from a maid.

Daisy must have noticed the colour draining from Olivia's cheeks. "A marriage of friendship, that's all he offered. On account of him acting in her brother's stead. To protect her, ma'am. Nothing more. He said they could live in separate houses."

Gabriel's proposal surged into her mind.

A relationship based on friendship and mutual respect will suffice.

The truth struck like a bolt from the heavens.

He hadn't been so enamoured he'd say anything to marry her.

She wasn't the first.

She wasn't special at all.

"Would you—" She tried to speak, but her mouth was dry,

her throat closing. "Would you ask Mrs Boswell to come to my chamber?"

Daisy paled. "I'm sorry, my lady. Have I spoken out of turn? I was just about to say his lordship is different around you. We've never seen him—"

"It's fine, Daisy." She was seconds from crying, the words like splinters in her throat. "If you could just do as I ask."

The moment the door clicked shut behind her, the tears came. Hot. Unstoppable. They streamed down her face, dripping from her nose and chin. She pressed her palms to her eyes, but it was too late to stop the ache inside.

What a fool she'd been.

What a stupid fool.

To believe what existed between them was anything more than lust. Their rampant coupling in the theatre was proof enough—this was want, not something profound.

In fairness, he had tried to warn her. Desire was fickle. His heart made of stone. He lacked the capacity to love. The words a testament from his own mouth. Words she had knowingly ignored.

A knock on the door broke the silence.

Mrs Boswell entered a moment later, breathless, her eyes wide with concern. Her chin trembled slightly as she spoke. "My lady, Daisy told me what happened. That she feared she caused some upset. She's a young girl whose mouth works faster than her brain."

Olivia gathered herself, drawing up what composure she could. She trusted Mrs Boswell to speak plainly. "Is it true? Did Gabriel propose to the countess? Did he make her the same offer he made me? Friendship? A safe haven from trouble?"

To fight to the death to protect her?

Mrs Boswell's hesitation was answer enough.

"I've known him since he was a boy, my lady. And I swear to you—he's in love with you. I've never seen this kind of devotion. It's you, only you. Whatever was in the past meant nothing."

For a second, she almost believed it.

So desperately wanted to.

But doubt had already taken root.

"You're avoiding the question, Mrs Boswell. Just tell me, did Gabriel ask the countess to marry him?"

The housekeeper wrung her hands, as if the gesture might soften the blow. "He did, my lady. But only because he feared she'd ruin her life with Mr Chance. In the absence of family, he felt a duty to her brother. And his lordship …" Her voice wavered. "His lordship never expected to find love."

The drum of her heartbeat drowned out everything else.

A single tear slipped down her cheek. Then another.

Mrs Boswell stepped closer, her voice gentle. "It's clear you love him too, my lady. I beg you, please don't let his noble gesture taint what's happening between you."

Olivia straightened, her mind in tatters, her emotions frayed.

He was waiting for her, making love the only thing on both their minds. Now, those intentions seemed painfully naive, swept aside by the weight of uncertainty.

"Thank you, Mrs Boswell. It's late. That will be all for tonight."

The housekeeper dipped her head but hesitated at the door. "At least let him explain. I assure you, if he hasn't mentioned it, it's because it doesn't matter. Nothing matters more to him than you, my lady."

And how quickly he'd become her world, too.

Olivia nodded. "I just need time to think."

"But you do love him?" Mrs Boswell asked, hope shining in her rheumy eyes.

More than she could express in words.

"Yes, but please don't mention this to him. I prefer to speak to him myself."

"Of course, ma'am."

Alone now, she tried to make sense of it.

It might have stung less had their circumstances been different. But Gabriel's reasons for offering marriage were practically identical. Was she merely a convenient replacement for a man whose life had been marred by rejection?

She paced the room, arms wrapped around her middle, but nothing eased the hollow ache in her stomach. She wouldn't sleep until she'd spoken to him, and he was already waiting for her in bed.

It was more than lust.

It had to be.

The only way to know was to ask him.

That's what they'd promised. Honesty above everything.

Tightening the ties on her wrapper, she pushed her feet into her slippers and crept down the servants' stairs, the quickest route to his chambers. The stone was cold beneath her soles, each step echoing slightly in the hush.

At the foot of the stairs, the corridor stretched, dim and narrow, the sconces unlit. She moved towards the door that led from the servants' passage into the main house—

"I seek an audience, my lady."

The voice, edged with winter's chill, stopped her cold.

"Who's there?" The hair on her neck lifted.

The shadows stirred. "You're in grave danger. You think

you know the man you married. You don't. You can't trust him, and I can prove why."

A soft flare cut through the dark. Miss Bourne raised a lantern, her features bathed in gold. An angel with the devil's cunning.

"How did you get in here?"

"The servants' door is always open."

"No, it isn't. The staff were told to keep all doors locked."

Someone had let her in. But who? Who had betrayed Gabriel?

Miss Bourne gave a careless shrug. "I stole the key."

"That I can believe."

Was there no end to this woman's audacity?

She answered the question when she drew a pistol from inside her cloak and levelled it with expert aim. "Is there a limit to what you would do for love? Would you die for the man whose name you took? Would you lie, cheat, and steal if it meant sparing him the noose?"

Olivia didn't need to think.

She would protect Gabriel with her last breath.

The very thought of him waiting, unaware of the danger as he poured wine and smoothed the sheets, twisted like grief in her chest.

"Killing me won't solve your problem, Miss Bourne. Gabriel will never forgive your treachery."

Miss Bourne's sigh carried genuine sorrow. "I wish I hadn't hurt him. And I wish I didn't have to hurt him now. But the man I love will lose his life if I fail to deliver you to the destination tonight."

Olivia stilled. The words weren't laced with spite, only fear. This wasn't vengeance. It was desperation. A woman backed into a corner, trying to barter one life for another.

The truth of it hung between them, heavier than the threat.

As her heartbeat thudded in her throat, the confusion began to clear. "You work for the fraternity. You came back for the valise, not to claim your inheritance."

Miss Bourne couldn't hide her relief. "You have it? The valise?"

"Not here. It's hidden for safekeeping." Perhaps she could bargain, buy some time. "But I can arrange to collect it and deliver it to a place of your choosing."

Miss Bourne's mouth thinned. "It's too late for you." She shifted her weight, her hand tightening on the pistol. "You should never have come here."

Olivia's heart kicked against her ribs.

Then a noise behind her.

A soft scuffle. The creak of a board.

Relief fluttered in her chest. A servant entering through a different door, or Mrs Boswell making her nightly rounds. Thank heavens.

But when she turned, it wasn't Mrs Boswell.

A man stood in the shadows, face half-obscured by the lantern light.

A stranger.

She barely had time to gasp. A rush of footsteps. A shadow lunging.

Something heavy cracked against the side of her skull.

Pain exploded behind her eyes, bright and searing.

The last thing she saw was the pistol still raised, and Miss Bourne's face, unreadable in the dim light.

The world tilted.

The light blurred.

Then everything went black.

Chapter Nineteen

Gabriel woke to a pounding in his skull, his friends Dalton and Gentry gathered at the foot of the bed, Mrs Boswell fussing, and the unmistakable taste of betrayal on his tongue.

He was naked beneath the sheets, the space beside him cold and undisturbed. His wife's name hovered on his lips, a question he couldn't quite form.

"It's the brandy," Gentry was saying, amid the faint clink of crystal and the sound of someone sniffing. "It's the only thing he's touched since returning home from the theatre."

Yes, he remembered.

Passionate kisses on the carriage seat. Swallow wallpaper. Brandy. The heat of anticipation. The slow haze that had dulled his senses as he waited for Olivia.

"Do you think she did this?" Dalton asked, never one to soften a blow. "Did she drug him?"

Mrs Boswell bristled. "Of course not. Lady Rothley went straight to her chamber to change for bed."

"Then where the hell is she?" Dalton shot back.

A spike of panic split the fog in his head. Gabriel tried to sit up, but his limbs were sluggish and leaden, his skin clammy, and the room tilted like a boat with a broken keel. His stomach lurched at the effort.

"O-Olivia?"

His mouth was dry. His pulse raced. Was this some fractured dream? Voices in the room. The space beside him vacant. The weight of absence where she should have been.

Where was she?

Why wasn't she here?

And why the devil were his friends in his bedchamber, watching him like a man on the brink?

"My lord." Mrs Boswell was at his side, wringing her hands, the same anxious expression he'd seen countless times before, back when his parents entertained. "Thank heavens. You're awake."

Barely.

"There was no need to send for the doctor." He met Gentry's gaze and saw the tension pulling every muscle tight. "I'm alive. Now will someone tell me what the blazes is going on?"

Mrs Boswell's mouth twisted. "I'm sure it's not how it looks."

"Then tell me. How does it look? Because we clearly have company. It's a half-hour ride to town, which means I must have spent at least two passed out in bed."

"Someone drugged your brandy," Gentry said.

Gabriel's blood turned to ice.

"Someone?" Bile stung his throat. Fury surged like a second heartbeat. "Someone with a death wish. There's a traitor in this house."

He tried to rise but froze, remembering he was naked

beneath the sheets. Mrs Boswell averted her eyes, hovering like a hen.

"Assemble the staff." He forced the words through the rasp in his throat. "In the drawing room. And fetch me a robe."

No one moved, except Mrs Boswell, who fetched the silk robe and tossed it onto the bed.

"Who's going to tell him?" Dalton said.

Mrs Boswell raised her chin. "I'll tell him. It's best he hears it from me, but you might want to leave the room."

Gabriel stilled. "Tell me what?"

She drew a breath. "Lord Rutland is questioning the staff, my lord. He's in the servants' dining room. Threatening them all with the full weight of the law."

A few drops of laudanum, and the whole household was in uproar? "Good God, woman, you summoned my friends because someone tampered with my brandy? I'm quite capable of handling my own affairs."

She didn't answer right away, but winced as if called before the magistrate. "No, my lord. I summoned them because Lady Rothley hasn't been seen since I left her upstairs ... three hours ago."

He blinked, praying he'd misheard.

"Three hours ago?"

Three damn hours.

The words echoed through his mind, tolling like a bell that wouldn't stop. He stared at Mrs Boswell, waiting for her to retract them. She didn't.

He was already on his feet, robe barely tied, the floor tilting beneath him. "Where's her maid? Has anyone searched the house?"

Hang it all. That alone would take a day.

"Lady Rothley was distressed, my lord. She believes you weren't entirely truthful. That you married her because all your friends have settled, and you felt obliged to do the same."

Dalton and Gentry stepped back.

Was this some sort of ill-timed joke?

"She knows exactly why we married." His voice rang with disbelief. She was his wife. His lover. His dearest friend. There could be no doubt. Not after tonight. Not after the way they had touched each other.

"Daisy mentioned you offered for the countess before she married the earl. To save her from the noose. To protect her. A marriage of friendship." Her words were clipped, her eyes sharp with censure. "Lady Rothley was upset you hadn't told her. And now that knowledge has tainted any blossoming feelings."

Gabriel opened his mouth to explain, but every sentence that formed rang with uncomfortable similarity. The same promise. The same protective instinct. With one distinct difference.

He had never wanted Joanna.

He'd wanted Olivia almost from the moment they met.

"It's not the same. If she'd come to me, I would have told her." He exhaled sharply, dragging a hand down his face. "Joanna was a friend in trouble. Nothing more. I love Olivia. From the moment I saw her, it's always been her."

If he'd hurt her by not explaining sooner, then the fault was his.

But his heart had never been divided.

"She's taken her clothes," Gentry said, regret plain in his voice.

Mrs Boswell was quick to contradict him. "Not all her clothes. Just the grey dresses, undergarments, and half boots."

"Everything she came with, then?"

"She didn't take her books."

"You're certain?" It was like saying she'd left her soul behind.

Perhaps she'd left them for him. A reminder of what he'd let slip through his fingers. Or worse. To torment him with morbid lines of poetry.

"She confessed to loving you," Mrs Boswell added, rubbing salt in an already raw wound.

But the comment triggered another memory. Their blood pact. The sting of the hatpin. Her solemn vow never to profess love and leave the same night.

After everything they'd endured, she wouldn't walk away without confronting him. Without demanding he account for his lapse in judgement.

But as doubt gnawed at him, a colder thought settled over the heat of regret.

"No." Something fierce ignited in his chest. "She didn't leave." He looked up, voice hardening. "My wife was taken. By this damned fraternity."

It was all he could do not to grip the bedpost and curse his own stupidity. Why hadn't he insisted she come straight to his room?

The devil's own fury rose inside him.

There was a reason he could kill a man with his bare hands.

And that reason was now.

"Summon Kincaid. I'm going out. Tell him to ready the carriage. The one bearing my crest." He faced his friends.

"Go home. Protect your wives. These people will stop at nothing to hide their identities. No one is safe."

They didn't stare as though he belonged in Bedlam.

Dalton spoke first. "We'll not leave you to deal with this alone. But you'll need to tell us what the blazes is going on."

Gentry nodded. "Don't make us list the times you've saved our necks." He turned for the door. "I'll send my coachman to collect our wives and take them somewhere safe —the home of the Earl and Countess of Berridge."

"I won't have you die on my account."

"That's not your decision to make," Dalton said.

"You'll need weapons."

"We have them."

With no time to spare, Gabriel dressed in black, pulled on the Hessians with the concealed blades, and marched to the servants' dining room.

He entered the dimly lit room to find the entire household gathered around the long table, most dressed for bed. The maids still wore their white caps, the footmen their dressing gowns, all of them staring blankly, as if awaiting judgement.

They froze at the sight of him.

His head still swam faintly, the edges of the room softening before sharpening into focus. He braced a hand against the doorframe, just for a moment, then straightened to his full height.

Daisy sat near the end of the table, her eyes red and puffy. She was wringing her hands and muttering between sobs, "I never meant to upset her ladyship. I didn't think—"

Her voice cracked and faded when she saw him.

Not one of them moved. Not one dared speak.

Gabriel's gaze swept the room of familiar faces, loyal staff, people who'd served this house and his family for years. But tonight, trust was a fragile thing. Tonight, anyone could be the traitor.

"No one leaves here until I have answers." His voice betrayed none of the panic that thrummed beneath.

Rutland turned to him, arms folded, expression grim. "No one packed Lady Rothley's clothes. No one saw her leave."

"She didn't leave. She was taken." Gabriel's voice was like steel, measured only by force of will. "And someone here is an accomplice to kidnapping." His gaze cut from one servant to the next, searching, judging. "You may wish to consider that abducting the wife of a marquess is punishable by death."

Jane spoke up, voice shaking. "I overheard the earl and countess talking when they came for Mr Gentry's wedding, milord. I told Daisy you'd offered marriage. It's me what's to blame, not her."

No, he was to blame. For not realising it would matter.

Gabriel gave a tight nod. "Thank you for your honesty. But that doesn't answer the question. What the hell has happened to my wife?"

Rutland drew him aside, lowering his voice. "None of them know. Is it possible she left of her own accord?"

Gabriel didn't hesitate. "No."

He'd stake his life on it.

A discreet cough drew his attention.

Alfie hovered in the doorway, cap clutched in his hands. "Mr Kincaid sent me, milord. I need a quiet word about the carriage. Outside, if you've a moment to spare."

Kincaid knew better than to interrupt without good reason.

"No one is to leave," Gabriel barked, before striding after Alfie down the basement corridor. They stopped outside the pantry door. "I assume this isn't about the carriage."

"No, milord. But Mr Kincaid said I'm to tell you what I've seen."

His pulse stuttered. "You saw Lady Rothley?"

Alfie shook his head. "I saw the cook last night, out in the garden. He met a woman down by the fountain. He was meant to be locked in the pantry, calming his temper, only he wasn't."

Gabriel's fists clenched at his sides.

"You're certain it was Molière?"

Alfie nodded. "And it ain't the first time, neither. I saw him out there the other night, meeting the same lady who came across the field."

"From the direction of Wynbury Hall?"

The lad shrugged. "That's what Mr Kincaid thinks."

Gabriel laid a hand on Alfie's shoulder. "You've done well. Tell Kincaid we're leaving in five minutes."

He turned on his heel, striding back to the servants' dining room.

The moment he entered, every head snapped up.

He didn't waste time. "Molière will be leaving us tonight. Though if he's lucky, he may yet save himself from the gallows."

Molière's eyes darted to the door, then back to Gabriel. His fingers fumbled at the edge of his chair, white-knuckled and trembling.

"Raise your hand," Gabriel said, his gaze sweeping the table, "if you've ever seen him slip out of the house at night."

One by one, the staff slowly raised their hands.

Molière surged to his feet, chair scraping against the floor.

"Imbéciles," he spat. "Stupid traitors!" He bolted for the door.

Gabriel was faster. He caught the cook by the scruff and slammed him against the wall, hard enough to rattle the sideboard.

"You've been feeding information to Miss Bourne," he growled. That woman was the bane of his existence. "I don't give a damn that you drugged my brandy. Who has my wife?"

Molière's lips clamped shut.

Gabriel shoved him again, fury coiled tight in every muscle. "Answer me. Or you'll be begging for the noose."

Molière winced, hands raised. "Please … I had no choice."

"Wrong answer."

"They have my brother," the cook cried, his accent thickening as panic overtook him. "In Lyon. In gaol. Miss Bourne, she said if I did not help, he would rot there."

Gabriel's grip tightened. "Help how?"

"She wanted information. To know when the lady was alone, when the house was quiet." He swallowed hard. "I never meant for her to be harmed. I swear it on my mother's grave."

It took a saint's will not to throttle the man.

"Where would they have taken her?"

"I don't know!" Molière stammered, shrinking back, his feet slipping from underneath him. "I was never told. Only when. Only that it must be quick, and at night."

And to make sure he couldn't follow.

Gabriel cursed under his breath. "Get up."

When the man hesitated, Gabriel seized him by the collar and hauled him upright. "You'll be our guest in the pantry until I decide whether to hand you to the authorities or deliver justice myself."

He dragged Molière down the corridor, shoved him inside, slammed the door shut, and turned the key, leaving it in the lock.

Facing the servants gathered in the hall, Gabriel's voice rang like steel. "He doesn't leave this house. Not for a piss or a prayer. The men are to guard the door until my return."

The staff nodded, wide-eyed.

God help anyone who defied him now.

He gestured to Rutland. "We're leaving." But he was already striding down the corridor when his friend caught up with him.

"Was it him, dead in the watch-house?" Rutland asked. "Was it Lovelace? Gentry said he went to identify the body, but the resurrectionists stole it."

Gabriel mounted the stone stairs, the image an unwelcome distraction. The similarities were uncanny: bone structure, hair colour, height, frame. Yet he would stake his life that it wasn't him.

"I want to say yes."

"But every instinct says it's not," Rutland finished.

Gabriel nodded. "Had I looked into his eyes, I'd have known. I'm afraid we're no closer to knowing whether our friend is dead."

Their footsteps echoed down the corridor, the truth still shrouded in doubt.

His thoughts turned to Olivia.

Where was she? Was she afraid? Had she fought, cried out? Did she know he would find her, whatever the cost?

Miss Bourne hadn't taken her in a fit of jealousy. This wasn't some reckless impulse. It was cold. Premeditated. The work of revolutionaries, not a woman scorned. Molière had used the word *they*.

But he couldn't think about losing her. Couldn't let the fear take hold. If he faltered now, he might never see her again.

They wouldn't kill her.

Not yet.

Not until they got what they came for.

He had time. Time to get her back.

In the mews, Dalton was the first to press for answers. "Where do we start? We don't know why they took her or what they're after."

"Or why you married her without telling your friends." Gentry gripped Gabriel's shoulder. "Why you've kept us in the dark."

For the same reason he did anything. To protect those he loved from the faceless devils who hunted in shadows.

"I'll explain on the way," he said, already moving.

He noticed Alfie atop the box, swamped in a heavy coat, cap pulled low. The boy might like to think he was invisible.

"Alfie."

The boy jerked upright. "Yes, milord."

"Loyalty is the only currency that matters here. You've earned your place, and can ride with us tonight." The boy's smile took the chill from Gabriel's heart, if only for a moment. "Still, you answer to Kincaid."

"Aye, milord."

The horses stamped and snorted in the dark, breath clouding in the cold. Kincaid steadied the team of muscled Friesians pulling the elegant black carriage emblazoned with the dragon crest. "Where to?" he asked.

"Wynbury Hall." He'd strike the obvious places off the

list first. There was no time to search the house for swallows and spend hours hunting down the next clue. "Then to World's End. I have questions for Mrs Hodge, and may want to call on the rector."

The drive to Wynbury Hall took ten minutes, just long enough for Gabriel to give his friends a quick recount of all that had happened.

Rutland shook his head. "And you think Miss Bourne is part of this fraternity? That means she knew Olivia's father."

Gabriel didn't know what to think. "Without the full picture, we're groping in the dark. But I'm convinced she took Olivia, and not because she wants me." The carriage rattled through Wynbury's rusted gates. "Hopefully her aunt can shed light on the matter."

"It's gone four," Rutland muttered as the carriage wheels crunched over gravel. "They'll all be abed."

"Then we'll wake them," Dalton said, sneering.

Wynbury Hall loomed ahead. The house was silent, every blind drawn, every window black. An eerie mist clung to the place, creeping low to the ground, weaving up the stone steps like it knew the way.

Gabriel alighted, scanning the facade where ivy clung like rot. Something in the air told him he wasn't wasting his time. But only an amateur would bring Olivia here. And Kate Bourne was as devious as the snake that tricked Eve.

"Kincaid, keep your eyes peeled. There's a slim chance Miss Bourne is here. But have a care. Don't fire blindly in the dark."

The coachman gave a sharp nod and drew his pistol.

Gabriel mounted the steps, slammed the brass knocker against the plate, each hammer echoing like a summons for the dead.

No response.

Not even a whisper of wind in the trees.

A second knock failed to rouse a sleepy-eyed servant.

Gabriel stepped back from the door and searched the windows for a twitch of curtain or sudden flicker of light.

"Dalton, you and Rutland take the rear. Force your way in if you must. *Caesar* is the code word. So I know it's you if I encounter a figure in the dark."

"You think we'll need it?" Dalton asked.

"I think we won't get a second chance to wonder."

Dalton nodded brusquely. He and Rutland moved off without a word, skirting the house and vanishing into the gloom.

While Gabriel contemplated which windowpane to break, Gentry shifted beside him, face grim. "Something isn't right. Maybe Miss Bourne wished to draw you away from Studland Park. Assuming she's the one responsible."

He had thought the same and dismissed it. "She's responsible. Everything about her return to Islington feels wrong. Besides, she had Molière drug my brandy. Miss Bourne could have searched every room without my knowledge."

"But why join a band of revolutionaries? What is she hoping to gain? Certainly not wealth. She's about to inherit this estate."

"Is she? Perhaps her aunt had other ideas." He refused to waste time grasping for answers. "We'll discuss it during the journey to World's End. There's a chance Olivia has been taken there."

He pictured her, defiant, trying to hide her fear. She wouldn't have left willingly. The thought of someone hurting her was a slow, sick twist in his gut, and he forced the image away.

The scrape of bolts snapped his attention to the door. He reached for the blade in his boot as it creaked open.

A figure appeared, his candle held high. "Can I help you?" The butler squinted into the dark, hair mussed, his waistcoat unbuttoned.

Gabriel stepped forward. "I know the hour, but this can't wait. I need to speak with Mrs Culpepper."

The butler's mouth thinned. "I'm sorry, milord. Mrs Culpepper passed two days ago. Mere hours after you left. A dreadful coughing fit led to her heart giving out. I thought you'd have heard."

Gabriel didn't quite believe it. Not that she'd succumbed to illness, but that the timing was so convenient.

"Then I'd like to see her. I assume she's been laid out in the drawing room." He'd have Gentry check the body and look for anything out of place.

A muscle in the butler's cheek twitched. "No, milord. She was laid to rest in the family plot by the west wall this afternoon. The physician was certain of the cause, and Miss Bourne saw no reason to delay."

Already six feet under. Why was he not surprised?

"Is Miss Bourne at home?"

"She left after the funeral and hasn't returned."

"Then you'll step aside. I need to search this house."

Gabriel barged past the butler, took the stairs two at a time, and threw open every door along the corridor. He scanned the armoires, looked beneath the beds, into every damn shadow.

Miss Bourne wasn't upstairs. Neither was his wife.

He did the same on the ground floor and in the cellar. Nearly demanded they dig up the grave, afraid of what he'd find beneath the earth.

He stormed from the house with Gentry in tow, heading for the west wall. His stomach churned as they neared the garden and its cluster of old headstones. As God was his witness, he'd never read another graveyard poem again.

He stood before the mound of freshly turned earth and the homemade wreath of lavender, rosemary, and sprigs of bay, bound with torn muslin and thrown together in haste.

Reading his mind, Gentry crouched and pressed his hand to the soil. "It would take an hour to reach the coffin. And if what you say is true, the fraternity needs something from her." He stood, brushing the dirt from his palms. "Olivia's not here. I'd stake my life on it."

"I know."

He felt it in the marrow of his bones.

They returned to the house. He had one last question before they left for World's End. A thought that came from nowhere but took root fast.

He found the flustered butler in the front hall. "Fetch Carrow. He was the coachman here when my father was alive, and I believe he still serves you now."

A few minutes later, Carrow appeared in a nightshirt and trousers, grey hair flattened to one side, eyes still fogged with sleep.

"Answer one question. Do so honestly, and you'll be spared prosecution when the magistrate learns of Miss Bourne's criminal deeds."

Carrow paled. "I'll do my best, milord."

Gabriel prayed the man had a good memory. "Ten years ago, the night Miss Bourne left Islington, did she leave with someone? Did you take her to the stage? Or ferry her to Dover?"

Carrow gave a half-shrug and stared at his boots.

"She didn't just disappear. You took her somewhere. I advise you answer. I've no desire to whip an old man. But I've reached the end of my tether."

"She met a fellow at a coaching inn in Rochester. I left her there."

"And this fellow? Do you know him?"

Carrow shifted, clearly rattled. "I never got his name, milord. But he wasn't a stranger."

Gabriel firmed his jaw. "I'm in no mood for games."

"No." The coachman's hands twitched at his sides. "He was a friend of yours, milord. Handsome fellow. A visitor at Studland Park."

Gabriel cursed inwardly. Yet relief slackened his shoulders like a rope cut from a winch. "Justin Lovelace?"

"I didn't ask no names."

And he didn't need to hear more.

Minutes later, he was back in the carriage with Rutland, Dalton, and Gentry. The door slammed, Kincaid cracked the reins, and Wynbury Hall disappeared behind them.

No one spoke.

Gabriel looked between them. "Did anyone here know Lovelace and Miss Bourne were lovers? Say now, and I'll stop the carriage. You'll have my forgiveness—God knows it wouldn't have been easy to tell me—but you'll no longer have my friendship."

Too much had already been lost to silence.

He'd lived with half-truths while the rest of it rotted in the dark.

He couldn't stomach more lies.

Not from those he trusted most.

Rutland met his gaze without flinching. "Had I known, I'd have told you. Loyalty is everything between friends."

Dalton scoffed, shaking his head. "Do you think I'd keep something like that from you? I know the price you put on betrayal."

Gentry held his gaze, a shared pain behind his eyes. "I'd have dragged him through gravel if I had."

The ache in Gabriel's chest eased.

He hadn't doubted them.

"Then we'll not mention it again."

The rest of the journey passed in silence.

They arrived at Mrs Hodge's cottage to find the front door open, the frame splintered, a side table overturned, and the woman sprawled on the floor, clutching her middle.

A silver hilt jutted from her abdomen, glinting faintly in the dark. Blood soaked her white nightgown, the crimson stain spreading fast, the coppery scent already rising in the still air.

She was alive—barely. Her chest rose in shallow jerks, her lips parted in a faint, breathless moan.

Gentry tore off his cravat and crouched beside her, gently moving her trembling hand aside to press the bundled silk to the wound. "Hold this," he said quietly. "Keep the pressure. Let me see what we're dealing with."

Her hand slipped. Gabriel dropped to his knees, catching the silk and pressing it down. "Who did this?"

Her eyes fluttered open, vacant at first. Then they found his and filled with fear. "No," she muttered through cracked lips.

"I'm not here to hurt you."

She looked beyond him, her voice a croak when she

uttered Olivia's name. "Where is she? You didn't leave her ... not at the house?"

Pain burned low in his gut. The blade of fear was still lodged there, impossible to ignore. "They've taken her."

Mrs Hodge cried, a soft, broken sound, Olivia's name lost in the pain. "No. No. No. Do they have the file?" She gasped. "Did you find the evidence?"

"No, on both counts."

Rather than dismay, her sigh carried relief. "Then all is not lost. There's still time."

Hope flickered to life. He didn't trust it, but clung on, refusing to let it die. "Do you know where they took her? Do you know where her father hid the evidence?"

She reached for him, a trembling hand on his coat sleeve. "Follow his clues. He was convinced you would help her find it." Another ragged breath. Her hand slipped from his sleeve, her eyes glassy with pain. "They'll kill her once they have it ... you too. They'll not risk your wrath."

Gentry leaned over her, voice low but firm. "Conserve your energy, ma'am. If we're to save you, the blade has to come out." But when he looked at Gabriel, he gave a slight shake of his head.

Mrs Hodge's gaze drifted. She knew every second counted. "All you need is the file ... but I don't know where it is. No one does."

Gabriel bent lower. "You must know where they've taken her. Who's involved. For heaven's sake, woman, give me something."

Seconds passed.

"The man in the bed ... it wasn't Mr Lovelace."

The truth hit like a punch, but there was no time to dwell.

"The watchman ... he did this. He was paid to get rid of the body."

The devil's own fury rose in Gabriel's chest.

"Sir ..." Her voice rasped. "Sir Randall. His sister knew."

Gabriel stared at her, blood thundering in his ears.

But the woman had one final message as her life ebbed away. "Trust no one. Go home, my lord. Find the file before it's too late."

Chapter Twenty

The air was so cold, Olivia could see her own breath, short bursts of white mist against the gloom of the cell. Beneath her, the cot was damp. The musty blankets weren't fit for a dog. The pounding in her head refused to cease, and the lump behind her ear was the size of a plum.

Yet her thoughts were not for herself, but for Gabriel.

He would have heard how upset she'd been, that in a moment of jealousy, she had packed her valise and left Studland Park. Left him. Left him for good.

The ache in her chest hurt more than the one in her skull.

If she died here, among this band of revolutionaries, he would spend the rest of his life wondering, never knowing the truth.

That she loved him.

That the days with him had been her happiest.

That she would trade her life for his.

She pulled her wrapper tighter across her chest, closed her eyes, and willed him to find her. He had come to her aid when she'd needed him most. She had every faith he would do so again.

Except how would he know where to look?

She could be a hundred miles away.

She could be a stone's throw in Islington.

The echo of booted steps beyond the iron door stilled her breath. Since her arrival, she'd seen no one but Miss Bourne and the hulking brute who had struck her with a cudgel.

The clatter of metal on stone said her gaoler had dropped the key. His biting curse told her to expect a man.

She clutched the edge of the coarse blanket.

Her captors had tried the soft approach. Miss Bourne had swept into the room, her hair a halo of gold, grasped Olivia's hands, and pleaded, "Tell me where to find the valise, and I swear no harm shall come to Gabriel. Tell us, and you have my word you'll walk free."

It was the greatest lie she'd told.

Her tone had lacked conviction. She was not so confident now, like a predator who'd become the prey.

What options were left to them?

Threats? Torture?

God help her if they chose the latter.

The man who entered the cell stole her breath. She'd expected the flat-nosed brute, not someone with kind eyes and a sculpted jaw. Not someone who looked remarkably like the corpse in the watch-house.

Recognition slammed into her, hard and bitter.

Rage followed close behind.

"Mr Lovelace. You look considerably better than the last time I saw you. Though clearly that wasn't you dead in the box."

His hair was more golden than straw blonde, his ears

smaller, his brow less heavy. The likeness was uncanny, but now she understood why Gabriel had reservations.

She came to her feet as he shut the door, waited for him to step that bit closer, then slapped his face with all the strength she could summon.

His head whipped to the side. The crack rang through the stone chamber, her palm throbbing with the force of it.

"That's for my husband. For ten years of lies and cowardice. For letting a better man suffer while you hid like a worm underground."

Mr Lovelace rubbed his cheek, red from the sting, but when he faced her, tears welled in his eyes. "He deserves satisfaction. Has every right to call me out. My death was staged to save him questions, not cause more."

"Then you don't know him as I do." Emotion gathered, swelling in her chest. "He believed you betrayed him, yet still fell asleep at night hoping he might save you."

Ever desperate to put the world right.

Mr Lovelace glanced away. He couldn't meet her gaze. "I did betray him." His voice broke, his throat working. "I stole Kate's heart. Though I swear I never meant to."

The confession came as no shock. The two people closest to Gabriel had left within months of each other. One dead. One vanished with his father's bribe. No wonder he was so guarded.

"He would have understood. He would have stepped aside. He wouldn't have married a woman who didn't want him."

Yet he had married her.

A woman who had refused his first offer, who had bargained the second time he asked. Yet the spark had been there since the start. He'd felt it too, and somehow found the faith to trust her. To trust in them.

She touched her wedding ring, her thumb tracing the band.

What had he inscribed inside?

She couldn't look.

Not now.

Not when she needed her wits.

"Rothley would have shot me at dawn," Mr Lovelace said.

"Wounded you, not killed you. You know the value he places on honour. The truth would have served you better in the end."

Silence filled the cell.

She wished Gabriel were here to see the sorrow in his old friend's eyes, to feel the regret that hung in the air. If she survived this, she needed answers. Not to see these villains punished, but to ease Gabriel's restless mind.

"And now you're part of this fraternity of fools who waste their days trying to destabilise the government." She thought of her life with Gabriel, a cosy night reading by the fire, the heat of their bodies in bed. "You let Miss Bourne risk her neck to cause civil unrest. Is that what you call love, Mr Lovelace?"

He reeled from the bite in those words. "Kate is my wife. I joined this godforsaken group to protect her. So yes, my lady. I've sacrificed much in the name of love."

His wife? They'd spent years wrapped in each other's arms while Gabriel had denied himself the pleasure? She felt like taking her fist to his face.

But her mind jumped to the only question that mattered. If Miss Bourne had joined the fraternity before him, who had recruited her? Because that person had likely signed her father's death warrant.

"So your wife lied. She hasn't recently returned from France."

"That's not your concern," he said sharply, casting a quick glance at the door. Suddenly, he leaned in, his voice dropping to a whisper. "We were permitted to leave as long as we returned when summoned. To prevent Rothley from pursuing the matter."

The pieces were falling into place, none of them pleasant.

Had Miss Bourne been part of this fraternity for a decade? Had she taken the bribe to ensure Gabriel would always blame his father for their separation?

"What do you want from me?" she snapped, in case anyone had their ear to the door.

"Your father's valise. The evidence that implicates us all."

She almost told him the truth—that there was no evidence, or none they'd managed to find. But she refused to die in a gaol cell. If they wanted answers, she'd give them just enough to survive.

"The evidence is a series of complex clues. I'm the only one who can decipher them. Gabriel has the items, and I have the knowledge. He can't do it without me. I can't do it without him." A wave of panic rose. What if the fraternity killed them both and buried the truth forever? "We're close to solving it. You need us alive, unless you're willing to risk someone else getting there first."

Mr Lovelace fell silent. He seemed to debate the possibility that she might be of use, but he delivered a stark warning instead.

"They'll kill us if we give them the evidence," he mouthed. "They'll kill us if we don't. Either way, there's little hope. In a bid to save you, your father has doomed us all."

A chill threaded down her spine. There was only one man who might protect them now. One man her father trusted. One man who had risked everything for her, and would again if only she could reach him.

She had to get back to Gabriel.

Somehow, she had to convince them to let her return to Studland Park before it was too late.

Gabriel paced the study, the draught slipping under the door, as cold and insidious as the one weaving through his heart. Rain pelted the windows. A darker storm was coming. A tragedy waiting to unfold.

"Swallows?" Mrs Boswell frowned. Doubtless, she thought he'd lost his faculties, that grief had clouded his mind. "A room of swallows? Like an aviary?"

"No, not like an aviary." Cursed saints. Every second mattered. "On the wallpaper. Failing that, an old painting or tapestry."

The weight of Gentry's hand on his arm was a calming force. "Give her a moment. There are two hundred rooms. And she hasn't slept since Olivia was taken."

"We have a Peacock Room," Gabriel said. The thought of Olivia weeping there pierced something vital. "Do we have a room of swallows?"

"Your grandmother was fond of birds," Mrs Boswell muttered. "And there was an aviary in the garden when you were a boy."

"I recall the aviary."

God help him. Time was running out. There had been no contact, no demands. He could only pray Mrs Hodge was right. That while the evidence remained within their grasp, Olivia might still be alive.

"Wait. I locked the sample in the desk drawer." He crossed to the desk, vowing to curse her father if it led to another clue. "Perhaps it might jog your memory."

He was out of options. Mrs Hodge was dead. Reverend Clay had been no help. The man had been visibly shaken when Gabriel roused him from bed to search the rectory, under the guise of hunting her killer.

He dug into his waistcoat pocket for the key—but paused at a sudden sound.

A woman's voice.

Faint, but unmistakable.

She was calling his name.

"Quiet for a moment." He motioned to his friends, who were devising a plan to search every room. "Do you hear that? A woman speaking?"

They all cocked their heads and listened.

Dalton shook his. "Sounds like the wind."

"It could be a maid," Mrs Boswell offered.

Was he so steeped in grief he'd taken to hearing voices?

While his housekeeper opened the study door and peered into the corridor, he turned to the window. Rain blurred the glass, the garden beyond slick and shifting in the early light. He strained to see, certain he'd heard it again, somewhere beyond the manicured topiary, near the fountain.

Then he saw it. A flutter of grey. Perhaps the hood of a cloak.

He blinked hard.

Was it the laudanum? Or the brandy still thick in his blood?

Or not the drink at all, but a vision born of longing.

A desperate, aching hope playing tricks on his eyes.

"Excuse me for a moment." He was at the door before they could question him. "When I return, we'll begin searching the house."

Gentry stood. "I'll accompany you."

Gabriel smirked. "To use the pot?"

And then he was gone, picking up the pace once out of earshot, racing through the corridors and bursting out the servants' door into the herb garden.

He stopped. Rain soaked him in seconds.

Cold water ran down his collar, sharp as pins.

They'd think he'd lost his mind.

And he had.

Because until Olivia was home, nothing in his world would be right again. He'd hunt down every last member of this damned fraternity. A lone assassin out for blood. A stone-faced—

"Gabriel." Gentry appeared behind him, using his given name for the first time in years. "Come inside before you catch your death. You heard what Mrs Hodge said. We need to find the evidence. It's the only way to save Olivia's life."

He turned, wiping rain from his face, knowing Gentry was right.

But something pulled at him.

An impulse he couldn't ignore.

"Give me a minute."

He didn't need a minute.

He heard his name carried on the breeze.

Then he saw her, just a flicker in the corner of his eye,

gripping the raised hood of her grey cloak to shield against the rain. Her hair was loose, fiery strands whipping in the wind like flames.

Olivia?

She was home.

But she was moving, ambling across the lawn.

Away from the path.

Away from the house.

Away from him.

Had she been drugged? Injured? Returned under their noses to serve the fraternity's next wicked plan?

"Olivia? Olivia!"

He was running, sprinting through the rain, calling her name to lure her back, afraid she couldn't hear him.

She stopped. A statue for a second. Then she turned and headed towards the small copse of trees, moving like a puppet through someone else's nightmare.

She stopped again. Dazed. Disoriented. He couldn't tell.

What the devil was wrong with her?

"Run, Gabriel!"

A sharp crack pierced the morning air. Pistol fire, not thunder. The shot came from the cluster of trees.

He fell to his knees, instinct taking over.

Olivia didn't. She jerked from the impact but didn't scream, just collapsed hard onto the wet ground, limbs slackening, the grey cloak spreading around her like a shroud.

He froze. Pain tore through him, as if the bullet had struck his own chest.

"No! Olivia … No!"

Gentry was suddenly there, grabbing his arm, forcing him to his feet, dragging him forward. "She's still breathing. Move."

They reached her in seconds. Gabriel sank down, rain soaking through his trousers as he turned her gently onto her back.

He stilled, disbelief knotting in his gut.

Not Olivia.

His breath caught. For one irrational second, he couldn't make sense of what he was seeing.

Miss Bourne stared up at him, ghostly pale, her wig askew, revealing the familiar golden hair beneath.

Gentry crouched beside him, parting her cloak, his skilled fingers finding the wound. "It's her shoulder. Clean shot, I think. But we must get her inside before the shock takes hold."

Miss Bourne's weak fingers found Gabriel's. "Run. Run before he shoots again. I ... I was meant to lure you to the trees, but I couldn't. I couldn't hurt you again, Gabriel."

His grip tightened around her ice-cold hand.

None of it made sense. Her presence. The cloak. The warning. The sacrifice.

He wanted to ask *why*. To ask how far this betrayal went, how long it had festered under their noses. But Olivia was out there. And every second's delay was a gamble with her life.

"Where is she? Where have they taken my wife?"

Another shot rang out, missing them but shattering a windowpane behind, shards spraying the flagstones.

"Take this." She pressed a folded note into his hand. "You'll find her there. With Justin. She's alive. He'll do what he can to keep her safe. Hurry. Take the valise. They may agree to a bargain."

Her eyes fluttered shut.

Gentry pressed his fingers to her throat. "She's losing consciousness. I need to get her somewhere warm." He cast a glance at the trees. "But doubtless that bastard's already reloading."

Shouts rang out beyond the copse, muffled, frantic, followed by the sharp snap of undergrowth and a sudden crack of gunfire. A man's groan followed, pained and guttural, chased by a stream of curses in a rich Scottish brogue.

Kincaid emerged, ruffling Alfie's hair and grinning like his horse had just won the Derby. "The lad hit the beggar with the first shot," he called. "I wouldn't believe it had I nae seen it myself."

"That boy was wasted at the seminary." Gentry hauled Miss Bourne into his arms, the strain etched into his features. "If you're planning a rescue attempt, should you not wait until Daventry arrives?"

One of Daventry's men had returned to Mrs Hodge's cottage, breathless and bloodied. He'd found her wounded and chased the devil, but lost him near the Thames bend.

He should wait.

Wait for reinforcements. Wait for a plan.

But love made fools of sensible men.

Gabriel stood. He opened the note, now damp in his hand, and read the address, one he knew all too well. "Give this to Daventry." He shoved the paper into Gentry's pocket. "Tell him to follow with his men. And have Rutland look for that damned swallow wallpaper."

The rectory stood tucked back from the road, half-swallowed by trees, its weathered gables just visible through a screen of tangled branches and ivy. Carts and carriages rattled past,

A Marquess Scorned

unaware a woman had been seized from her home and held prisoner within.

Gabriel cursed his own stupidity. He'd searched this house hours ago. Every room. Every cupboard. And come away with nothing but the rector's stunned grief and the nagging sense he'd missed something.

Dalton scanned their surroundings as they crouched low behind the hedgerow. "You're sure you trust Miss Bourne? That we're not walking into a trap?"

He wasn't sure of anything. Except the love that burned in his chest. And the fear of what awaited him inside this godforsaken place.

"It's undoubtedly a trap." They'd sent Miss Bourne to Studland Park to kill him in the woods or force him here at gunpoint. To make him hand over the evidence while they tortured his wife. "But we have the advantage."

"We should wait for Daventry."

"And have them silence her when they see the cavalry amassing?"

That had always been the fraternity's plan. Bury the truth and dispose of the witnesses.

Still, Dalton erred on the side of caution for once. "If they're expecting you, you can be sure we're not just dealing with the rector."

Having met the man, Gabriel knew the Reverend Clay was nothing more than a fool out of his depth.

"Do you think Lovelace is in there?" Dalton's tone held the bitterness of someone who'd spent a decade believing a lie. "That he's been alive all these years and never bothered to tell us?"

Gabriel wanted to think the worst of Justin Lovelace. That

he was a liar, a cheat. Cruel. Conniving. What sort of man let his sister identify a body, believing it was him?

Only a desperate one.

"He's in there." Whether as friend or foe, only time would tell.

"But why bring her here? Why not somewhere less conspicuous?" Dalton glanced back along the road. "Mrs Hodge died practically on the doorstep."

"Because clever villains hide in plain sight. This whole business is a case of smoke and mirrors. Clues hidden within clues. The evidence is there, if one knows how to decipher the messages."

"Olivia's father led her here for a reason." Dalton's hand moved to the sheathed blade at his side as a cart trundled past on the road. "He gave her the key to the mausoleum. Why do that if it's nothing more than a meeting place?"

Gabriel considered the clues. The cross, a symbol for the church. The message carved into the back, saying the truth lay in poems. The compass pointing west of the mausoleum. All of it led to the rectory.

But something still didn't fit.

"The answer is in the poem, but we've spent hours analysing every line." Gabriel raked his hand through his hair, tension coiling beneath his skin.

Maybe he was too close. Too emotionally invested.

He thought of those first few days after their wedding, how every moment spent with her fed his obsession. He began reciting lines he could remember, nothing standing out at first, until one made him stop dead in his tracks.

> *"This crypt, built to entomb the dead,*
> *Is now a prison for a living thought."*

He turned towards the road, the graveyard visible in the distance, his heart thudding. "A prison? Perhaps it's not a metaphor. Some old churches had hidden tunnels. What if the men gathering at the mausoleum weren't footpads, but fraternity members, meeting beneath the rectory?"

Dalton eyed the graveyard. "It won't hurt to look. Our only other option is to knock on the rectory door. And we've no idea how many men are inside."

They followed the road back to the graveyard and entered through the rickety gate. Gabriel stole a glance at Olivia's cottage, recalling the sharp ache of regret when she'd refused his proposal. He'd ridden away, his heart heavy, yet something had compelled him to turn back.

It was different now. That ache no longer stemmed from uncertainty, but from love. Whatever lay ahead, he knew she felt it too.

Someone had fixed the lock on the mausoleum door. Thankfully, Dalton had brought a ring of skeleton keys and made quick work of the mechanism.

"Is there no end to your talents?" Gabriel teased.

Dalton gave a knowing grin. "My wife often says the same."

Inside the mausoleum, nothing had changed.

Gabriel removed the lid of the wooden coffin, expecting to find a sack of rotting meat, shocked to find an actual corpse.

"Someone who knew the fraternity's secrets?" Dalton asked.

"It's not anyone I recognise." He quickly replaced the lid and brushed his hands on his trousers, then scanned Dalton's solid frame. "Let's hope you're still a decent pugilist, and married life hasn't dulled your footwork. I need that brute strength to help open these tombs."

Dalton arched a brow. "After all those late nights reading poetry, are you sure you have the stamina?"

"Take hold of the end, and we'll move on the count of three."

They took their positions at either end of the stone coffin. The lid was cold and smooth beneath their fingers.

"Ready?" Gabriel said.

Dalton gave a curt nod, bracing himself.

"One," Gabriel counted. "Two ... three."

With a groan of effort and the grind of stone against stone, they heaved the lid sideways. It shifted an inch. Then another. One last push, and it slid free enough to reveal the hollow interior.

As Nesbit suggested, it was not some poor soul's final resting place but a theatre's prop basket—clothes, hats, rope, wooden staves. A few sacks of coins in denominations smaller than sovereigns.

Gabriel sighed. "Well, that sends my theory to the dogs. We'll check the other, then return to the rectory and kick down the back door."

The lid on the next tomb was lighter and easier to move. With a final shove, it shifted, dust rising in a thin plume. Inside lay a body bound in linen, the image more fitting for an Egyptian crypt than an English churchyard.

Gabriel stared down, unease creeping up the back of his neck.

The cloth was discoloured, but something caught his eye. The linen was darker in places, not just with age, but with the faint smudge of sooty fingerprints.

"Someone moved this body recently." Gabriel reached in and tugged the edge of the linen. "Help me lift it out."

Together, they moved the wrapped figure. It was so light, he doubted it was a body at all. Beneath it lay a coarse roll of hessian. Beneath that, wood, not stone.

"It's a trapdoor," Dalton whispered.

"Yes, secured by nothing but a latch."

"You think it leads to a tunnel?"

"There's only one way to know for sure." Gabriel hesitated, meeting Dalton's eye. He couldn't lose another friend, not like this. "Wait here. Stand guard until Daventry arrives."

Dalton caught his arm. "I'm coming with you."

"You've a wife at home. She'd—"

"Understand why we risk our lives for each other."

Gabriel looked at the man who'd stood beside him for over a decade. It was easy to dwell on what was broken and forget what still held fast.

"You've been a loyal friend to me."

Dalton gave a crooked smile. "And love's made you sentimental. Now open the damn door so we can find your wife and be done with this."

The tunnel was narrow and airless, swallowing all light the moment they descended. Damp clung to the walls, the scent of soil and decay thick in the dark.

They walked for a minute before spotting the glow, a lantern hanging from a hook on the stone wall. To their right, a row of studded iron doors.

All stood open but one.

"These are cells," Dalton muttered.

But Gabriel's heart was in his throat. He quickened his pace, checking each cell in turn, hope and fear waging war within him as he reached the end of the row. The final one. Closed. The key still lodged in the lock.

He daren't call her name. He held his breath, turned the key and pushed the door slowly open.

A man sat slumped in the corner, face bloodied.

Justin Lovelace looked up.

Time stilled.

Memories surfaced. The last time they'd spoken. The laughter, the slap on the back, the lie that said everything was fine.

Relief surged through him, not anger, not even confusion.

Just relief.

Relief the man wasn't dead.

That he'd never again have to wonder, or carry the weight of it in silence. That part of his past no longer clung to him like a coat lined with lead.

"Where the hell is she?" Gabriel whispered through gritted teeth. Olivia was his only focus. "I'll kill you if you've harmed her."

But Justin staggered to his feet, panic sparking in his eyes as he looked past Gabriel. "Where's Kate?"

"One of the fraternity's thugs shot her." Gabriel paused, letting the blow land, the same low punch he'd felt when he learnt Olivia was missing. "It's a shoulder wound. Gentry's tending to her."

Justin shuffled forward, one hand pressed to his ribs. "I did what I could to save your wife. But they—"

"If she's dead—" Gabriel lurched, clasping the man by the throat, the sudden chill in his body at odds with the fire in his voice.

"They have her upstairs," Justin rasped. "They're waiting

for Kate to return, to confirm you're dead. They'll use her to find the evidence, then kill her. Us too."

"Did you not warn them?" Gabriel released him and turned for the door. "Never underestimate the devil when he has everything to lose." He paused. "How many men are there?"

"Five. And one woman. You'd best shoot her first."

Gabriel nodded. Then said the words he never thought he would. "The trapdoor is open. Miss Bourne is at Studland Park. Tell Gentry the code word is *Caesar*. It might be best if you both disappear. Abroad. You may be certain I'll never look for you again."

They crept up the narrow wooden stairs, boots soft on the worn treads.

The cellar was packed tight, crates stacked to the beams, burlap sacks spilling grain, a rusted cider press hunched in one corner like a forgotten relic. Wooden barrels crowded the space, leaving barely room to turn.

There were no guards at the door. None in the corridor either.

Dalton exhaled. "They never expected you to find the hatch, and certainly not the tunnel."

"They underestimated Olivia's father." He peered into the dining room, then the butler's pantry as they prowled through the house. "And the power of poetry."

They stole into the main hall, pausing when they heard raised voices.

"This has gone far enough," Reverend Clay said, the strain clear in his tone. "When did this stop being about reform? About bringing the government to account? About helping the poor and needy?"

"When one of our members betrayed us," came Sir

Randall's faint Scottish burr. "Reform will nae happen unless we weaken those peers who control the House of Lords."

"Yet while others shouted in the streets, you were buying up half the high street in Melford, three months before the borough was granted its own Member of Parliament."

"Aye. To make sure the people are charged a fair rent."

"Yet you killed my mother years ago."

Gabriel froze.

Olivia!

Her voice was clear, steady. She was alive.

He'd never heard a sweeter sound.

"Your mother died in a house fire," Sir Randall countered.

"I have evidence to suggest otherwise."

Pride rose in his chest. He'd never known a woman so courageous.

The mention of evidence sent the rector into a panic. "Where is Miss Bourne? She should have returned by now. This will all end badly. Mrs Hodge said as much when—"

"Well, she'll nae have much to say anymore."

Olivia gasped. "Is that what you do when members disagree? Silence them by any means necessary?"

"The cause is all that matters."

"And lining your pockets in the process."

"When will this madness end?" the rector whimpered. "Do you really think there's a list out there? Perhaps it was nothing but an idle threat."

"And the lass happened to find her way here from Cambridge? Poking her nose around the graveyards and visiting The Burnished Jade?"

"But you've abducted a marchioness," the rector cried. "If we don't hang for sedition, we'll hang for that."

"Miss Bourne packed her clothes. Rothley will think she's

left him. 'Tis a familiar pattern in his life. One he's come to expect."

Gabriel felt the sting of those words.

The past threatened to surface like an undead corpse.

"Gabriel knows I would never leave him," Olivia said, laying a mortstone over any doubt, burying history with it. "I made a vow to him, and to Mrs Boswell, not to leave without speaking to them first."

Mrs Boswell.

He was curious to know the details of that conversation.

"You're all fretting unnecessarily." A woman spoke, the words ringing with certainty. "Rothley will be dead in the woods. Katherine will have the valise. When she returns with it, we will deliver the traitor's daughter to Studland Park and raze that monstrosity to the ground."

Gabriel smiled to himself, satisfaction slithering through his veins. He glanced at Dalton, drew the blade from his boot, and entered the drawing room.

Olivia sat on a crude wooden chair, her hands bound in her lap.

Their eyes met. Anger surged at the bruise on her cheek.

It took everything in him not to go to her first.

Instead, he turned to Mrs Culpepper, who looked the picture of health. "I suggest you reconsider, madam. I believe there's a flaw in your plan."

Chapter Twenty-One

Olivia caught sight of Gabriel, standing in the doorway, eyes dark as Erebus, only softening when they landed on her. In that split second, she saw it: relief, the well of emotion he was struggling to contain. Then his gaze shifted an inch, to the bruise marring her cheek, and a shadow passed over his features.

A tear rolled down her cheek. "You came."

"I'd go to the ends of the earth to find you."

He scanned the room like a predator deciding who to slay first. The quaking rector? The conniving baronet? The three men with necks as wide as mooring posts? The aunt who had made a miraculous recovery? Treachery her only ailment.

"We can do this the easy way." Gabriel cracked his neck. "Surrender and face trial for your crimes. Or I hurt you." He glared at Mrs Culpepper. "Every last one of you."

Mrs Culpepper moved closer, the tip of the blade she concealed pricking Olivia's nape. "There is an alternative. You surrender, or watch your wife die before my men kill you."

A Marquess Scorned

She saw him stiffen.

"Miss Bourne is in custody and ready to give names. The evidence is locked away safely at the Order's office. Hurt my wife, and none of you will leave here alive."

Sir Randall laughed. "You bluff well, Lord Rothley. But you're alone and outnumbered. And my comrades would die to protect the fraternity."

Something occurred to her then. There were other people, *important* people, involved with this group. It was unlikely anyone here would live long enough to stand trial. They'd either die protecting the cause or risk becoming the fraternity's next victim.

"I'm not sure your comrades will survive much longer than you." Gabriel scanned the men, doubtless searching for the weak link. "Reverend Clay. The Lord forgives those who repent. Be sure to choose the right side."

Gabriel employed the clever tactic of divide and conquer.

It worked. Perhaps fearing the Lord's wrath, the rector raised his hands. "All I wanted was to help the needy. But once these devils sink their teeth in, there's no getting free."

According to Mr Lovelace, that's exactly what had happened to Miss Bourne. Olivia might have suffered the same fate, had her father not given his life to protect her.

"And Sir Randall," Gabriel began, "are you aware Mrs Culpepper has faked her death? That she left her house to a fictitious relative abroad? That she plans to leave for France tonight?"

"Liar!" Mrs Culpepper cried. "Don't believe a word, Randall."

"I saw the grave," Mr Dalton said.

Sir Randall turned, as sharply as if he'd seen a snake in the grass. "You've been acting odd of late. I feared you were planning something. You want the evidence so you might blackmail us all."

"Fool. Can't you see what he's doing?"

Olivia ignored the angry exchange. She used the distraction to work at the knot on her bindings, as she had been doing for the past half hour.

Clearly weighing his odds, Sir Randall nodded to the three gormless brutes. They puffed their chests and approached Gabriel, one's knuckles still cut from the beating he'd given Mr Lovelace.

Mr Dalton seemed amused by the situation. "Remember the brawl in that tavern near the docks?"

"The Slipper?" Gabriel slid the blade back into his boot. His sardonic smile would give Lucifer pause. "Where the dockworkers placed wagers against us? Yes. If only we could bet on ourselves now. I could purchase a new Arabian." He flexed his fingers. "Which one of you bastards hit my wife?"

She wasn't sure which brute threw the first punch, only that he missed. Her elegant husband. A gentleman by birth, a warrior by heart, a pugilist by necessity, delivered a blow that knocked the wind from the thug's sails. He staggered back, landing on a side table, splitting the wood in two.

While the rector darted into the hall like a frightened doe, Mr Dalton proved just as adept with his fists. He was quick and lethal, using both brains and brawn, while his opponents swung like men with straw for wits and fists like mallets.

Two came for Gabriel at once.

The first blow caught his jaw, not enough to fell him, but enough to remind him this wasn't a sparring match. He ducked the next, drove his elbow into the man's ribs, then pivoted and kicked the other square in the knee.

Mr Dalton took a hit to the shoulder that would certainly

bruise, but he answered with a head-butt that sent his opponent staggering back, clutching his bleeding nose.

And then Mr Lovelace arrived, one hand gripping an iron bar, the other his ribs. He brought it down across one man's back with a sickening crack. The thug let out a howl and crumpled, arms flailing like a felled ox.

Mr Dalton grinned, a trace of blood on his teeth. "I do enjoy a dramatic entrance."

"Yes, if only we hadn't had to wait ten years." With a wolflike grin, Gabriel beckoned his opponents.

But one lay groaning on the floor. The other two hesitated, bloodied, winded, and far less certain of their odds.

Mr Dalton straightened, reached into his coat, and drew a blade with a soft hiss of metal. "I suggest you reconsider. We've men surrounding this house. Leave now while you still can."

That did it. One glanced towards the doorway, the other swore under his breath. The fight drained from their eyes. They stepped back and slipped into the corridor before vanishing through the front door.

Gabriel turned to Sir Randall. "I trust you've kept your membership at Jackson's, and your courage matches your fellow Scots."

Sir Randall adjusted his cuffs, chin lifted with a pride that bordered on delusion. "You think me a villain, but the people dinnae rise on their own. They whimper. They wait. We gave them something to roar about. And when they did, the House listened."

"Yes, and lined your pockets in the process." Gabriel shifted his gaze to Mrs Culpepper, perhaps aware of the blade pressed to Olivia's nape. "Release my wife. You won't escape this house. And once the investigation is underway, I've no doubt they'll discover you've profited from other people's misfortune too."

"How easy it is to speak from such an elevated position," Mrs Culpepper mocked. "Your mother knew how it felt to be trapped by convention. Why do you think she chose to work for me?"

Olivia noted the twitch in Gabriel's eye, the tightness in his mouth, the way his fingers curled into fists. She wished she could run to him, wrap her arms around him, tell him nothing mattered but their future.

But he needed to hear this.

And she had almost undone the twine binding her wrists.

"So that's what they argued about." He swallowed hard as recognition dawned. "The real reason they entertained. Doubtless, she persuaded peers to vote with their cocks, not their heads."

"She was an excellent agent, until your father died, and it was clear you weren't so easy to manipulate. If only Katherine hadn't fallen in love with Justin Lovelace. History may have repeated itself."

Gabriel turned to face his old friend.

But Mr Lovelace had gone.

So had the rector.

"I suddenly have a newfound respect for my father," he said with a wry grin. "I'd wager your niece used the money to run. To escape the life you mapped out for her. You didn't allow them to live abroad. You found them and forced them to come home."

Mrs Culpepper laughed quietly to herself. "When I heard Miss Hawkins had visited The Burnished Jade, I knew her father had sent her there. The plan was to recover the evidence, and you'd have been none the wiser. Katherine was insurance. Meant to turn your head. The fact you're alive, standing here, says she failed in every regard."

Gabriel didn't snap back. His gaze found hers, his dark eyes softening. "No woman alive could turn my head. I'm in love with my wife. My heart is hers. And always will be."

A breath caught in her throat. Of all the words he could have said—harsh retorts, threats, demands—he'd chosen that.

Love.

Freely given, when she'd braced for fury.

It stirred in her, rising like warmth through her chest. And if they died here, if this was their final stand, she wanted him to know how deeply she loved him.

"I'm in love with you, too, Gabriel." She blinked hard, willing back the tears. "I knew you'd find me. I was afraid you thought I'd left."

"You'd never break our blood oath."

She shook her head. "No. Never."

Mrs Culpepper groaned. "Give me the evidence. Let me walk out, and you'll never have to worry about the fraternity again."

"And what of me? You forget we both swing if the truth gets out." Sir Randall's burr sharpened the words. "What of our bargain?"

"It's every man for himself. And I've got a blade to the girl's neck."

"Does the lad know you killed his mother?" Sir Randall let out a mirthless laugh. "That you had men hunt her down and leave her to rot in that French hovel?"

"Traitors must pay. Else we'd all be for the gallows."

Gabriel went still.

Olivia caught the shift, the way his breath stopped, shoulders tensing like a bow drawn tight.

A chill swept through the room, sharp as an arctic storm that settled in the bones and never left. He slid the blade slowly from his boot, his expression so vengeful Satan would have cowered.

"Release my wife." His tone was hard, unforgiving. "Or I'll throw this blade so it lands between your brows, witch."

"And risk the life of the woman you love?"

Perhaps Mrs Culpepper meant to put her blade to Olivia's throat or wave it at Gabriel. Either way, the tip was no longer at her nape. She caught the glint of steel as the woman's hand dropped and knew it was her one chance to act.

She yanked hard at the twine binding her wrists, and it snapped.

In the same breath, she lunged from the chair and struck Mrs Culpepper across the face, sending her reeling, the blade skittering across the floor.

Mr Dalton was already moving, charging at Sir Randall like a battering ram. The front door burst open and Mr Daventry stormed in with half a dozen armed men at his back.

"What the hell kept you?" Gabriel said.

Mr Daventry grinned. "Timing is everything. And I could hear the conversation from the doorway. You've been in the dark too long. Now, you have the truth."

Gabriel didn't reply. He was already crossing the room, his eyes on no one but her.

She rushed to meet him, falling into his warm embrace, resting her head on his chest, relishing the feeling of being home.

"You're so cold," he said.

"I'm warm now you're here."

He stroked her hair, kissed her forehead, and held her so tight she could barely breathe. "Forgive me."

She looked up at him, tears blurring her vision, emotion rising. "For what? You saved my life. You've saved my life again, Gabriel."

He smoothed the backs of his fingers along her cheek. "You've saved mine. You rescue me with every touch, every kiss."

He ignored the raging Mrs Culpepper being dragged away in wrist shackles, and the grumbling Scotsman swearing he'd been misled and was only there to help a friend.

His mouth found hers, a kiss that curled her toes and turned her blood molten. He knew how to make a woman forget everything but the heat of his lips, the silken glide of his tongue, the hard press of him against her belly.

He broke away, his breath unsteady. "I'm in love with you. Desperately so. Forgive me if I failed to make that clear. If I left you in any doubt."

She cupped his cheek. "I love you. I'm sorry if you thought I'd left Studland Park. Left you. It killed me, knowing you were lying there, waiting in the dark, wondering why I never came."

He closed his eyes briefly, thumb brushing her jaw. "Don't think I wasn't half out of my mind. But you're not the sort of woman to make an oath and break it."

"I was coming to see you when Miss Bourne appeared in the corridor." She touched the tender lump behind her ear. "A brute clubbed me with a cudgel, and I hit my cheek when I fell."

He cursed under his breath. "No one will hurt you again."

She wished she could promise the same, but he needed to hear the truth. "Mr Lovelace and Miss Bourne are—"

"Lovers. I know."

"They're married. Mr Lovelace took a beating because they caught him trying to help me escape." She'd been forced to watch every cruel blow. To listen as he begged for his wife's life. "There's a trapdoor inside the mausoleum. In the tomb."

"Yes. That's how we found the tunnel. We followed a clue in your father's poem." He exhaled slowly. "I wish I'd known him. I think we'd have understood each other."

She laid her hand on his chest. "He made a mistake. He tried to put it right with me, though I wish he'd made finding the evidence that bit easier."

"Yes, I left Rutland at Studland Park, searching for swallows. Let's hope he's had some luck." He glanced at the door, at the men gathered outside. "Daventry will need the evidence to help secure a conviction."

She wondered how many people were involved. How long they'd been meddling in politics. Who had enough influence to escape a trial and the gallows.

"Perhaps we should keep the evidence when we find it, or at least some of it. To make sure the fraternity can't hurt us again."

Gabriel nodded. "Hopefully there'll be enough information to confirm Sir Randall and Mrs Culpepper are the ringleaders."

Mr Dalton returned, though she hadn't noticed he'd left. "Daventry needs our statements but said it can wait until tomorrow. Though Mrs Culpepper is convinced she'll be free by midday."

"One has to admire her optimism," she said.

"Did Daventry arrest Reverend Clay?"

"Yes, and the hired thugs."

"What of Lovelace?"

The corner of Mr Dalton's mouth twitched. "He escaped."

Gabriel sighed. "Good. We'll linger here, give him time to reach Studland Park. Daventry will want to know every detail. And then we've a call to make before we return home."

Olivia frowned. "We do?"

He ran a hand down his face, weariness etched into every line. "Someone needs to tell the Countess of Berridge her brother isn't dead."

London was a hive of activity by the time they reached the Earl of Berridge's townhouse on horseback. Carriages rattled past, hawkers called out their wares, and errand boys weaved between ladies with parasols and gentlemen in polished boots.

Olivia drew more than her share of stares. It wasn't every day one saw the Marquess of Rothley riding in shirtsleeves, his wife nestled against him, wearing his coat over a nightgown and silk wrapper. At least she'd tied her hair in a braid.

But she kept her chin high, relieved she'd lived to see sunrise.

The butler answered promptly, welcoming them in as if they were expected. Then Olivia's friends emerged from the dining room—the wives of Gabriel's friends. Once assured their husbands were safe, the questions came in a breathless stream.

"Where have you been? We were so worried."

"Why didn't you confide in us?"

"Joanna said you married Lord Rothley. Is it true?"

Olivia clasped their hands in turn, though hers were cold. "I'll explain everything when you visit Studland Park. For now, know I stayed silent to protect you."

While Mr Dalton was persuaded to take breakfast, Gabriel touched her gently on the back, his mouth close to her ear. "We must tell Joanna the truth. She's in no condition to hear it from Daventry and his men."

They were shown into the drawing room. Joanna sat curled beside her husband on the sofa, her head on his shoulder, his arm wrapped around her, one hand covering hers as she cradled their unborn child.

She looked up through teary eyes. "Gabriel." She didn't seem surprised to see Olivia in her nightgown. "Olivia. Thank heavens Miss Bourne saw sense and told Gabriel where to find you."

One didn't need the wisdom of Socrates to work out how she knew.

"Justin came here," Gabriel said.

"You've just missed him." Joanna gestured to the sofa opposite and urged them to sit. "Aaron gave him money, use of an unmarked carriage, and the suggestion he collect his wife and leave for the Americas. He has a man in Liverpool who can help."

The earl sighed. "We agreed to keep the details to ourselves."

"We can trust Gabriel. He's like a brother." Joanna met his gaze, hesitation in her eyes. "You're not angry? Justin said you let him go. That you urged him to save his wife and leave London."

"I'm not angry." Gabriel sat beside Olivia on the sofa, his thigh solid against hers. Yet he took her hand, as if he needed help calming the storm inside him. "It was evident he was a pawn in Mrs Culpepper's game."

Joanna pursed her lips and swallowed hard. "He's sorry for the pain he caused, Gabriel, that for the past decade, we've both lived with questions, never knowing if he was alive or dead."

It was clear from her tone that she saw Gabriel as family. And when she looked at her husband, the love in her eyes was unmistakable. Fierce, enduring. The kind Olivia had found too, by some miraculous twist of fate.

She squeezed Gabriel's hand gently, the weight of the past days finally beginning to lift. "All he's ever wanted is answers. An end to the uncertainty."

And all she wanted now was to go home with him, close the door on the world, and take comfort in the fact they were safe, together.

"We won't see him again." Joanna's breath hitched. She looked at her husband, reached for him, drawing strength from his touch. "And perhaps that's for the best."

"What about his grave at St Michael's?"

Joanna managed a smile. "The grave you refused to visit? Some poor soul is buried there. I'd rather not disturb him."

The earl glanced at their clasped hands, a flicker of amusement in his eyes. "And what will you do, now there are no ghosts left to chase?"

She felt the subtle twitch of his fingers and knew exactly what he planned to do once they returned home, aside from hunting for swallow wallpaper.

"Give my wife a thorough tour of the house," he said smoothly. "Make a list of what we intend to do in every room."

Heat crept up her neck. Two hundred rooms to explore.

Two hundred days and nights where he would worship her, ruin her, love her completely.

"Make Studland Park a home again?" Joanna said hopefully.

"Indeed. It will be quite the undertaking."

Olivia bit back a smile. "We'll begin with Gabriel's dressing room. There are things in there that need taking down."

They stayed for tea and a late breakfast.

"At least allow us to lend you a coach," Joanna said as they made to leave. "Olivia can't ride all the way to Studland Park on horseback, especially not in her nightgown."

Gabriel didn't argue. She was already stifling a yawn, exhaustion setting in now that the danger had passed.

They sat together on the same seat. He drew her close as the carriage pulled away, tucking the blanket around her shoulders, his mouth brushing her temple.

"We'll be home soon. Where you belong."

She looked up at him. "That's not the first time you've called Studland Park home. I remember how cold it was, walking into that grand hall. But now, the house feels warmer somehow."

"You've changed everything." The chill that had once haunted Studland Park was gone. With her, he saw more than shadows and stone. His heart was open now. And for the first time, the future looked glorious.

"I don't suppose you remember our conversation about hope."

He gave a dry snort. "Which one? We've had several."

"When I said I'd rather our days be filled with hope than regret." Her hand settled on his thigh. "You said—"

"I know what hope looks like to me," he finished.

"What did it look like?"

He didn't need to ponder the question. It was there at the forefront of his mind. "Hair like the burnished leaves of autumn. A mouth made for poetry, though I wasn't thinking of verse. A heart so generous, mine longed to beat in time with it. That's what hope looked like to me. You, Olivia."

She sighed. "That's very romantic."

"I know. I surprise myself."

"Mine falls terribly short now, no pun intended."

He arched a brow. "Why do I suspect your version of hope will have me behaving like a lustful buck in our friends' carriage?"

"Yes, I'm afraid it's not very poetic." She paused, letting the silence tease. "I rather hoped to catch you at the washstand—after you removed the towel."

Chapter Twenty-Two

"I gave them clean clothes, a basket for the journey, and some linens and brandy to help keep the wound clean." His housekeeper was busy recalling the items she'd packed into Justin Lovelace's carriage. "Some blankets and a bottle of laudanum. And I gave them—"

Gabriel raised a staying hand. "Is there anything you didn't give them, Mrs Boswell? Will we be eating with our fingers tonight? Drinking from crude tankards? Must I ride a lame mare into town?"

Mrs Boswell pursed her lips, then laughed. "Oh, it's so good to have you back, my lord. And while you're in such a fine mood, Parker, the undercook, can't prepare dinner. The traitor's still locked in the pantry."

Damn. He'd forgotten about Molière.

"Pack his things. Tell Kincaid to secure him a seat on the next stage to Dover, and make sure he's on it."

Mrs Boswell nodded. "Consider it done. Will you be dining in the formal room or your private chambers tonight?"

A vision came to him, an intimate supper, the food untouched, but a different hunger sated.

"Our private drawing room. But expect changes moving forward." They'd discuss it properly once the swallows were found and the evidence handed to Daventry. "I don't suppose you've had an epiphany since Rutland left? Recall seeing any birds?"

"No, but Lady Rothley did. Had an epiphany, I mean. She said to tell you she's checking the upper floor in the west wing. What with swallows being birds, and the compass pointing in that direction."

His heart softened. He knew her search amounted to more than a list of names. She hoped to find a note from her father.

"Then I had best join the search. As they say, more hands make light work." And he planned to have his on her body within the next ten minutes.

He found her pulling a dust sheet from an old pianoforte, sneezing as the particles tickled her nose.

She didn't hear him enter, and almost jumped out of her skin when he slipped his arms around her waist. "Gabriel. Good Lord. You scared me out of my wits."

He drew her close, burying his face in her hair, breathing her in. "We've been home a few hours, and still you're on the hunt."

She turned in his arms, brushed hair from his brow, and wound her hands around his neck. "I'm eager to put this all behind us. To focus on our future, not the past."

He touched his lips to hers, seeking the comfort only she could bring. But need overtook them, a chaste kiss turning into something hot and wild and hungry.

He crushed her to him, one hand fisting in her hair, his

mouth claiming hers in fierce possession, the need to be inside her like the beat of a drum in his veins.

God help him, but he was a slave to this, to the burning mix of love and lust, to the ache she stirred in his blood.

"I can't wait, Gabriel." She was panting, against his lips, then against his jaw, her gaze flicking to the fall of his trousers. "I can't wait until we're alone in your chambers. I need you. I need this ... I need us."

"It will be quick," he warned her, already freeing himself, the first bead of arousal glistening at the tip. "But I'll spend the whole night making love to you."

She glanced behind her, but decided there was no time to drag the dust sheets from the poster bed. She wrapped her fingers around his length and stroked him, kissed him open-mouthed, her tongue doing all the things he would do to her once he was buried inside her.

Somehow they ended up on the floor, him holding himself rigid, her hiking up her skirts and straddling his thighs.

"Merciful Lord," he groaned as she sheathed him so slowly he thought he might die. "You're so warm. So wet, love." His eyes flickered shut. He'd never felt anything so exquisite.

He grasped her hips as she began to move, every roll of her body stoking the fire between them. Hell, this is what he'd waited a lifetime for—a love that knew no end.

He watched her, transfixed. The fall of her hair. The flush rising on her throat. The soft, bitten-back sounds that undid him more than anything she could say. Anything, except *I love you*.

He slid a hand between them, fingers finding the tender spot that made her gasp. Her rhythm faltered, then deepened, hips sinking onto him again and again, each motion more desperate than the last.

"You're nearly there," he murmured, his own climax building.

He stroked her gently, deliberately, watching the pleasure break across her face like sunlight through a storm. She clenched around him with a cry, her body shuddering in his arms, and he held her through it, breath ragged, heart hammering.

He was already there, right on the edge, holding himself still with the last of his strength. She must have felt the tension of his body, the falter in his rhythm.

She took his face in her hands, her thumbs brushing the stubble along his jaw. Her eyes held his, steady and sure.

"You don't need to withdraw," she whispered. "Not unless you want to. I have faith in the future. Faith in us. But if it's too soon, if it's not what you want, then just—"

"It is," he said, voice hoarse. "It is what I want."

And then he let go—a groan torn from him as he spent inside her, giving everything of himself. His forehead dropped to hers, the tension in him uncoiling all at once.

They sat together in silence, their bodies still joined, hers soft against his, their breaths gradually slowing. He brushed his hand along her spine, fingers drifting in idle, contented strokes.

Neither of them spoke. There was no need.

She shifted slightly, lifting a hand to push the hair from her face, and then stilled. "Gabriel. Good heavens. Look."

He followed her gaze to the high panel above the bed.

A sky full of swallows stretched across the wood, painted in looping arcs, wings extended, frozen in flight, like they'd been waiting for someone to find them.

"It's not wallpaper."

"No. What made you search this room?"

She didn't answer at once. Instead, she pressed a last kiss to his mouth, then eased off his lap, smoothing her skirts as she stood.

He handed her the clean handkerchief from his pocket and tucked himself away.

"This is west. Swallows are a sign of luck, and this room overlooks a bank of white heather. You can see Wynbury Hall from here. And Mrs Boswell said your mother used to stand at the window for hours."

"I should have known where to look?"

But he'd fought to suppress every echo from the past.

"How could you? There must be thousands of items spread across two hundred rooms." She gestured for his hand. "Help me onto the bed."

She knelt on the bed, craning her neck for a better view of the painted canopy. "Five panels make up one mural. The detail is remarkable. Every feather, every wing. But ..." Her brow furrowed. "That one's different."

Gabriel knelt beside her, the mattress giving beneath his weight.

She pointed. "One swallow's flying the wrong way."

He saw it, near the centre panel. All the others looped westward, but one turned east, its wings angled sharply, as if caught in a crosswind. Just beneath it, the edge of one panel sat ever so slightly askew.

Olivia reached up, fingertips testing the seam. "This one's loose."

The panel shifted beneath her touch, sliding back with a faint scrape. Behind it, nestled in the hollow, lay a flat bundle, wrapped in waxed linen and tied with a faded blue ribbon.

Dust drifted as she eased it free.

She looked down at it, then at him, eyes wide, her excitement barely contained. "I think we've found it. We've found the evidence."

They sat together on the bed. He watched as she untied the ribbon and peeled back the linen. Inside were letters, documents, receipts for bribes paid. A note from her father—a simple apology, and a message to look forward, never back.

She dashed tears from her cheeks. "This proves Mrs Culpepper is involved. She wrote to my father, instructing him to—" She stopped abruptly, the colour draining from her face.

"What is it?"

"Mrs Culpepper answered to someone else."

She handed him a letter.

The blood roared in his ears as he read the name.

A cold fury had him gritting his teeth. "Daventry needs to see this. We need to take it to him now."

Two days later

Daventry was waiting on the corner of the street when Gabriel arrived. He stood alone, though his men were stationed at key points along the row in case the traitor bolted.

The sun shone, the city bustled, but someone's world was about to come crashing down around them.

Gabriel caught the gleam of satisfaction in Daventry's dark eyes. A quest for truth and justice was something they shared. But how could justice prevail when those sworn to protect it were corrupt?

"The last few weeks have been full of surprises," Gabriel said. "None more so than this."

"Corruption usually begins at the top."

"I assume we have the Home Secretary's approval."

Daventry grinned. "We have the King's approval."

"Do you want me to enter alone and mention the evidence? Hope he tries to offer a bribe. You could listen from the door."

This devil had been manipulating events for over twenty years, ruining lives while lining his pockets, presenting one vision while hiding another.

"That won't be necessary," Daventry said. "We found documents buried in the grave at Wynbury Hall. Mrs Culpepper's insurance policy."

"If her plan to take a new identity abroad failed?"

"Once they'd placed the headstone, no one would have looked there." Daventry glanced at the steps of Bow Street Magistrates' Office. "And there was a foiled attempt to free Mrs Culpepper from Newgate last night. My men waited until she looked heavenward and gave a relieved sigh before pouncing."

Let her rot. He'd make certain they all paid for what they'd done to Olivia. "I wish I'd been there to witness it." But he'd been at home with the woman he loved, memorising the feel of her skin, the sound of her laugh, the way she whispered his name in the dark.

"You'll be there to witness the shock on Sir Basil's face when he realises the game is up. I'm confident it will be just as satisfying."

Sir Basil was leafing through a case file when Sergeant

Reid showed them into the cluttered office.

He stood, a show of deference to Gabriel's position. "Ah, Lord Rothley. I trust all is well, now that sorry business is behind you." He acknowledged Daventry with a nod and gestured for them to sit. "You'll be pleased to know Reverend Clay gave a detailed confession last night. The man has been preaching politics from his pulpit for years."

"After hours, I presume."

"Yes, it seems his bid to help the needy extended to secret meetings at St Luke's by night. The watchmen had seen some strange goings-on but failed to report them. And the sexton had his suspicions."

Gabriel's temper simmered beneath the surface, but he remained composed. "The sexton? I'm not sure I'd give much weight to a drunkard's ramblings."

He saw it then, the slight tremble of the magistrate's lip.

"Perhaps not, but it all leads to the same theory."

"Any news on the person who killed Mrs Hodge?" Daventry asked.

"Yes, good news." Sir Basil reached across his desk and handed Daventry a signed document. "Robbery was the motive. A man who frequents The Bear was caught trying to sell stolen goods. Among them was a locket Mrs Hodge had kept. You've the murderer's confession in your hand."

Daventry read it but didn't hand it back. "We've had some luck ourselves. However, it may mean questioning the suspects and witnesses again. To determine who's lying."

The magistrate's brows rose. "I can't speak for your men, Daventry, but I've heard the confessions from the principals themselves." He gave a small shrug. "I'm in no doubt who's at fault here."

Daventry didn't blink. "Nor are we." He paused, letting

the silence stretch, just long enough to carry the hint of accusation. "We have the guard in custody. He arranged to have arsenic added to Sir Randall's broth. And he smuggled Mrs Culpepper out of her cell with the kitchen delivery."

With puffed cheeks and a deep frown, Sir Basil tried to look confounded. "Why is this the first I'm hearing of it? Still, I'm not surprised. The guards in Newgate are underpaid and overworked."

"Spoken like a true revolutionary," Gabriel said.

"All suspects and witnesses have been moved to a secure location." Daventry delivered the line like a man who'd watched countless liars squirm. "The documents recovered from the grave at Wynbury Hall confirm who will be charged with murder and sedition, and who might receive a lighter sentence."

Gabriel watched Sir Basil carefully. No flicker of surprise. No outrage. Just the measured silence of a man calculating the damage.

"Grave? Documents? You went to Wynbury? I said my men would search the suspect's property."

Daventry shrugged. "I answer to the Home Secretary. I imagine a detailed look at your property portfolio might offer some clues. As will the list of bribes you took to sow division in government."

Sir Basil rose in a rush, outrage stiffening his posture. "This is preposterous. You'd give weight to some dust-covered papers and the ravings of those villains found at the scene?"

Gabriel stood, cold fury sharpening in his chest. "Villains acting under your orders." He wanted to drag this fool across the desk and force a confession from him. "You tried to have me killed. Worse. You had my wife abducted and beaten. For that, you'll find out what it's like to dance with the devil."

Daventry was on his feet. "Sergeant Reid."

The footsteps came at once. Sir Basil turned, blanching as the door opened and the sergeant stepped inside, four constables in tow."

"Sir Basil Malden," Daventry said calmly, "you're under arrest for conspiracy to commit murder, abduction, sedition and the corruption of public office."

"On whose authority?" Sir Basil countered.

Daventry smiled. "The King's."

Sergeant Reid stepped forward, taking Sir Basil firmly by the arm. "Best you come quietly, sir, save—"

"Unhand me, you fool." The magistrate shirked out of his grip with a sneer. "This is a mistake. A damned mistake. I've served this city for twenty years—"

"And in that time," Daventry said, unmoved, "you've profited from every lie you helped conceal."

Sir Basil opened his mouth to argue, but said nothing. Perhaps even he sensed the futility of denial in the face of ruin. Sergeant Reid took hold of him again, more forcefully this time, and led him from the room.

Gabriel watched them go in silence. The door closed, not just on a traitor, but on every wicked lie that had nearly cost Olivia her life. That chapter was over. She was safe. And that was all that mattered.

Daventry gave an amused snort. "No matter how many criminals we put behind bars, nothing satisfies quite like those who believe they're invincible."

"Or those who got away with murder for twenty years." Gabriel considered the hours Daventry had spent as master of

London's finest enquiry agency, relentlessly pursuing justice." "But at what cost to you, personally?"

Daventry's smile softened. "I do it for my wife, who's the heart of everything I am. And for my sons, to show them that a man doesn't walk past what's broken. He does everything in his power to fix it. And I've every faith your sons will learn the same from you."

The remark drew his mind to Olivia and the future they might build, the life they would share. If the wheels of fate were already turning, she might soon be with child. He'd be the father he'd once needed. The man he'd spent his whole life trying to become.

Daventry pulled his watch from his pocket and checked the time. "On the subject of being a better man, I promised my wife dinner at Marcello's tonight. And I've an important call to make in Kingston."

"Kingston? Are there not enough rogues in the city?"

"This one's personal. A deal I made with Dominic Hawke."

Gabriel jolted. "You're riding to Shadowmere?"

"To deliver a document. Hawke and his friends need very little help from me." Daventry laughed, almost to himself. "If you want to see the foundations of the *ton* rocked to its core, accept the invitation to the Templeton ball next month."

Gabriel watched him with mounting curiosity. One thing was certain. Whatever document Daventry had for Dominic Hawke, it would send the man's life veering in a different direction.

Daventry checked his watch again. "Well, I'd best deal with Sir Basil before heading to Kingston. Nothing will make me late for dinner with my wife."

Gabriel didn't doubt it. In Daventry's world, rogues came

and went—but love endured. A man didn't earn a reputation as a matchmaker without understanding what truly mattered.

He thought of his own path, every loss, every hard lesson. The road had been merciless. But it led him to Olivia. And he would crawl a thousand miles, gladly, if it meant finding her again.

Chapter Twenty-Three

Two months later

There had been nights in the cottage when peace seemed a distant dream, happiness little more than an idle wish, and family just a fading memory. But here, now, laughter and music filled the ballroom at Studland Park. The house pulsed with life, their friends' voices echoing through rooms once silent, the lonely days behind her.

The Chance brothers made playful bets on who might lure their eldest brother from his wife's side for five minutes. Mr Daventry and his agents waltzed with their wives, while her friends from The Burnished Jade remarked how a single year could transform everything.

"Who knew we'd be dancing at Studland Park?"

"And that Lord Rothley enjoys a party."

He didn't, but he'd done it for her. For their future.

Mr Dalton and Lord Rutland passed by, champagne flutes in hand, lost in conversation. Yet Gabriel had slipped from view.

"I last saw him heading for the terrace." Mr Gentry pointed as if she didn't know the way. "He said he needed air."

Perhaps the memory of his parents' parties still haunted him. Or perhaps the joy in the room was simply too much.

"I'll see if I can coax him back to the ballroom." She smoothed her hands over her midnight-blue gown and made her way to the terrace.

He stood gazing out over the manicured garden, hands braced on the balustrade. She took a moment to observe the rise and fall of his shoulders beneath the black evening coat, tracing the elegant line as it tapered to his narrow waist, and those solid thighs she loved to straddle.

His presence always left her breathless, yet she knew the tender man beneath the surface. Tonight, she sensed he was measuring the life he had left behind against the one they had created together.

"A penny for your thoughts," she said, resting her hand on his back as she joined him on the terrace.

He turned towards her, sliding his arm around her waist, drawing her close. "I thought we might escape into the garden. I seem to recall seeing a nymph lounging somewhere near the fountain."

The memory of them making love brought every nerve to life. "She might be there later, when all our guests have gone. I believe she has a penchant for bathing naked in the moonlight."

"And I have a penchant for her." He bent, pressing a tender kiss to her temple. "And, it seems, for nighttime romps, which we'll resume the minute we have the house to ourselves."

"Is that why you're out here?" She rested her head against

him. "So our friends don't get too comfortable and outstay their welcome?"

He laughed as he stared at the shadow of Wynbury Hall on the horizon. "No, I was contemplating what we might do with the house."

She frowned, following his gaze. "The house? What could we possibly do? It's been seized by the Crown, the money from the sale meant for almshouses in World's End."

"I insisted we have first refusal. And I was thinking we could have an enormous bonfire, roast a hog, and invite the whole parish to dance on Mrs Culpepper's grave."

She caught his arm and turned him to face her. "Memories live in the mind, not in bricks and mortar. Burning the house won't change that."

A muscle in his jaw ticked. "I'll not have crooks living so close again. I'd rather see it turned to pasture."

"We'd have to be rather unfortunate to suffer a similar fate. Besides, our attention will be elsewhere." She had meant to wait until tomorrow to tell him the good news, but the sky was clear, the stars were out, and love filled her heart. "There's something I wanted to discuss with you."

He straightened, giving her his full attention. He took her hand, tracing the edge of her wedding band with his thumb. "You've read the inscription? When? Today, when you went to town?"

"Not yet, no." She had tried once or twice, but he'd written it back when they'd agreed to a marriage of friendship, and fear stopped her from reading it now. "But perhaps this will be a night of surprises."

"You have a surprise for me?" His lips curved in wicked amusement. "Should I wear a blindfold ... guess where you might touch me next?"

"No." She laughed, though the memory of her mouth on his fevered skin stirred the embers of desire once more. "There'll be time for that later." She hesitated, the news pressing at her lips like a secret too large to hold. "I think I'm with child. I've missed two courses, and have been plagued by nausea for days."

He stilled. For a long moment, he simply looked at her—as though she were something rare and unexpected, a jewel amongst a handful of pebbles. When he spoke, his throat was tight with emotion.

"You're certain?"

"As certain as I can be." She laid her hand over his heart, which thumped in time with the music. "I know it's a shock—"

"Not at the rate we make love. And I'm not shocked." He covered her hand with his. "I just didn't expect life could be any better."

She gave that teasing smile he claimed spelled trouble. "I'd count on it getting considerably better. We have a lot of rooms to fill."

He pulled her close and kissed her, her belly tightening with each slow slide of his mouth.

"Read the inscription, Olivia." His voice was as rich as brandy, his dark eyes fixed on hers. "You have my heart, my soul. What is there to fear?" He kissed her again, a promise in every touch. "Read it, and I'll tell you what wish I made with the halfpenny."

It was the enticement she needed. She eased it to her knuckle. "I'm not sure it will come off."

"Let me help you." He caught her hand and wiggled the band loose, though his gaze kept drifting to her face. When the ring came free, he placed it gently in her palm.

She peered at the tiny inscription, squinting in the candlelight, but it was almost impossible to read. "I can see it starts with *Who* ..."

"Shall I tell you what it says?"

"Please do. It would feel more personal if spoken aloud."

He took the gold band and positioned it on her finger, sliding it slowly back to her knuckle. "*Who ever loved that loved not at first sight?*"

The quote caught her off guard, not the words, but the way he said them, as if he'd made her his world the moment they met.

"*Hero and Leander*," she said, a little breathless. "You believe our connection is fated?"

"For me, it was immediate. Unforgettable." He pressed the ring into its rightful place. "I married you because I wanted you. There wasn't a week, day, or hour when you weren't uppermost in my thoughts."

Tears blurred her vision, the plump drops falling onto her cheeks. "But you said a marriage of friendship was—"

"Forget what I said. I threw a halfpenny into a murky pool months ago, and my one wish was you."

"Me?"

The word came out quieter than she intended, more wonder than question.

She had felt it too, simmering just beneath the surface. Attraction. Anticipation. And something else she'd been too afraid to name.

"Thank heavens your wish came true."

He smiled faintly. "I knew it would, even before the coin touched the water."

She studied his face, his eyes steady and sure in the

moonlight. "You've wasted a decade avoiding romantic liaisons. What gave you faith in the future?"

He leaned in, brushing her lips with his. "I haven't wasted the last decade, my love. I've spent it waiting for you."

I hope you enjoyed reading *A Marquess Scorned.*
That may be the end of one love story, but another begins
with a shocking encounter in a ballroom.

He's the scandalous son of a wastrel.
She's a baron's daughter trapped in a gilded cage.
Why does he plan to ruin her in front of the *ton*?
What if revenge leads to something unexpected?

Find out in …
The Sins of Shadowmere
Rotten Scoundrels - Book 1

More titles by Adele Clee

Gentlemen of the Order

Dauntless

Raven

Valiant

Dark Angel

Ladies of the Order

The Devereaux Affair

More than a Masquerade

Mine at Midnight

Your Scarred Heart

No Life for a Lady

Scandal Sheet Survivors

More than Tempted

Not so Wicked

Never a Duchess

No One's Bride

Rogues of Fortune's Den

A Little Bit Dangerous

Temptress in Disguise

Lady Gambit

My Kind of Scoundrel

The Last Chance

Printed in Dunstable, United Kingdom